Fear in Buckskin Forest

Eburne leaned forward for a better look around the notched logs. Suddenly his gaze encountered a woman's face. Then he saw that she was leaning against a sapling—that her arms were tied behind her.

A fury rose in Eburne. He forced himself enough to wait. At that moment he heard heavy footfalls on the steps, and his breath caught. Then Dyott took another step that brought him within reach of the woman. She shrank as his big dirty hand neared her breast.

Eburne leaped from his shelter and discharged his rifle over Dyott's head.

"Don't move, you on the log," he said.

"I ain't movin' and I ain't goin' to," replied the man.

"Turn around."

The burly form moved around as on a pivot.

"Eburne, the deer stalker?" he muttered in surprise.

"Yes. I've a mind to kill you...."

HarperPaperbacks
by Zane Grey

ZANE GREY

THE DEER STALKER

HarperPaperbacks
A Division of HarperCollins*Publishers*

This is a work of fiction. The characters, incidents, and dialogues are products of the author's imagination and are not to be construed as real. Any resemblance to actual events or persons, living or dead, is entirely coincidental.

HarperPaperbacks   *A Division of* HarperCollins*Publishers*
10 East 53rd Street, New York, N.Y. 10022

Cover photo courtesy of Culver Pictures

First HarperPaperbacks printing: February 1991

Printed in the United States of America

HarperPaperbacks and colophon are trademarks of HarperCollins*Publishers*

10 9 8 7 6 5 4 3 2 1

1

*T*HAD EBURNE rode slowly down a trail through the forest of Buckskin Mountain. It led from his lonely cabin to one of the ranger stations called V. T. Park. He had blazed and trodden it himself—a winding trail, made to dodge the automobile roads that during recent years had extended too far, he thought, into the wilderness of his beloved deer sanctuary. He loved the great herd of deer on Buckskin, and though he did not hate civilization, he feared its encroachment into what should always have been kept virgin forest.

Afternoon was far advanced, and the warmth of the early summer day was fading. Shafts of golden sunlight slanted down through the giant pines and spruces of the open forest. Big blue grouse flew up from the thickets along the trail and sped away in noisy flight; and every open glade showed at least one of the squirrels peculiar to that forest plateau. They were black as coal, had tufted ears and huge furry white tails.

Eburne paid more attention to these than to the deer

that he encountered everywhere along the trail. It hurt him to look at them because of late he was always taking stock of their leanness or counting their ribs. For the deer of Buckskin Forest were starving and that was the deer stalker's great concern.

In a way, Thad Eburne had sacrified himself to the cause of forest conservation. True, he had first sought the ranger life to regain rugged health, but having achieved it years ago, he had not returned to the home and advantages he had left back in New England. A life in the open had always been his dream, and the West had claimed him. He was past thirty now. His ambition had been to work himself up in the service to the point where he could travel from one national forest preserve to another, fostering his ideals of conservation. But that long since had become only a dream. His very love of the wild animals, his antagonism to the killing of even wolves and wildcats, and especially cougars, had incurred the enmity of men above him in the service. Besides that he had fought the building of roads and the overtures of lumbering and mining men who would have exploited the beautiful preserve for their greedy ends. There were cattlemen, too, who hated Eburne for sternly holding them to their prescribed grazing permits. Graft had not worked with this ranger, and men of little brief authority found him a hard nut to crack. Wherefore he had remained merely a ranger, and had been advised that even his present situation was none too secure.

Thad had not worried himself by dwelling upon this implied threat; still, as he rode down the trail, on his return to V.T. Park, where he knew he must encounter one or more of his enemies and deliver reports that he knew would be disliked, his thoughts were far from pleasant.

Next to the great herd of deer, he loved this vast plateau, upon the level summit of which Buckskin Forest stretched its dark growth of virgin conifers. He felt that probably no living man, certainly none in the service, knew this vast, silent place so well as he. For eight years he had ranged it, sometimes alone for months, exploring, mapping, studying the deer, the snow, the water, the timber, the grass.

The wonder of that plateau country never lost its enchantment for the deer stalker. It was Grand Canyon country. Buckskin Forest occupied the highest eminence for many miles around. To the north the dim round dome of Navajo Mountain peeped above the red ramparts across the intervening desert; to the south, equally distant, the sharp San Francisco Peaks notched the azure sky.

The plateau itself was geologically a fault—an abrupt crack and upthrust of the crust of the earth. A hundred miles and more of its southern edge formed the wild and sublime north rim of the Grand Canyon. Its long black-fringed line, sloping imperceptibly, extended almost to the Pink Cliffs of Utah. On the desert side it broke, and its yellow wall and dark-spotted slope gave way with a wonderful and majestic concord to the gray level of the barrens.

"It's made me well, changed me, gripped me, yet it's not a home," mused the ranger as he rode along the shadowing trail. "I've let the years roll by....Still, what does that matter? I'll drift to another forest preserve, I suppose, and to another until—"

But he did not conclude the wandering thought. Morbid self-pity never abided long with him. Material success in life, so often worshiped as a false ideal, did not mean much to Eburne. His wants were few and his needs simple. Moreover, he had a strange undefined faith in his destiny, in something that was going to happen to him. Failure to advance in the forest service had not killed his zest for life nor the latent love of romance in his soul.

The forest was growing dark when Eburne rode into V. T. Park. Troops of deer, as tame as cattle, showed indistinctly in the gathering dusk. They had come down to water. A light shone brightly from the cabin. The hum of a motorcar droned out of the woods, gradually dying away.

The ranger reflected that he must have missed someone, but whether tourists or service men, he had no regrets. The roads, though soft in spots, were already open to the summer traffic, an increasingly growing factor in a ranger's life. Most of the rangers welcomed the coming of the tourists, but Eburne did not care for it. He had no self-interest, and he had a clear vision of what the opening of Buckskin Forest would bring. To his reflective mind, the day would come when automobiles must inevitably prove fatal to the wild life and beauty of the forests. Snow had not yet melted off the north slopes of the woodland ravines, yet the influx of tourists and travelers already had begun.

Eburne attended to his horse and then entered the log cabin, burdened with saddlebags, pack, and gun. The big rude room was bright with the glow from blazing red logs in a stone fireplace. Blakener, a companion ranger, one of his few friends in the service, was the only occupant, and manifestly he had been interrupted in the process of eating supper. He was a mature man from the Middle West, rather stout, and of genial aspect.

"Howdy, Thad, you're just in time for grub," was his greeting.

"I'm hungry, all right," replied Eburne as he deposited his burden. "Who's been here? I heard a car."

"Cassell. Judson was with him. They came yesterday mornin'. 'Pears like Judson is gettin' in with the boss.— Better come an' eat while it's hot—an' before what I have to tell you spoils your appetite."

"Ahuh.—Any mail for me?"

"A lot this time. Papers, magazines, letters. But you come an' eat before I throw it out."

Blakener was indeed full of news, the first of which pleased Thad immensely. The day before, Jim Evers had passed by V. T. Park on his way to see how his herd of tame buffalo had fared during the winter down in black Houserock Valley. Jim had once been a Texas ranger and later a predatory game hunter for the government. He was another one of the deer stalker's few friends. They had been much together in former years during that period when Evers had been hunting cougars along the canyon rim.

"Jim was sorry to miss you," said Blakener. "But he said he'd stop in on the way back to Fredonia. He talked a lot about the starvin' deer an' blamed the government a lot for killin' off the cougars. Jim recalled his old friend Buffalo Jones, who you know hunted an' lassoed cougars here some fifteen years ago. It was Jones who left Jim the pack of hounds an' the herd of tame buffalo. Well, Jim was talkin' about how true old Jones' prediction had come. Kill off the cougars an' deer would multiply so fast they'd eat off the range an' starve to death. Or else die of disease."

"That's just what's going to happen," declared Eburne. "This last trip convinced me of that more than ever. The deer have had a hard winter.... Yes, I remember how Jim and I used to talk about it. But we never expected the calamity so soon."

"Deer multiply like sheep," returned his companion. "We know that. When I told Cassell we'd estimated around twelve thousand increase this year, he didn't believe it. Fact is only us rangers who live on the ground know anythin' about the numbers of deer. I say there's fifty thousand in the forest."

"I wouldn't wonder," assented Eburne thoughtfully. "Something must be done to save the herd."

"Cassell said there was a movement afoot to permit hunters to shoot deer this fall."

"Oh, no!" exclaimed Thad sharply. "Surely they're not thinking of that?"

"Humph. They just are. Judson was keen about it. He has a lot of friends in Utah an' he'd like to see them drive their cars down here to hunt. 'Pears to be some feelin' between Fredonia an' Kanab about this."

"No wonder. Fredonia is in Arizona and Kanab in Utah," replied the deer stalker.

"Sure. But just the same they're most all Mormons on both sides of the line. Funny they'd clash."

"Blakener, we don't know all we'd like to," said Thad bluntly. "But it's a fact that this Buckskin preserve—the Grand Canyon National Forest—lies in northern Arizona yet is actually governed by Utah."

Eburne learned presently that during the coming summer an investigating committee was to visit Buckskin to inquire into the condition of the deer herd and to make a report to the Secretary of Agriculture in Washington. Among the organizations from which representatives would be sent were the American National Livestock Breeders Association, the Boone and Crockett Club, the National Parks Association, the Audubon Society, and the American Game Protective Association.

"Well, I'm glad to hear that," declared Thad. "Surely, good will come of it."

"Sure sounds O.K. to me," went on Blakener. "You an' I have been detailed to guide that committee an' cooperate with them. Suits me better than entertainin' a lot of tourists."

"Suits me too. We can help that committee. Any fair-minded man will see how the deer have overmultiplied and have eaten all the forage off the range."

"Thad, I'll bet other orders Cassell left won't suit you so well," returned Blakener dryly.

"And what are they?" queried Eburne sharply.

"You're to trap deer alive," responded his comrade deliberately. "Fawns, does, bucks. You're to trap deer alive an' study how they react to captivity."

"Trap deer alive! Fawns, does, bucks!" exclaimed the ranger. "For Heaven's sake—why?"

"They want to see if deer can be captured an' shipped."

"Ahuh! They want to deplete the herd that way—I think it's impossible, deer will kill themselves in traps."

"Well, there's your written orders," rejoined Blakener.

"Cassell was pretty sore that you hadn't got in. He waited till near dark for you. Then he wrote these. You've got a job on your hands."

Eburne disliked the idea so thoroughly that he forthwith dismissed it from his mind; and after finishing his supper and sharing the chores with Blakener, he devoted himself to a perusal of his mail. Letters from home were rare, and when cheerful and full of good news, as were these, they were exceedingly welcome. His sister expected to be married sometime near Christmas—a bit of information that was hard for him to realize. She had been twelve years old when he had left home. How time flew by! Then his mother wrote at length, and some of her statements were thought-provoking. "You should come home to visit us. I am getting along in years and your father is ailing.... After your sister is married and settled we'd like to move to a milder climate—California, for instance, where we could see our son occasionally.... Your father has retired from active business.... And when, pray, do you intend to get yourself a wife?"

This last query roused both mirth and a slight edge of irritation in Eburne. Nevertheless, it made him think. How far indeed had he drifted from the old normal ways of life! Yet he had never definitely settled for himself the question of marriage, except to avoid dwelling upon it. But confronted by it now, in his mother's letter, he suddenly realized how futile and useless his future must appear in the eyes of his family, who had not understood him even when he was at home. Marriage, considered as an actuality instead of a dreamy possibility, seemed not for such as Thad Eburne. Where could he find a wife? His acquaintance with marriageable girls was absurdly limited. He knew several Mormon girls at Fredonia, and Clara Hilton, a young woman employed at the El Tovar Hotel across the Canyon. She had left no doubt in his mind as to her eligibility and willingness, in fact during Thad's several visits at the El Tovar, she had rather embarrassed him by her too obvious interest. Clara was good-looking, vivacious, but the idea of her as wife was just plain ridiculous.

"It's funny," he declared, thinking aloud.

"What?" queried Blakener, rising from his task of replenishing the fire. "You don't look funny."

"My mother writes I should be getting a wife," replied Thad with a laugh. "And I was thinking about all the desirable ladies of my wide acquaintance."

"Thad, that's not funny," returned his partner seriously. "You're still a young man. Now, I never entered the service until I lost my wife. That was years ago. You're surely not goin' to stick to this rotten job forever?"

"I don't think it's a rotten job," said Thad soberly.

"But it is, all the same, an' especially for a well-educated man like you who could get somewhere."

"Blakener, I consider forestry as a splendid calling for any man who loves the open," protested Eburne. "The future of our forests is a mighty important thing. It must develop. Some men of brains have got to devote their lives to conserving the timber and wild creatures."

"We've argued that out before," rejoined Blakener. "It's true. But you can't ever get anywhere in this forest service. You've made enemies. An' I'm givin' you a tip that even your ranger job won't outlast the year."

"That's true, too," replied Thad with a sigh. "Well, sufficient unto the day! My failure to succeed in the service makes it just that much easier to dismiss the idea of a wife."

"Eburne, you don't do yourself justice! Everybody knows you're the best forest man in the whole service."

"Thank you, Blakener," said Thad in quick and grateful surprise.

"No thanks comin' from me," replied his comrade gruffly. "But there ought to be some from the government. You get all the hard jobs. Cassell really took pleasure in the idea of makin' you trap deer. He said you'd have them eatin' out of your hand. An' say, he grinned like a chessy cat. He sure hates your guts.—Thad, I'd chuck the job if I was you."

"It's a temptation. But for the sake of the deer I'll stick as long as they let me."

"You've saved money, haven't you?"

"Yes. Perhaps half of what I've earned here. But you don't get much in the service! Why did you ask?"

"Well, I'd chuck this trappin' deer job an' beat it," replied Blakener with slow earnestness. "Things are bound to get worse. An' this fall they'll sure let hunters in to kill these tame deer."

Eburne thoughtfully turned his friend's advice over in his mind. He was bound to confess there was a good deal of sense in Blakener's words. On the other hand he knew that if deer had to be trapped he should be the one to do it; and if an investigating committee was really coming to Buckskin, in the interest of the great herd he was the ranger best qualified to show them the true situation. He eliminated his personal feelings and fortunes and sat there watching the fire and pondering this new task that had been assigned him.

Outside, the night wind began to rise and mourn through the pines. It brought the faint yelp of a coyote. A branch swished against the roof of the cabin. The fire blazed and crackled, lighting the room with a ruddy glow.

"I've more news," spoke up Blakener presently as he removed his pipe and thoughtfully gazed at the fire.

"Out with it, then," retorted Thad, startled from his reverie. "It never rains but it pours."

"Well, several days after you left I rode over to Quakin' Asp," began Blakener slowly. "But I didn't ride in. I happened to get a glimpse of some horsemen actin' rather suspicious. So I got off an' slipped ahead through the woods an' hid where I could see. Well, sir, I'll be darned if I didn't fall into somethin' queer. I'd been right about the horsemen—Bing Dyott an' four of his outfit—an' my instinct to spy on them had been right, too. For it wasn't long till Judson an' Settlemire rode in. The meetin' had been planned. That was as plain as the nose on your face."

"Bing Dyott! Judson with Settlemire! Well, I'll be a—" exclaimed Eburne in genuine amazement.

"Humph! I thought it'd strike you queer. Well, Dyott an' Settlemire drew off to one side an' had a long confab. It was serious, an' they were sure acquainted with each other. Judson acted uneasy, as if he'd be glad when the council was over. Dyott's men lounged around whisperin' together mysterious like an' laughin' among themselves. . . . Well, presently Settlemire went back to his horse an' called Judson. They rode off toward the valley, no doubt makin' for Lower Pools where his cattle outfit is now. Then some of Dyott's men fetched up their pack-horses an' they started to make camp. Judgin' from the look of their horses an' packs, the gang had come a long way. Now, Eburne, can you make anythin' of this meetin'?"

"No, not offhand," replied Thad gravely. "But it doesn't look straight."

"Well, some things you'd call crooked are just plain business dealin'—with a big cattleman like Settlemire," rejoined Blakener. "We can think what we want, sure, but if we're goin' to make reports we've got to be careful. Let's keep mum about this. An' let's get our heads together right now to see what we can make of it."

Settlemire was at the head of the Houserock Cattle Company, which operated in southern Utah and northern Arizona. He was known to get along well with the Mormons, and it was suspected that he had influence with some one high in the forest service. His cattle outfit had broken about all of the forest regulations, and there was strong feeling between the rangers and his cowboys.

This prosperous cattleman had always bitterly resented the developing of the great deer herd upon Buckskin. He had government grazing permits to run his cattle all over the forest. Since the over-multiplication of the deer, these permits had been gradually reduced and withdrawn until this year they had been revoked entirely and Settlemire had been ordered to drive his cattle off the preserve.

"That was the order," declared Blakener. "I saw it myself this spring in Kanab. But Settlemire still has three thousand head runnin' over on the west side. An' he's makin' absolutely no move to round them up an' drive them off. He's not goin' to move them while there's any grass left. Now it's sure plain he's got a pull somewhere. An' we always knew why he opposed the spreadin' of the deer herd. But where do Judson an' Dyott fit in here?"

"That's a stumper, I'll agree," answered Eburne. "You see, in the case of Judson, we're somewhat in the dark as to his actual status. He's not a ranger or a supervisor. He claims to be an inspector. Anyway, we know he has always catered to rich cattlemen and dallied around with the tourists, especially when they're women. In this instance he's probably favoring Settlemire's schemes, whatever they are."

"Sure. Settlemire wants to regain his grazin' permits an' to see the deer herd depleted by killin'. Judson is for both of these plans."

It was not so easy for the rangers to fix Dyott's part in the situation. Dyott had a bad name. Some fifteen years back he had been a rustler, and before that, as a boy, he had ridden with the notorious Hash Knife gang of the Mogollons. Of late years he had been making small deals in cattle, chiefly among the Mormons. Eburne had long suspected that Dyott killed deer on the preserve and sold the meat. His outfit was a hard-riding one that kept to the rough canyons and brakes of the forest. Rangers as a rule avoided contact with Dyott's men.

"It occurred to me that Settlemire might hire Dyott to drive the deer back from where his cattle are grazin'," suggest Blakener.

"Would that pay Settlemire?" asked Thad doubtfully.

"Well, it might save what cattle he has left."

"There must be something more, though that hunch is not to be overlooked," returned Thad. "If in addition to this, Dyott is in here to kill deer ... You say the preserve will be open to hunters this fall? That means thousands of deer killed and packed out. It wouldn't be impossible for Dyott's gang to clean up rich on some kind of a butchering deer job. Still, to find a market for a lot of meat! It'd be difficult."

"Maybe there's something in the wind we've not hit on yet," suggested Blakener.

"Right. Let's go to bed and sleep on it," rejoined Eburne, rising with a yawn.

EBURNE'S slumbers did not clarify in any degree the rather dubious relation between Dyott and the cattleman or inspire him with any wonderful ideas as to the best method of trapping deer.

He got out before sunrise and walked around the station, through the edge of the forest. Not one deer rewarded his roving eye. The morning was clear and cold. Bluebells peeped up wanly from the frost-whitened grass that he brushed as he strode along. There was no sound. The forest seemed a dead wilderness. He found his horse at the far end of the pasture and was glad to see that the grass there afforded better grazing than in the open forest.

The sun came up, rosy and bright, illuminating the steely blue scene. Thad returned to the cabin, where he helped get breakfast. His conversation with Blakener soon reverted to the deer question.

"Forgot to tell you," said Blakener with animation. "Cassell's goin' to send out two deer traps. Cleveland somethin' or other he called them—made in Michigan. Said he had some comin' from Ogden. Looks to me that he's had this trappin' stunt in his mind for some time."

"Probably he means to stick the dirty job on other rangers too," replied Eburne.

"Sure, I heard him tell Judson he'd had several orders for live deer."

"Humph! The more I think of it the more absurd it seems," said Thad forcefully. "Still, to be honest, I really don't *know*. I think deer will kill themselves if trapped in close quarters. But thinking isn't knowing. This is a chance for me to find out. I've my orders and I've got to carry them out or quit. As I won't quit, I'll just have to swallow my feelings and meanwhile add to my knowledge of deer."

"Sure. Now you're talkin'," rejoined his comrade heartily. "I'll tell you what, Thad, I'll help you all I can. But you've got to do the figurin'."

Eburne was quite conscious that it would take a good deal of mental and physical effort if there were to be even anything approaching success. To that end he set out on the unwelcome task. In the shed he found several bales of wire and a quantity of old lumber, slabs with the bark on one side. These would come in handy when the time arrived to build fences and pens. Then he walked down the park to look over the ground around the spring. The season had been the driest for years. Water was far from abundant. The spring was lower than Eburne had ever seen it. As far as he knew there were only four other springs on that side of Buckskin.

After carefully getting the lay of the land, Thad decided to fence in the water and have the wings converge into a narrow chute that led into a corral around the spring. He did not know how many deer watered at this place, but he believed they might number over a thousand. There was no other water near, and the deer in the vicinity had become used to this spring and they would not readily abandon it.

He spent the day watching and planning. About three o'clock, deer began to come down into the park to drink. Often as Thad had watched them, he seemed never to have seen them as gaunt as now. They were as tame as cattle yet were really wild deer. They came in troops, by twos and threes, and in sizable herds; and now and then a lordly stag, almost as big and stately as an elk, walked in alone. The little fawns caught Eburne's eye and delighted him. Some does had twin fawns, graceful, beautiful spotted little creatures, as playful as kittens.

These deer were all lean, and they somehow lacked the sleek, velvety, rich gray usually common to deer on the plateau. The bucks appeared to be in the best condition, as was natural. Sometimes there would be forty or fifty at a time around the water hole. They did not linger long, however, and soon worked off into the woods, plainly aware of Thad's presence. The newcomers would come in, scent or see him, stand with long ears erect, motionless as statues for moments, and then go on for their drink. Still, they were uneasy. If Thad had been on horseback or even moving along on foot, they would have shown less interest.

By sunset, Thad calculated that more than six hundred deer had come in to drink. No doubt many more came after it was too dark to see them.

"Well, Blakener," announced Eburne upon his return to the cabin, "if deer *can* be trapped this is the best place ever, and the most propitious time. They are hungry and thirsty. With water and hay we can coax them anywhere. Oh, we can trap them easily enough. But what they'll do the moment they're trapped! That's the rub."

"I saw one old buck walk by here," commented Blakener. "Say, he was as big as a steer. Now, I wonder what he'd do in a trap."

"He'd make us climb the fence," replied Thad. "An old buck is bad medicine, unless you're on a horse....Well, tomorrow we'll begin to stretch wire. I don't believe we'll have to put in many posts. There're a lot of trees except down in the meadow. And I think it'll be best to do this work only in the mornings. I don't want to scare the deer before we get the trap built."

Next morning, while the deer stalker was laboriously stretching wire, a horseman rode into the park. He was leading a pack-horse, behind which trotted a number of hounds. The ranger did not need to look twice. The visitor was his old friend Jim Evers, the former predatory game hunter for the government.

"Hello there, old-timer," called the ranger heartily as his friend rode up.

"Howdy, Thad," drawled Evers, reaching out to grasp the proffered hand.

The Texan was a striking figure, despite the bowed shoulders that told of encroaching age. His face was lean, red, keen as an Indian's, and remarkable for the long sloping lines and the narrow slits from which his blue eyes flashed. His garb, his weapons, the trappings of his horses, his pack—all showed long service in the open.

"Blackener told me you'd ridden down to look over your buffalo," said Thad. "I'm glad I didn't miss you today. How'd you find the herd, Jim?"

"Wal, they wintered fine," replied the hunter. "Got twelve new calves. But I reckon I'm aboot ready to sell out. I cain't take care of thet herd. They shore ain't never been nothin' in it for me. I'm goin' to sell—one hundred dollars a head. Mebbe I can get the government to take them off my hands."

"Jim, I'm inclined to think the government already has one white elephant on its hands here—this tame deer herd."

"Great guns, yes," mildly exploded Jim. "It's a shame aboot these deer—Thad, I'm invitin' myself to eat with you an'stay all night."

"Old-timer, you're welcome as the flowers in May," responded Thad warmly, "Let's go up to the cabin and throw your pack. You can turn the horses loose in the corral."

"What you all doin' with this heah wire? Son, don't you calkilate fences is as bad as them automobiles?"

"Indeed I do, Jim. But I've my orders. And I'm supposed to trap some of these deer. Trap them alive to ship out of Arizona!"

"Wal, jumpin' juniper!" drawled the old hunter. "Who and what and why now?"

Eburne briefly explained the situation and was not a little gratified to have Evers forcefully deliver himself of views that coincided with his own.

"Wal, it's this way," continued the hunter, "these government fellars air all right an' want to do good, but they jest don't know. It takes a lifetime to learn anythin'. Now, I've been huntin' on Buckskin for twenty years. I've seen this deer herd grow from five to fifty thousand. You rangers say twenty thousand, but you don't see the deer us hunters see. Why, down in the brakes of the Siwash, where you never get, there's ten deer to one thet's in heah. . . . Wal, killin' off the varmints, specially the cougars, has broken the balance of nature so far as these deer are concerned. Herds of deer, runnin' free, will never thrive whar the cougars have been killed off. The price of healthy life in the open is eternal vigilance—eternal watch an' struggle against death by violence. Man cain't remove thet balance an' expect nature to correct it. These heah deer ain't had nothin' to check their overbreedin' an' inbreedin'. They jest doubled an' trebled. Buckskin is a queer sort of range. Canyon on one side an' bare desert all around. The deer cain't migrate as they do in other places. They just eat up everythin'. An' now they're goin' to starve or die of disease."

"Something must be done before it's too late," asserted Eburne.

"Wal, Thad, it's most too late now. For part of the herd, anyhow. Conditions ain't favorable. There wasn't much snow last winter. Thet means poor grazin'. An' it'll be a dry summer. The deer air eatin' the aspens, junipers, buckbrush. You cain't find an aspen saplin'. Why, the deer seem turnin' into beavers. Then the government's goin' to let a jam of hunters come in this fall to kill deer."

"So Blakener told me. But I can't believe it, Jim. That would be such a rotten thing to do. After developing this wonderful herd, taming them almost to eat out of your hand, advertising them to thousands of tourists as the greatest sight in the west—to let hunters murder them! It's pretty low-down."

"Shore is. An' I'm not thinkin' much of the kind of hunters who'd shoot tame deer for sport. But I'm givin' you a hunch, Eburne: thet very stunt is comin' off. I'm on the inside. I've got friends in Kanab—they're Mormons—an' they tipped me off. They're all smackin' their lips at the prospect of venison all winter. An' laughin' up their sleeves because Arizona hunters won't be permitted to shoot on Buckskin."

"Well, I'll be hanged!" ejaculated Eburne, confounded. "Jim, you're hinting that the government will permit hunters to shoot deer this fall and the State will oppose it."

"Shore. An' the funny part will be to see you rangers helpin' the hunters avoid arrest."

"I'll do nothing of the sort," declared Thad stoutly.

"Wal, then you'll get fired," drawled Jim complacently. "It'll be a healthy mess, an' you can gamble I'm glad I'm out of the service."

"Come along. Let's go to the cabin," said the ranger shortly. He strode off, leading Jim's pack-horse. The long-eared hounds trotted beside him, wagging their tails and begging with solemn eyes. They had visited Eburne before. When the men reached the cabin, Blakener called out a cheery welcome to dinner. Thad helped the old hunter unpack and carry his effects inside. They had dinner, and an interesting talk in the pleasant living room. Later, as the afternoon advanced, Evers accompanied Eburne out to watch the deer come in.

"Wal, Thad, the particular reason I dropped in on you today I ain't told yet," said the hunter.

"Oh, you haven't?" returned Thad with curiosity. "Out with it, Jim. I hope to goodness you've saved the best for the last."

"Wal, it's only an idee, an' it's not mine, but it shore is amazin'," rejoined Evers thoughtfully.

Eburne did not importune the old hunter, though he sensed something out of the ordinary. They found a seat under a pine tree above the spring, so situated that they could watch the deer come to the spring without being seen. Already a few deer had entered the meadow and at the moment were standing motionless, long ears erect, gazing at the edge of the forest where the men were hidden. Evers lighted his pipe.

"Thad, you're well acquainted with Bill McKay?" he queried finally, with deliberation.

"Indeed I am. We're good friends. I think a heap of Bill. But I haven't seen him since he began boring for oil out on the Indian reservation."

"Wal, thet fell through like so many things Mac has tackled. He's onlucky....I met him yesterday packin' across Houserock Valley. He's workin' a mine down in the canyon. Somewhere near the foot of Tanner's trail, but on this side of the river. Says there's copper, gold, an' silver. Wal, me an' Bill had a bite of grub together, an' we talked a lot. Naturally I touched on this heah deer problem, which is really close to my heart. I told Bill the conditions an' how they had riled up government, forest officers, rangers, Mormons, an' everybody generally. Then Bill whacked me with his sledgehammer fist so hard he near knocked me flat. 'Jim,' he says, 'I've an idee!'"

"McKay always was full of ideas," rejoined Eburne as Jim paused to take a puff on his pipe and to allow time for suspense to take hold of his listener. "In fact he's a far-sighted man."

"Heah is what he said: 'Jim, you know the deer herd

splits in winter, part goin' down off the mountain in the west brakes, an' part on this east slope. There's ten or fifteen thousand deer winter on these cedar an' sage slopes. Now you know there's a wall of rock reachin' from the Cocks Combs to the Saddle Gap, an' another wall runnin' off the other side under Saddle Mountain. These heah walls form a fence up which no deer can climb. An' they head up where the Saddle trail goes through the Gap an' down into the canyon.'—Mac dropped down on his knee when he was tellin' me all this, an' he drawed maps on the ground. An' I said yes, I agreed aboot the lay of the land."

Here Evers paused again, but he was too thrilled or obsessed by the information he had to impart to remember his pipe.

" 'Jim ' says Mac, 'give me a hundred Indians an' fifty cowboys an' I can drive ten thousand deer through the Saddle Gap, down the canyon, across the Colorado River, an' up Tanner's trail to the rim—right into forest ranges where feed an' water are aplenty.' "

Eburne stared. His jaw dropped. The idea was amazing.

"Drive ten thousand deer!" he exclaimed finally.

"Shore. Thet's what Mac said. First off I gave him the laugh. But the idee got me. It's great. I know the country. The deer are tame. They might drive. The more I thought aboot it the bigger the idee got. An' now I'm stuck on it. Shore it's grand."

"Drive ten thousand deer!" echoed Thad incredulously. "Through the saddle—down the canyon—up the rim."

"Shore. You're locoed now. But wait till thet idee soaks in," replied Jim with glee, nodding his gray old head. "It'll shore get you. Because it's a way to save the deer without trappin' or killin'. An' it'll be good for other ranges on the south side. Deer used to be thick in the Coconino Basin,

around the San Francisco Peaks, an' south toward the Mogollons. Now they're gone. This drive would restock those
ranges."

"Wonderful, but impossible!" ejaculated Eburne,
breathing hard.

"No it ain't impossible," returned the old hunter
stoutly. "I'd bet a million dollars if Buffalo Jones was heah
he could drive them deer. He understood wild animals.
But McKay will have the Indians to help. Navajos he
wants—drivin' on foot with cowbells to ring."

"Jim, I tell you it's impossible," protested Thad, re-
gretting that he must take this negative viewpoint. "Deer
won't drive. You might move them, gradually work them
into a great herd. But then! The instant they found you
wanted them to go in any one direction, they'd bolt. They'd
spill like ants over the ground. They'd scatter like a flock
of quail. They'd run over horses and men. No, deer won't
drive."

That was Eburne's intuitive reaction to McKay's as-
tounding idea.

It was what he felt. He had been a deer stalker for
many years, at first as a hunter, and then as a watcher,
and finally as a lover of nature and of the most beautiful
and graceful wild creatures in the woods.

"Wal, now, how do you know they won't drive?" demanded Jim persistently.

"I don't know. I just feel they won't," replied Eburne.

"Let's stick to what we know. Take for instance last
month when Lee Daley an' a couple of cowboys drove
them ten buffalo yearlin's of mine into an automobile truck.
Who'd have thunk it could be done? Wal, it was, an' them
buff calves went clear to Mexico where I sold them. Look
how cowboys can drive wild steers. I reckon a bunch of
wild steers is wuss than a herd of elephants. I remember
them Stewart boys, wild hoss hunters years ago. They
could drive anythin' on four legs. Wal, we never heerd of
deer bein' drove, an it's good figurin' to believe it can be

done till we find out for shore."

"Jim, you're right. I've nothing to stand on. I admit it *might* be done. How I hope it could!"

"Wal, McKay wants you to submit his proposition to the forest service an' to the government, with your approval," drawled Jim confidently, as if there were no question of Eburne's stand.

"By thunder, I'll do it!" burst out the ranger, suddenly elated. "Sure as you're born they'll fall for it. And then what a row with the opposing side who'll want to kill the deer! It tickles me, Jim, it's fascinating. It grows on me."

"Wal, I was plumb shore it would," replied Evers mildly. "Now let's get down to brass tacks. McKay wants to make money on the drive. He wants to ask the government two dollars an' fifty cents a head for deer drove across the canyon, an' thet much more a head for deer drove to other ranges."

"Little enough. He can get it," said Eburne.

"Wal, it's going to cost a lot to make the drive. The Indians an' cowboys will have to be paid wages an' fed. Outfits will have to be packed. Trucks to haul grain for horses an' supplies for camps. Mac's no hand at figgerin', but I calkilated somethin' like five hundred dollars a day."

"That's a lot of money," replied the ranger, seriously.

"Shore is. An' Mac hasn't got a dollar. He'll have to have backin'."

"He's welcome to all I have. But it's not enough."

"I'll chip in a little to help Mac. An' his friends in Flagstaff will donate. Shore he'll raise the money. You jest go ahead an' get a strong bid ready for the drive."

"Jim, wouldn't it be wise to go slow on approaching the government?" queried Eburne thoughtfully. "It's over four months till time for the deer to work down off the mountain. If we sprang this idea at once wouldn't that give our opponents too much time to work in their propaganda?"

"Reckon I'd wait till you've given this trappin' deer a

good tryout. It's shore bound to be a failure, an' when you send in your reports to thet effect you can inclose McKay's proposition. Thet'd be a favorable time to hit them. But on the other hand you don't want to wait too long an' give the deer-killin' crowd a chance to get set. For that matter, they are set, but this new idee may throw them out. I shore hope so."

"Well, it's settled," returned Eburne with satisfaction. "Now Jim, let's sneak up closer to that bunch of deer coming in. Let's watch them. And you can work out your idea of what a trap corral should be like."

The ranger and the hunter spent the remainder of that afternoon spying upon the deer. By sunset about five hundred had come in to drink. The wire fence Eburne had already erected did not appear to interest the deer to any appreciable extent. It was evident that they would come in to drink if they had to pass through open gates and down a narrow aisle. The matter of their entering a trap, then, as Eburne had surmised, was not a difficult question. Indeed, though he had no definite plans formulated for traps, he had not been in the least concerned about his ability to construct them. Jim Evers hit the nail on the head when he drawled out, "Wal, it shore ain't gettin' deer alive in a trap thet'll stump you; it's gettin' them out alive!"

Traps and deer occupied the fireside talk for an hour after supper. Then Blakener sounded out the old hunter on the well-known controversy between cattlemen and forest service. Evers had served on both sides. He had lived on and around Buckskin for twenty years. It was his humble opinion that the government should never have coddled the deer herd to grow into such unmanageable numbers. The little ranchers and sheepmen, of whom there had formerly been many and now were few, had been dependent on the grass of the plateau. Many of them had been ruined by the multiplication of the deer and the consequent restrictions. Then, for fifteen years, nonnative cattle companies had obtained the best of the grazing that had once belonged to the local ranchers. The company that at the present time and for the last six or eight years held the balance of power on Buckskin was composed of absentee owners and headed by the Californian, Settlemire. According to the hunter, Settlemire had neither legal nor moral right to the privileges he enjoyed. Apparently he was not a Mormon, which fact made his influence all the more astonishing. It had been Settlemire who had claimed he would see to it that the deer preserve should be opened to hunters in the early fall.

"Jim, why is it when the rangers order Settlemire's cowboys to drive their stock off the range they roll their cigarettes and grin and say: 'Reckon we gotta ride out on that job pronto,' and then never even make the attempt?"

"Wal, boys, don't ask me thet," drawled Evers. "But I've always wondered why you rangers didn't get together and drive Settlemire's stock off the range."

"We act under orders. We have but little leeway," replied Eburne. "I put that very proposition up to headquarters."

"An' what come off?" queried Evers, knowingly.

"I got disliked for my pains and called down for my suggestions," replied Thad tersely.

"Wal, boys, it's no wuss heah than anywheres," said Evers. "Reckon life is aboot the same wherever you go. I remember Texas when I was a boy. This heah Utah, is a picnic to live in compared to my home State then. Rich men do things that poor men cain't. There's always men in high positions thet oughtn't to be there. Or so it seems to us poor devils who have to hold the sack. But after you live a long while, like me, an' can look back a ways, you see thet everythin' happens for the best an' things work out better than if you done it yourself."

"Jim, your philosophy is fine," rejoined Eburne. "I wish I could accept it. But I'm still full of protest and fight—at this particular time against both the forest service officials, high and low, and the outside cattlemen."

"Thad, where'd it ever get you?" asked Evers with blunt kindness.

"Nowhere, materially. But I don't live just to get on and up in the world. If my conscience tells me a thing is wrong I'm against it. That's all. And I'll say so."

"Wal, a fellar's conscience can feel somethin's wrong, like what we was hintin' aboot Settlemire. But thet ain't proof. An' thet's why it'll be wise to keep your mouth shut. No one ever caught Settlemire even on the edge of a shady deal. Either he's honest or hard business or just slick."

"Jim, you know Bing Dyott, don't you?" queried Thad.

"I shore do. I knowed him in Texas thirty years ago. If all I know aboot thet hombre was told he'd go to jail for the rest of his life an' then hang. . . . But what's Dyott got to do with this argyment? He's different."

"Blakener saw Dyott meet Settlemire in these woods and hold a conference that was sure serious, if no more."

Evers looked astounded and had to hear Eburne's account of the rendezvous witnessed by Blakener, after which he lapsed into silence.

"Wal," he said at length, "thet has a queer look. There's no mebbe aboot it. Dyott was foreman of an outfit in Utah some years ago. Settlemire bought it. He let Dyott run it. Then, a year or more ago, when the law went off grazin' permits, Dyott showed up heah on this range. Looks queer!"

*I*T TOOK nearly two weeks for the two rangers, working during the mornings, to put up the wire fences as planned by Eburne. It was an experiment and not at all satisfactory to the men. But wire and lumber were scarce and must be replenished from Kanab before any further plans could be attempted.

The wide end of the corral, which extended by wings down along the meadow, was left open. The head that surrounded the spring had a gate for the deer to pass out. At a point close to the water, Eburne planned to place the traps to be sent by Cassell, and if these proved unsatisfactory he would construct one of his own design. The question as to how the trapped animals would act kept the ranger awake at night.

At length the Cleveland-Cliff traps arrived, and the driver who had packed them in his rickety Ford had also guided two automobiles loaded with tourists. He had not lost the opportunity to enlarge upon the wonders of Buckskin, the thousands of deer, and the hospitality of the rang-

THE DEER STALKER • 27

ers. Soon he departed, pocketing the generous tips bestowed by the sight-seers and leaving the rangers in an awkward situation.

One of the rules of the forest service demanded courtesy to visitors. An old slogan was that the national parks belonged to Americans. Eburne and Blakener greeted the strangers with a certain amount of reserve. Now that the vanguard of the summer tourists had arrived, the rangers realized that in addition to guarding their country's natural resources, they would have to serve as guides, cooks, and information bureau.

Thad did not have time to examine the traps until the visitors had left. Then he found them to be boxlike constructions, nine feet long, eight high, and between four and five wide. The entrance was a trap door. Manifestly the idea was to leave the door open for the deer to enter and pull at the bait of hay, which action would release the catch and close the door.

"Well, these traps won't do as they are, that's certain," declared Eburne.

Blakener, too, was doubtful of the traps' practicability, but he expressed himself in quite different language. They carried one of the contraptions up to the cabin porch, where, after supper, they studied it. It was easy to see where they could be improved.

Next morning they set about the task of lengthening the boxes and adding another trap door to each. When completed, they were rather heavy; and packing them out to the fenced-in water hole taxed the strength of the rangers. Finally they were set and baited to suit Eburne, and he repaired to his hiding place above the spring.

The crudely reconstructed traps did not look very enticing; however, they were made of old lumber and had nothing conspicuous about them. Thad had not the slightest doubt about deer going into them to nibble at the hay.

On this day the deer appeared slow in coming, and Thad grew tired of waiting. At long last, however, a whole troop filed across the meadow and entered the corral. Thad's position was such that he did not have a good view of the traps, and he crawled to a more advantageous, though less comfortable, place. The bucks were plainly curious about the traps, but the does and fawns gave them a wide berth. Eburne's instruction had been to make a speciality of the latter. Young bucks would be acceptable, but the tough old stags were not wanted.

It turned out that the desirable deer were not likely to be captured in this sort of trap. The older, bolder bucks, however, plainly showed they were going after that hay. Eburne espied one, presently, warily enter the trap. He waited, but nothing happened. If the buck was pulling on the hay, which Eburne doubted, it certainly did not spring the trap door. The failure of the trap to spring nonplused the ranger. At the same time he was pleased to see the other deer grouped around the trap which contained the buck. The fawns were especially amusing. They imitated the actions of their mothers, yet they seemed to have a good many ideas of their own as they flipped their short tails and kicked out with their hind legs.

There were probably twenty-five deer in this group, and their excitement over the buck in the trap seemed to make them forget why they had come to the spring. They forgot to drink or to exercise their usual caution.

Suddenly a crack and a bang sounded from the second trap, which Eburne could not see very well from where he sat. This was followed by a clattering and scraping, mixed with solid thumps. It was obvious that a buck had sprung the door of the trap.

Eburne was rising to get a better view when a crashing sound from the first trap warned him to expect violent action in that corner. The box trap rocked; and then, right out of the top of this eight-foot pen shot a big buck deer. Thad yelled with delight to see that magnificent leap. "Good boy!" he shouted.

The deer was unhurt but pretty badly scared. He

bounded straight against the wire fence, staggered back, then, recovering himself, ran with prodigious leaps down into the meadow, followed by the whole troop, They halted at the edge of the forest to look back. Then one by one they trotted out of sight into the brown and green forest.

Meanwhile the trapped buck in the box was making a battering ram of himself. He could not break out, however, or scale the side of the trap. Eburne ran toward the spring, yelling for his partner Blakener to come. It did not take more than a glance to see that the deer had injured himself. Blood dripped from his mouth. Eburne was afraid the jaw was broken. But the deer would not stand still long enough for Eburne to make closer observations. As he stood there, Blakener came running from the cabin.

"Say, Blake, we've got one—a big buck," shouted Thad. "He sure raised the dickens. There was another buck got in the other trap. For some reason the door didn't work at first. Maybe he didn't pull on the hay. But when he did spring the trap—wow, he leaped right out of the box!"

"Stop your—kiddin'," panted Blakener.

"Honest. Look, see the trap door down—the hay pulled off the wire."

"By golly—" exclaimed Blakener, peering into the trap. Then he was interrupted by a terrific commotion in the other box. The captured buck had begun to thrash and crash around again.

"He'll kill himself. I knew this would happen," declared Eburne in distress. "We'll let him out into our pen."

Suiting action to word, Eburne lifted the slide door at the back of the trap. They had set the trap against an opening of appropriate size in the fence. The buck rushed out blindly, colliding with the wire of this small round pen, bounced back, and then began to circle. Eburne closed the slide door in the trap. They now had the buck captive, but in quarters where he could see and move. Thad had built this little side pen for the does and fawns he hoped to catch. It was soon evident that the buck would not further injure himself. Eburne feared, however, that serious harm already had been done. The buck limped; he had skinned his knees and breast; his lower jaw hung down, dripping with blood.

"Bad hurt," said Blakener regretfully. "What'll we do? Let him go?"

"No. Not unless he kicks up more fuss," replied Eburne. "I'm afraid he's done for. We'll hold him a while, anyway."

"How about the traps?" queried Blakener.

"I'm afraid they won't do," replied the ranger. "Certainly not for big, strong deer. They'd be fine for fawns. But the foxy little things wouldn't go in. One out of a hundred might, but that would not make this kind of trap of any use to us. We'll try my pen trap idea."

On the other side of the corral Thad had constructed another small wire enclosure with a trap gate. There was water inside. A board pen, ten by twenty feet, had been built alongside this, into which deer could be quickly driven after they were captured. By shutting off access to the spring in the larger corral Eburne felt confident that even does and fawns might be induced to seek the water in the small pen.

While the rangers were talking over the advisability of trying this trap on the next herd of deer, a motorcar came humming out of the forest and halted before the cabin. The discordant honk of a horn disturbed the forest stillness. It frightened the captured buck into renewed frantic efforts to escape.

"Blake, there are some of your tourist friends," said Eburne banteringly. "I think I see a lady with red hair."

"Humph! So you do," replied Blakener. "Well, I don't see that you have anythin' on me. The fame of my sourdough biscuits has penetrated to the outside world, an' also your fame as the ranger who loves deer. Strikes me you get off easier than I."

"Yes, when you have to dispense biscuits and I merely sentiment," replied Thad, laughing.

Together they returned to the cabin. This time Eburne was rather agreeably surprised. The tourists turned out to be a family from Boston touring the West and sensibly and happily appreciative of the country and the rangers. The deer stalker was not a little thrilled to hear the well-remembered Yankee twang. The red-haired lady was an attractive girl, neither handsome nor plain, neither aristocratic nor common, and her appearance, talk and action stirred a strange regretful emotion in Eburne. He was almost sorry to see the pleasant family depart soon afterward.

"Well, they fooled us," ejaculated Blakener. "Didn't even want no biscuits!"

"I'm kind of ashamed of my remarks about tourists," confessed Eburne. "They were nice people. And the auburn-haired girl—"

"She took my eye all right," interrupted Blakener as his comrade hesitated. "Not too pretty! Not stuck on herself!—Thad, some day there'll be a girl; she'll ride up here to V. T. Park—an' you'll be done with rangerin' forever."

"Could be," rejoined Thad musingly.

"Some day, Thad, you'll have to choose between stalkin' deer and trailin' after another kind of dear. For your sake I hope it comes soon."

"Right now is a good time to change the subject," said Eburne and went out to watch his deer trap. He approached by way of the knoll above the spring and kept out of sight. A number of deer had come in, none of which appeared unduly excited by the sight of the captured buck in the side corral. Soon Thad ascertained that the buck was lying down. He espied also two other deer inside the opposite pen—a buck and a doe, of a size and age that he did not want to experiment with. It would have been an easy matter to pull the string arranged at hand for this purpose and thereby shut the trap gate. But he waited for these deer to go out and hoped others more suitable for capture would come in. He was, however, doomed to disappointment. The does and fawns were extremely cautious, and though they evidently were thirsty, they left without getting a drink. The ranger watched for two hours longer, during which time many deer came as far as the new trap he had erected around the water. Not many fawns, however, were included in the number; and it was the young deer that Eburne wanted to take. It occurred to him that some other watering place, where does and fawns were more plentiful, might yield better results.

Before sunset that day he had planned a more elaborate trap, on a large scale, which he intended to build after giving the present one another tryout. The ranger's new idea was to extend the fences clear beyond the meadow, taking in a hillside. These fences would be narrowed into a chute, with a gate attached that could be shut behind the deer. Then the animals could be separated by some means or trick he had not yet worked out, and the deer he wanted to keep could be let into a round corral with a very high fence. Here they could be fed and watered until tame enough to handle.

Next morning the ranger was not surprised to find the captured buck dead. It had a broken jaw and leg and many contusions. He dragged it to the cabin, removed the skin, and saved most of the meat. The autopsy failed to reveal the least sign of fat around its ribs. Though Eburne had expected that the matured deer might do themselves some serious injury when captured, the actual realization of this first tragedy depressed him as if it had come as a surprise.

Early that afternoon, out of a small bunch of deer coming in for water, a yearling doe and a tiny fawn ventured far enough into Eburne's pen to permit him to spring the trap gate and capture them. He was elated and at once ran down to the fence. The other deer beat a precipitous retreat.

Eburne found the doe in better condition than most of the deer he had seen. It was badly frightened, yet ran round the pen instead of butting into the fence. The fawn was rather unsteady on its legs, either from weakness or extreme youth. It was red, fuzzy, with white spots, and the prettiest little animal Thad had ever seen. But for the antics of the doe, the fawn might not have been especially wild. At any rate, Thad had no difficulty in catching it and he packed it in his arms up to the cabin. Blakener was delighted. The two rangers had rescued and saved many a motherless lamb, and they were pretty sure this was an orphan fawn. Whether it liked milk or not was of little concern to them; they fed it by force. And when Eburne at last set it down on the floor, it did not make any wild efforts to escape. It seemed bewildered rather than frightened.

"You poor forlorn little thing," said Eburne compassionately.

"Thad, let him stay right in here," suggested Blakener. "He'll soon get tame. Why he's so young he's shaky on his legs—What'll we call him?"

"Say, Blake, you're as softhearted as I am," declared Eburne with a grin. "We forget we're capturing deer for our superiors to ship and sell somewhere. That reminds me, I've got a yearling doe out there in the trap. Let's go out and see if we can move her into the large pen. I believe if we open the gates she'll go out of one pen and into the other."

But the rangers found further proof of their meager knowledge of deer. The doe would not drive. Instead she ran so frantically and plunged into the fence so violently that they were forced to abandon the attempt. They left the gate open, but still the doe did not come out. Eburne concluded that she had hurt herself.

"Let's get out of sight," he suggested to Blakener.

"It's pretty discouragin'," admitted Blakener as they climbed the knoll to conceal themselves. "These wild deer can't be herded or trapped or driven."

"Seems so," agreed Eburne. "But I'm not satisfied yet that we can't catch them. We may hit on just the right way."

"But if out of a dozen or so deer we trap only one isn't bad hurt—that won't be a success."

"In any event it's far from humane. However, nothing

was said about that. We've orders to trap deer alive for shipment out of the preserve ... Hello! There goes our doe. She limps, she's going on three legs."

The rangers watched the sleek, graceful form hobble down the aisle into the open meadow and out among other deer working in for water. Her advent occasioned a halt. The deer took a long time to come in. Blakener went back to the cabin while Eburne kept to his post. Before time to quit arrived he might have pulled the trap gate on several deer, but they appeared to be of a size and age that he did not want. At dusk he gave up for the day and trudged wearily back to camp.

When Thad entered the big room of the cabin, it was bright with light from fire and lamp. As he strode in, he espied the little captive fawn edging behind a chair. The ranger halted. The fawn peeped out, with long ears erect and large dark eyes shining slowly drew its head back out of sight, and then very slyly peeped out again. The action captivated Eburne.

"Hey, your name's Bopeep," he called cheerily. When he moved again, the fawn darted to a far and dark corner of the room.

Blakener appeared in the kitchen doorway. "Thad, she's sure goin' to be a pet. Just before you came in I seen her standin' right here in the door. Big, gentle, soft eyes, like a woman's! It got me somehow. Hang this deer trappin'. Well, she stood here till I moved."

"Ahuh!" replied Thad, "you're figuring about the same as I, Blake."

"An' how's that?"

"Well, if Bopeep peeps at me any more as she just did, she's one fawn that'll never be shipped."

"You said a lot," replied Blakener soberly. "Come in here, an' I'll bet she peeps at you inside of five minutes."

Eburne complied with a laugh and thought he had divined why his partner was late in getting supper. While he washed his hands and face and then stood up to wipe them dry, Blakener remained stock-still, his hands white with flour, and an expression of infantile pleasure on his face.

"What'd I tell you?" he whispered dramatically.

Then Thad espied Bopeep almost on the threshold. What wonderful dark, mournful, eloquent eyes! They drew a pang from the ranger's heart. The fawn was exquisitely timid and shy, yet scarcely frightened.

"What do you know about that?" whispered Blakener. "Lookin' for her mother. Now ain't that cute?"

During mealtime and for an hour after, Bopeep occupied most of the rangers' attention. They decided to let her stay in the cabin. It seemed to Eburne that this dark-eyed little fawn somehow brought out the loneliness of their lives. Blakener was not only amusing but pathetic. Thad divined in this simple reaction the fact that they both needed something to love. It was melancholy realization and lingered long with him while he lay on the floor in his blankets, watching the flickering shadows of the dying fire. Outside the wind rose and soughed through the pines.

Next morning Eburne wrote letters to officers of the forest service, telling of the difficulties of deer-trapping and that he did not believe the plan would ever be practical or successful or humane. And if he was to continue his experiments, he should have a truckload of wire and lumber sent in at once. These letters were to be given to the first tourists who passed that way.

Eburne entered more earnestly into the business of trapping deer. He was convinced that the experiment would prove a failure, but he felt duty bound to do his best. That day resulted in several captures, only one of which appeared to be of any value. This was a yearling buck, which by dint of much effort and patience Thad finally got into the large corral.

Darkness had set in when he returned to the cabin. Blakener informed him that the important letters had gone to Kanab; also that Bopeep had shown unmistakable signs of becoming tame. Eburne was delighted and thought it made up a little for the unsatisfactory day. He was immensely curious to find out if these little fawns could be caught and tamed in sufficient numbers and to an extent that would warrant the labor and the sacrifice of other deer.

The following afternoon proved to be one of those times when more deer than usual entered the park. Not all of these came to water, but by midafternoon Eburne was sure several hundred deer had passed through the lane and out the corral gate. He had a number of chances to spring the trap gate, but he chose to let them go.

Then just before sunset a doe and a fawn unsuspectingly entered the trap. Eburne pulled the string that dropped the gate. He was congratulating himself on an easy capture when the doe became wild to escape and plunged around the enclosure. He concluded to remain where he was until she had quieted down. Presently, after a crashing thud into the fence, she did become quiet. Thad could not see very well. He waited a little while. Then, as he did not see any movement of gray forms or hear any sounds, he hurried down to the corral.

The doe was lying on the ground motionless, and the little fawn was standing beside her, shaking and bewildered. The ranger went inside. Examination proved that the doe had broken her neck. The accident shocked Thad more than any of the other tragedies, probably on account of the forlorn little fawn. He had no difficulty in catching it in his arms and at once strode off toward the cabin.

"It's a little buck," said Eburne to Blakener. "We'll call him Bo." Blakener was delighted with the new addition to the household, yet when he heard the particulars of the capture, he regretted the necessity of this work. The little buck was slightly larger than Bopeep, but not so brightly spotted. He was very thin and poorly nourished. "His mother was in the poorest condition of any deer I've seen," said Eburne. "We can't even use the meat. No wonder her fawn is thin. Let's feed him."

The two rangers had to use force. Blakener held Bo

between his knees and opened his mouth while Eburne poured milk down his throat. Bo squirmed and choked, but he had to swallow. Bopeep stood close by, tremendously interested in this procedure. When he was released, to stagger in terror away from his captors, she followed him and stayed close to him.

"He'll tame easier because of Bopeep," said Eburne. "Well, Blake, you look after our menagerie while I go back to the rotten job."

By the time another week had passed, many things had happened. Eburne was a sadder and wiser man. Out of four captured deer, three had died of injury or grief and one had shown some light indication of recovering. Another fawn had been added to keep company with Bo and Bopeep.

The matter of caring for the fawns was something entirely different. The rangers liked it immensely. Bopeep, especially, became lovable and as tame and playful as a kitten. Bo followed Blakener about the cabin as if he were his mother. And the third fawn was responding rapidly at least to kindness, if not to the kind of nourishment given him. In a few days more he became a pet like his comrades, but he did not thrive. And he died from no cause that the rangers could discover.

Bo and Bopeep grew to be such pets that they were permitted to go outdoors and follow the rangers around. One day Bo disappeared. Blakener, who was alone at the cabin when this happened, hurriedly searched all over the park, but in vain. Upon Eburne's return the two rangers decided that Bo had not become lost but had run off. They reluctantly gave up the search. On the morning of the third day, however, he came home and quite blithely pattered upon the porch and into the cabin, to the infinite amazement and pleasure of the rangers.

"Oho, you came back!" ejaculated Eburne. "Starved, hey? Lost all that fat we put on you?"

Bo manifested satisfaction over his return to the cabin

and the companionship of Bopeep, but he did not appear to be hungry. This worried Eburne, who remarked to his comrade that these little wild creatures were extremely delicate and hard to understand. That evening Bo drank heartily of cold water, behind the rangers' backs, as it were; and the overindulgence killed him.

This was a blow to the rangers. It absolutely convinced Eburne of the almost impossible task of saving any number of fawns, even if they could be secured. He wrote and dispatched a detailed report of all that had happened and his reluctance to go on with this deer-trapping work.

Beautiful summer weather had come, and every day more motoring tourists visited V.T. Park. Blakener resigned himself more or less gracefully to the inevitable, but Thad hated the sound and sight and smell of automobiles. Most of the tourists were agreeable and diverting, pleasant to meet, but he would rather have avoided them.

"Say, Thad, if I was you I'd go to Kanab an' lay that proposition of McKay's before the supervisors," suggested Blakener. "You've got a good excuse. That wire and lumber you ordered hasn't come. Reckon you can find out a lot of thing interestin' for us."

"Blake, it's a good hunch. I'll go," declared Eburne. "Take good care of Bopeep while I'm gone. I'll find out when that investigating committee is due. And about this plan for opening the forest to the hunters. If the time proves right I'll submit McKay's proposition to the authorities. And don't you think I won't look into the Settlemire-Dyott deal, whatever it is."

"Fine and dandy," replied his partner. "Reckon you'll be gone a week or so. It's gettin' on into June now, Thad. Soon you'll be leavin' for your summer station at Big Spruce."

"Yes, unless I get fired—which is altogether possible," rejoined Eburne. "Believe me, Blake, I'm going to let my hair down with these officers."

"Huh! It won't do no good," growled Blakener.

*N*IGHT had fallen when the Santa Fe train that was bearing Patricia Edgerton to a new and unknown future crossed the New Mexico state line into Arizona. The magic name Arizona dispelled for the first time on this long journey the gloom that had filled her mind. From childhood that name had been alluring. But now, when at last she had entered the region of enchanting colors and desert grandeur, she could not see anything for the mantle of darkness. Wearily then she sought illusive sleep. But she lay tossing in her berth until far into the night. She awoke to find the sun already high in the sky.

The train appeared to be straining and winding a grade. Patricia could hear the panting of the engine. When she looked out she saw rough gray and green hills, steep at the base, with a wide stratum of yellow rock. In the narrow valley through which the train was winding, rugged pine trees, strange to her, grew wide apart and spread gnarled branches over the thin soil.

She had taken this side trip to visit the Grand Canyon

for no other reason than that the ticket agent had suggested it. All she had wanted was to leave New York. To go and keep on going had been her motive, without regard to what she might see. Passengers on the train talked volubly and enthusiastically about the Grand Canyon. To them, manifestly, the sight of this place would be a long-awaited event. Several mild-faced old ladies had tried to engage Patricia in conversation. She wondered at their eagerness and envied them their age and the hearty enthusiasm with which they seemed to enjoy travel and each new experience.

After endless twistings and turnings the train arrived at Grand Canyon station. The building appeared to be set down in a pine forest. As Patricia descended from the Pullman and began pointing out her many pieces of luggage, she was struck by the wonderful keenness of the atmosphere and the warm fragrance of the thin air. It seemed dry and sweet with a piney tang.

She followed the grinning, uniformed bellboys up a wide wooden stairway, not at all steep, yet she soon found herself out of breath. She imagined the long train ride had exhausted her: then she was forced to deny the thought, as she was young and in perfect health. It had been strife and agony of mind which had taxed her strength.

At the top of the stairway the Hotel El Tovar appeared, a long, low, rambling structure, built of logs, yet pleasing to the eye and giving every indication of comfort. Broad roads and bridle paths led away from it, winding among the pines. From the porch she espied an odd flat-topped structure, it walls built of red stone, from which protruded rough poles. The thing had a primitive look, unmistakably Indian.

The sun shone intensely bright, she thought, for a May morning, and the sky appeared unusually blue and wide. As she crossed the broad hotel porch she was able to see beyond the line of shrubbery to where apparently the level ground ended abruptly. Beyond extended what seemed to be a pink and mauve and blue void. This, of course, must be the Grand Canyon. This must be the wonder of the world which people came so many miles to see. Abruptly she turned to follow the bellboys through the wide door.

Patricia found the interior of the El Tovar very pleasing to the eye, unconventional and western, with comfort the dominant note. The big stone fireplace with its smoldering red fire particularly appealed to her. As she took the pen from the clerk she found her fingers quite cold and stiff. After a moment's hesitation she suddenly remembered that she did not intend to use her surname and she registered under her middle name, signing Miss P. Clay, New York.

A room at the end of a long corridor on the second floor was assigned her, and from it she could see far out over an undulating green forest to dim, dark mountains on the horizon. Immediately she liked this room and view. The distant horizon awakened a vague sensation in her breast—something she had never felt before. Patricia gazed across the green distance and felt as lost as if she were alone in a gray-green world. How different from the East! Never before, except on the ocean, had she felt such a sense of illimitable space. She turned to unpack one of her bags when a tap sounded on her door. Upon opening it Patricia was confronted by a young woman, rather handsome in a dark, intense way, full-bodied and red-lipped.

"I'm Miss Hilton," she announced. "I've charge of the trail trips. Your train was late. If you are going down either the Bright Angel or Hermit trail you must hurry to get breakfast."

"Thank you," replied Patricia, aware of the woman's sharp, curious glance roving over her. "I'll make inquiry later if I wish to take any trips."

As she closed the door Patricia found herself wondering why hotel people chose to employ hawk-eyed women to attend to their guests. This young woman made her conscious of her appearance, or more than that—of herself. Another glance into the mirror acquainted Patricia with the fact that her face was pale and sad. Dark shadows lay under her eyes. "Once I was proud of my good looks," she mused as a wave of self-pity flooded over her. "Now I wish I were homely and old...Ah! I suppose I'll be that soon enough."

She went in to breakfast. The dining room was half-octagonal in shape, bright and cheerful, with polished floor and white tables. The waitresses were clad in white. Patricia was given a seat beside a window through which the rich late morning sunlight poured. Evidently most of the hotel guests already had had breakfast, for there were only a scattered few at the tables. Patricia heard one woman exclaiming about the Canyon, and a man, manifestly an Englishman, responded languidly, "Jolly fine hole in the ground!"

Patricia's appetite was like her thoughts, listless. She did not care whether she ate or not, and her mind seemed dully at tension.

After breakfast, Patricia went into the lobby and stood before the fire. Groups of people, some in riding costumes, others in blue jeans, were hurrying about, talking excitedly of prospective trips. Patricia believed she would not want to stay long at the El Tovar. Could she find any place where she would want to stay? She had asked herself a thousand questions since leaving New York. None had been answered; no decisions had been made. She was adrift. She realized only one thing—that she wished to be alone, where she would see no one and where no one would see her, for a long, long time. Yet even while she longed for solitude and escape, she realized that they were unattainable. One could not escape from people any more than from oneself. Wherever she went women would be curious about her, men would approach her, and she must inevitably be influenced by her surroundings. This unique hotel where she had come to be away from all the people she knew had been built on this once inaccessible spot because from it one could look down a mile deep to where a river ran. It did not rouse even a languid enthusiasm in Patricia; nevertheless she went out to look at it.

From the hotel porch she saw a stone parapet, which, she judged, marked the rim of the Canyon. Motionless figures of men and women, like statues, stood apart from one another along this stone wall. Their heads were bent and their postures indicated the awe and wonderment that had transfigured them.

Patricia walked forward, yet toward a point that would separate her from these absorbed watchers. As she approached the canyon rim, she could see beyond the parapet into the blue distance to where a black fringed line rose out of what appeared to be a belt of gold. Certainly that distant band of black and gold could not have anything to do with the Canyon!

A wind, cool as ice and strangely pungent, swooped up out of the void and tore at her hair. Patricia was temporarily blinded; and she had reached the parapet to lean her knees against it before she had a chance for one glimpse at the Canyon. She had had no preparation for the sight that was to meet her eye.

She put back her thick hair from her eyes and looked down. For a moment she was stunned. But for the parapet against which she leaned, she would have been drawn by some irresistible force into the awful vastness below. She wanted to cry out in wonderment over this gigantic spectacle, but she had been struck mute, powerless to move, powerless to feel. Was this a chasm of dreams? Pictures were flat surfaces; descriptions were dead things—they had not prepared her for this staggering phenomenon.

Patricia stood there for endless moments, slowly coming out of her stupefaction, slowly awakening to reality. The appalling power of the human eye, the infinite possession-taking sight, had never before been revealed to her. It was as if some stupendous monster, alive, merciless with age-old knowledge, had lain in ambush for her, suddenly to strip bare the truth of her heart, the love of beauty, of life, of love, of mystery, of the physical in her and the spiritual that glorified it. This charm of red and black and purple, with its blank impendency, its unintelligible depths and terrors, resembled the gulf of her soul, into which she had now her first glimpse.

Patricia almost fell upon her knees. A woman accosted her, which made her realize that she was not a sole spectator there. Not that she cared! But habit of life reasserted itself, and while she had the strength left she wrenched her gaze from the Canyon and turned away.

As she closed the door of her room and locked it, she had a strange thought that she was another person. It was absurd but would not yield to reason. The mirror showed Patricia Edgerton, whiter, darker of eye, exalted by emotion, perhaps, yet the same woman. It was the crowding of new thoughts behind the level brow, behind the inscrutable eyes, that seemed to make her different. She paced the room; she sat in the deep chair to face the undulating green forest; and at last she flung herself on the couch to cover her eyes: "I didn't know this was in me!" she whispered. "What is it that has happened?"

Scorn, ridicule paled before her consciousness. She could not accept as explanation that after months of ennui and disgust with her life in the East, after a wild and reckless act of sacrifice, and then days of morbid gloom, the sight of the Grand Canyon had broken her dark mood and kindled a white fire of emotion in her soul. True, this had actually happened, but it did not tell why. She was utterly amazed at herself. The transport, or whatever had happened within her, had been too exquisite, too enrapturing, too tremendous to be ephemeral.

Like so many of her class she had drifted away from the Church.

"I'm modern, materialistic, pagan," she whispered. "Could this—this amazement, joy, pain be that, in the Canyon, I caught a glimpse of God?"

Patricia hoped this might be true, but she doubted it. Yet every intelligent effort to understand herself, to master and explain this inexplicable emotion, left the miracle she had experienced more wonderful, bigger, more stable and far-reaching.

"Oh, I was sick of it all," she thought. "I had no real home. I seemed alone in the midst of luxury, idleness, uselessness, decadence. If I could have married . . . But that rich, childless, middle-class crowd, bah!—I grew to hate it. Drinking men who wanted me to drink—so they could paw me. I couldn't do it. I couldn't stand it. . . . Then those few men—real men I did like—they thought only of money, of power. They never heard the pathetic little cry of my soul . . . And the women—my friends, especially the girl-wife for whom I sacrificed my name—dancing, smoking, flirting, half-naked painted dolls . . . Oh! I welcomed the chance to flee from it all. But I thought life was over for me. I saw no future, no home, no husband, no love, no children. I saw only drifting, wandering from place to place. I saw no work, no good in myself or in anybody. I had given up. For me the times were out of joint. I abandoned my class. I despised the greedy, vile, war-worn, un-Christian world that I came in contact with. The dreams of girlhood were all dead and buried. I was twenty-four years old and sick of what I thought was life."

So she pondered, as thoughts and memories she had tried to forget now surged through her mind, released by the miracle of the Canyon.

"It seems I'm out west," her thoughts went on. "I've stood on the rim of the Grand Canyon. That is nothing. Places are nothing. Yet—what is it that has come over me? It is simple enough. There are marvelous things in nature—and in my heart—that I never dreamed of."

"Oh, I hope it lasts," she murmured after a while. "It must last. I will make it . . . I must do something . . . I feel on the threshold of a new life. It terrifies me with hope, with joy, with . . . Oh! What can I do? . . ."

Presently she moved to the desk in her room. She began to write swiftly, with a sure pen:

Dearest Alice,

I did not mean to write to you, but something has happened that makes it imperative.

When I saw this glorious canyon it seemed I faced my soul. I thought it was dead. Something lifted a burden from my mind. It is impossible for me now to leave you in distress of mind—to permit you to imagine longer that I chose ostracism and exile solely on your account. I meant to let you suffer under that belief. It was ignoble and morbid of me.

Oh, I'm so glad to tell you. Your husband will never know. It is utterly impossible, so strange were the circumstances. I dare to write you this because I know he went abroad believing it was me he caught instead of you.

But though my sacrifice was made for love of you—impulsive and heedless—all the time it must have been an unconscious selfishness. I had come to hate our set—that idle, luxurious, childless, dancing, drinking crowd. I was a part of it, yes, but not of it. You *know*. I didn't fit because in my heart, deeply buried, there was ever strife and antagonism. I wasn't big enough to cut loose and find myself—a man, children, work—but nevertheless I rebelled more and more until my heart sickened in my breast.

Allie, I welcomed that chance to escape, though I did not realize it on the impulse. You know what little home life I had—my mother dead, my father a clubman. He will not care. No one will care deeply, not even you. I have money, and no ties. I shall travel under my middle name, Clay. Don't grieve over me. It was a release. If only I could tell you . . . ! It seems ungracious for me to repudiate my friends, to disown my people, to abandon my home. That great, teeming, changing, hideous New York! It has changed since the war. The East has changed. Oh, I am not a hopeless cynic. I know there are good women and fine men back there. But as I had neither goodness nor nobility, none of them ever sought me out.

Strange—I saw none of the West on my way out. I lay blind, sick, clamped in my seat. Strange that my first sight of the West embraced this Grand Canyon of Arizona. It struck me like lightning. I cannot tell you what I saw. Just a rent in the earth. But such a rent and such an earth!

You will not understand me, Allie, yet you must believe. What does it matter *what* reached my soul and burned away my bitter doubt of self? It has happened. I have not one regret. I owe you infinitely more than you owe me. Yet I impose upon you a solemn obligation, which, if you have any womanhood left, you will keep forever. Let that be your last wild fling!

Patricia.

Just as swiftly as she had written, Patricia sealed and stamped the letter and went out to the desk to mail it. Her hand shook, her eyes dimmed, her ears did not clearly record what someone said to her. The hour had been crucial, the last moment one of exceeding strain. What had she irrevocably turned her back upon? Why had that letter been the means to an end? She could not say then, yet she felt that it meant her freedom. Hurrying back to her room, she flung herself upon the bed and wept as she had never wept before in all her life.

The paroxysm gradually subsided, and at length she turned on the pillow and wiped her tear-wet face and lay there spent and tremulous, motionless for many moments. She imagined she saw the retreat of a pale, deformed, and restless soul, beaten into subjection for all time. She felt the blood beat in her veins as if renewed, vivified by some magic current, clarified of taint and fever and poison.

"I shall stay here for a while," she mused, and the decision gave her unaccountable joy. She rose from the bed and gazed at her trunks and bags. Suddenly they seemed to contain useless burdens, endless monuments to her fashionable life, her craving for beautiful garments. Leisurely she unpacked some of them, divided between a melancholy retrospection and a sense of gladness that this unaccustomed task was to be hers from now on and that in this instance it meant she was settled here for days, weeks—as long as she liked.

In the afternoon Patricia went out to take her second look at the Canyon. She approached the rim as if it were an altar. She looked. The great gap seemed to yawn at her. Lights, shadows, distances of the morning had now vanished. The canyon was filled with a smoky haze, through which the millions of red lines and surfaces shone with softened accents.

Tourists were there on the rim, talking gaily, inventing banal witticisms about the Canyon, photographing each other in attitudes singularly out of harmony with the scene. The Grand Canyon of Arizona was but a place to them, another, and perhaps the greatest, addition to their accumulated sights.

Patricia passed them by. She could not stand there in awe, in rapture, in immeasurable gratitude, while carefree and shallow people mocked the thing she revered. A trail wound along the rim, soon leading Patricia away from the vicinity of the hotel. She followed it, now and then passing a woman on a bench or a man sitting on one of the rocky points. They, too, seemed to have sought seclusion. They did not glance at Patricia as she passed by. She wondered at them and thought she understood. Here was a shrine for the lonely soul, where one could face its agony or revel in its exaltation. Every human being must be powerfully affected in the presence of this spectacle. Perhaps the ignorant and the callous were excited to loquaciousness and self-consciousness by its majesty.

The trail zigzagged in and out of the fragrant cedar forest, sometimes on the rim, and again back out of sight of the blue abyss. The rim appeared to be notched like a saw, with little and deep cuts, and lengthy yellow points of rock running out alternating with tiny abutments and promontories. But everywhere the drop was perpendicular, a fact Patricia seemed to sense rather than see. She was aware of the void; it dominated every step, yet she did not directly look. Instead she feasted her eyes on unfamiliar green growths and the gray patches under the cedars and lavender-colored berries on thick bushy trees she could not name. She recognized her first cactus and had the proof of it by sticking her finger on a thorn. She saw flowers, too, a carmine blossom like a ragged paintbrush, and pale lilac-hued flowers, growing in close round patches, that smiled modestly out of the somber gray soil.

At length the trail ended. Patricia went on, finding the brush thick and the ground rough. She had intended to make her way to a vast promontory which extended out over the canyon, but she found that after all this walking it seemed no closer. Indeed, it was miles distant, and so she had her first lesson in the rarified, deceiving atmosphere. Moreover, to her surprise and dismay she suddenly found herself quite exhausted. She had walked briskly, as was her pleasure always, only to realize that her breathing had become difficult. Her heart labored under an oppression and she discovered that her nose was bleeding slightly.

After resting, she threaded her way through gnarled, spike-branched cedars, out to a point which jutted into the canyon. It was scarcely twenty feet wide, and the end was naked yellow rock, cracked and splintered, completely bare of foliage. Patricia put a hand on her breast. How her heart was pounding. The point she had chosen extended for some distance out from the main rim, and the approach to it was thick with brush and cedars. She was alone in solitude and silence such as she had never known in all her life before.

A cedar tree grew back a few yards from the bare rock of the canyon rim. It was small, darkly green, with low-branched spreading foliage. The ground under it was brown, clean, odorous, very inviting. Presently she would sit there, to look and watch and feel for hours, and then she would come back. This spot would be her sanctuary.

"Am I in my right mind?" she mused. "Do I intend to throw myself over this precipice? ... A few steps! It would be so easy. No one would ever know what had become of me. I am not afraid."

She stepped bravely to the very brink. The golden sunlit depths gave place to blue, and these to purple. Appalling bottomless abyss! Patricia gazed down, down, down. She was fascinated. But she had no longing to destroy herself. If only a short time ago life had seemed to be a thing of complete indifference to her, now it seemed to her something to cherish and to make over. She found herself trembling, but not from fear. The thing that shook her nerve was that here, on the very rim of one of nature's great miracles, she had become the master of her own destiny.

Then she sought the restful seat under the cedar and abandoned herself to her senses. It was as if she had all of life to absorb something forever beautiful, growing, illusive, and infinite.

The sky was such a blue as she had never seen, not sea-blue or azure-blue, but a blue of marvelous deep transparency, as if it were a penetrable cloud canopy through which she could see. Her eyes seemed to be able to penetrate it, but beyond there was only more blue, the endless and immeasurable heavens.

Almost as unfathomable and mysterious as the blue sky were the depths of the canyon. She could distinguish the canyon floor, pale bronze through a purple veil, yet it was as evanescent as the heavens.

The Grand Canyon was an appalling rent, and not the least of its greatness lay in the ageless slopes of multihued rock that revealed the structure of the earth crust. Up the far slopes across the gulf, dark shadows were creeping, encroaching upon the red, swallowing the chrome cliffs. The westering sun, sinking behind the peaks and domes and turrets, and the rim, cast these mystic shadows. The purple depths turned to twilight gray. Far above and across the canyon, in the sunset light, blazed a golden belt with its black fringe silhouetted against the sky. Color and light and shadow changed and moved imperceptibly.

Patricia listened for some sound to break the unearthly silence. At first it seemed as though there were no sound. The place was dead with the silence of the infinite. The canyon represented a wearing of rock by the action of water. Slower than an infinitude of time, and as silent! Yet, by straining her ears, she was able to distinguish sounds. Her heart beat, quick, soft, muffled. Then she heard a very low, very faint roar, far away and deep down like that of a train in the distance. That was the Colorado River at the bottom of the canyon. Then there was an accompanying moan of the wind through the cedars, almost imperceptible. A bird, purple and black in hue, pitched with soft swish of wings down over the rim; and a tiny squirrel, gray as the rocks, dislodged little pebbles that rustled and rattled. So there were actual sounds, possible to hear; yet to Patricia these only accentuated the silence and loneliness.

The Canyon had its peculiar fragrance that revealed itself intangibly to Patricia's sensitive nostrils. She was familiar with the evergreen odor of the Adirondacks, the smell of smoke of burning leaves in autumn, both of which were recalled to memory here. But this canyon fragrance was different. She gathered a handful of the dry cedar needles and then stripped some of the green foliage, and again she crushed sprigs of the pale gray sage growing close by. These lent something to the canyon fragrance, but only a part. How sweet, new, exhilarating, and marvelously dry! That dryness was its outstanding feature. Patricia remembered then that this country was Arizona desert.

The sun sank low, losing its white fire. Now there came a startling and marked change in the canyon. Patricia sat up quickly, suddenly alive to the imminence of a glorious transfiguration. Far below, shadows and shrouds obscured the walls, but now a moving mantle above the smoky haze cleared away under the dying fire of the setting sun. She saw leagues and leagues of the upper walls, a thousand million facets of chiseled rock, reflecting the deep red and rich gold of sunset. It was too beautiful for the eastern girl to bear, too glorious for her gaze. She closed her eyes. As she opened them again, the glory already was fading and dying. The sun slipped out of sight, and the canyon yawned dull red and drab, now appearing aloof and cold.

Patricia shivered, suddenly aware of the chill in the air. She must hurry so that she would not be caught out along the lonely rim after dark.

Once on the trail, she set out with swinging stride, buoyant and eager, thrilled yet anxious. Soon she found the exertion affected her like climbing a steep hill. It slowed her pace.

Meanwhile the shadowy mantle in the canyon seemed to rise to meet the dusk creeping under the cedars. A cool wind brushed through the cedars. The trail was deserted. At last the lights of the hotel gleamed out of the gathering darkness. Patricia found herself relieved at the sight of their friendly glow. She paused to catch her breath. She panted, her skin was wet and burning, her feet were heavy as lead, yet these sensations seemed good and strangely welcome.

She went on, at last to halt opposite the hotel and gaze at the Canyon. Now it was a black, windy void! It was full of night, mystery, terror. She hurried in to the lighted hotel.

CHAPTER
5

WHEN Patricia came to dress for dinner, she selected a gown from habit, without a thought of
the motive that always actuated her friends. But
her gowns were exquisite, and although she never approached any extreme in design or style, still they were
in the latest mode. The moment she entered the dining
room she was the recipient of flattering glances from tables
all over the room.

As she passed the table next to her own, she heard a
woman's whisper and then a girl's voice exclaiming in
delight in the voice of a girl. After she had seated herself
and given the waitress her order she casually glanced up
and around. The dining room was brilliantly lit and filled
with guests, presenting rather a social and conventional
atmosphere. She was surprised and more at her ease.

At the table near her were two women and a girl,
plainly dressed and undoubtedly westerners. The girl was
rather small of stature, though not slight, and probably
about eighteen. She was blond, with something attractive

about her strong, tanned face. She was staring hard at Patricia with big, frank, clear eyes, dark with excitement and admiration. She blushed guiltily, evidently believing she had been rude to stare. It amused the eastern girl. How unsophisticated and old-fashioned! Then Patricia made the astonishing discovery that the girl's hair was not bobbed, nor were her eyebrows plucked or her lips smeared with rouge. She tried to recall when she had seen a girl between fifteen and twenty whose face was not made up.

When the girl looked up again Patricia smiled at her. The response was instant—a smile of shy surprise that rendered her face sweet and pretty. Patricia decided that here was a western girl she would like to know.

After dinner she found the lobby full of guests and all the desirable chairs, especially those near the open fire, occupied. She strolled through the hall and then the picture room, fully enjoying the attention she was attracting. Casually she glanced over the groups of guests chatting together or moving about, until she espied the blond head of the girl she was searching for. Patricia approached and found her with her friends at the end of the long desk where Miss Hilton made arrangements with guests for the trail trips.

"Clara, I shore don't want Nelson to be our guide," drawled the girl in a low contralto voice, unmistakably southern and singularly charming to the ear.

"Now, Sue, I thought Nels was sweet on you and you'd like him as a guide," replied the woman with a hint of malice.

"Reckon you're wrong," retorted the girl. "Can't we go down with Tine Higgenbottom? He's a Flagstaff boy. My aunt's nervous about mules and trails. I know Tine. He'll take a special interest in us. Please do me a favor, Clara."

"Yes, I can arrange it, Sue," rejoined Miss Hilton, studying her book. "Higgenbottom. Leaves at eight forty-five. Down Bright Angel to Indian Gardens, you said. Here are your tickets."

"My niece was born on a horse," spoke up the aunt, addressing Miss Hilton. "But Mrs. Price an' me are not much on ridin'. We want safe, gentle horses."

"We use mules on the trails. They're perfectly safe, even for old ladies, which you two are far from being," replied Miss Hilton, smiling. "Don't worry. I've given you one of our best guides. And Sue knows every turn of the trails."

At this juncture Patricia stepped forward to confront the girl and said, "I beg your pardon. I was waiting to get a trail trip ticket from Miss Hilton and I heard the conversation. May I join your party?"

"Shore—we'd be glad to have you," was the girl's swift rejoinder. "Won't we, Auntie?"

"Indeed you're welcome," replied the woman, with practical interest. "I take it you're a tenderfoot from the East."

"Yes," said Patricia smiling. "This is my first trip west. I am Patricia Clay from New York."

"Well, we're glad to meet you. It's our first trip north, if not west. We're from Texas. This's my friend, Mrs. Price, an' this is my niece, Sue Warren. She's been two years at the normal school in Flagstaff."

"Auntie, you forgot to introduce yourself," spoke up Sue gaily. "She's my father's sister, Mary Warren."

"I'm very fortunate," replied Patricia as she acknowledged the several introductions. "It will be something to remember—a day with real western folks, especially when one of them is a Texas girl who was born on a horse."

"Do you want a ticket, Miss Clay?" interrupted Miss Hilton rather abruptly.

"Yes, thank you," replied Patricia, aware of a scrutiny not wholly pleasant. Presently, having secured the ticket, she turned to the eager girl. The two older women had moved away to permit other tourists access to the trip agent. Patricia did not need to be keen to divine that she had made a conquest of this young western girl, and it stirred a warmth of pleasure in her breast.

"May I not talk with you a little?" she inquired.

"You shore may," returned the girl gladly. "I'd be unhappy if you didn't. Let's find a place all by ourselves."

She quite proudly drew her new friend past the groups of curious guests to a vacant corner where they found chairs.

"Was I very rude, staring at you so at dinner?" she asked, with a soft flush suffusing her cheeks.

"I did not think so," returned Patricia. "In fact I was flattered. And I returned the compliment, didn't I?"

"Auntie saw you first, as you came in," went on Sue. "She said, 'Heah comes a movie queen.' But I knew you weren't. Movie actresses paint, and they look different."

"When I saw you I said to myself, 'There's a girl who isn't a flapper, and I want to meet her'—so we are even," said Patricia, laughing.

"No, we shore aren't," declared Sue with a blush. "But it's nice of you to say so. I'm so tickled that I persuaded Auntie to come heah for dinner. You see, we're staying at the Bright Angel Inn. It's cheaper there, but plenty comfortable. We could not afford to stay at the El Tovar."

"You'll be here at the Canyon for a few days, I hope," said Patricia.

"Tomorrow, anyway, and maybe another day—Sunday," returned Sue. "I must get back by Monday."

"You go to normal school at Flagstaff, I think your aunt said. Then you're studying to be a teacher?"

"Shore am, and it's no fun. I wish I could stay heah longer. One more week before summer vacation. I might come over then if—if you—"

"I would like that very much," returned Patricia. "I'm alone. The Canyon has me in its grip. I feel I'll stay—quite a while. It was really quite an accident that I came here. The West didn't mean anything to me. It was just a great wide unknown region where I could escape from New York. But this wonderful place is like a dream of an enchanted land. I know it'll do me good."

"You've been ill?" asked the girl solicitously, with her large clear eyes intent on the eastern girl's face. She was naive, warm-hearted; and her simplicity had a potent charm.

"Oh, no—at least not in body," replied Patricia.

Sue laid a kindly hand, strong and warm, upon Patricia's. The pupils of her eyes dilated, darkened with swift thought, with earnest compassion.

"You've had trouble," she whispered. "Lost someone you loved. . . . Death, I reckon."

"Why do you imagine that?" asked Patricia, curiously stirred.

"Your face is so pale. Your eyes are so dark and sad. . . . Oh, you're lovely, Miss Clay, but I—you—it was the sadness that caught me."

Patricia returned the pressure of that firm hand; and she averted her face slightly. "You are kind to a stranger," she murmured tremulously. "Yes, I have lost—a great deal—though not exactly by death. But today that loss has seemed a gain, as it sent me out to your West, to your wonderful canyon."

"If you're miserable, if your heart is broken—the Canyon. . . . Oh, how I wish Thad Eburne was here to tell you what the Canyon can do!"

"Thad Eburne! Who in the world is he?" queried Patricia in surprise.

"Excuse me, Miss Clay. I—I quite forgot myself in my earnestness. . . . But Thad Eburne is a ranger who lives across the Canyon. I've only met him twice, first in Flagstaff and then heah. I heard him talk about the Canyon to a— a—well, a friend of mine, Nelson Stackhouse. Nelson was a cowpuncher over on the Bar Z, and a wild bad boy if there ever was one. He drank, he gambled, he fought. And all the time he swore he was in love with me! . . . Well, he got into trouble and Thad Eburne helped him out of jail. It was then that I heard Thad talk about the Canyon. He persuaded Nels to take a job over heah."

Patricia was quick in turn to sense the pain and strife in the young girl's troubled heart.

"Well! Did the Canyon help your friend?" she inquired as the girl seemed to lose her train of thought.

"I'm shore bound to confess it did," replied Sue with effort.

"This ranger, Thad Eburne, what is he like?"

"Thad's a wonderful man. Built like one of these Arizona riders, only he's not as scrawny. He has a keen, fine, dark face, almost as brown as a Navajo's. And his eyes—well, I heard an old cowman say Eburne's eyes would make a dishonest man hate him and an honest woman love him. And shore that's so.... Reckon I might have liked Thad Eburne pretty well. But he never even noticed me. Called me child! And he's only about thirty. But he seems older. He's an eastern man, well educated, and hails from New England. You'd think he was western-born—until he speaks.... He's a deer stalker."

"You mean a hunter? Like the hero in Cooper's novel *The Deerslayer*?"

"No. He's a deer tracker, according to what Nels told me. He works for the forest service, an inspector of wild animals in the national parks. Clara Hilton, the trail clerk heah at the El Tovar, claims to know Eburne well. She says he's softhearted about deer. She made fun of him. I like him for that. Deer are such shy, wild critters."

Further conversation led to the subject of the town of Flagstaff, about which Sue waxed eloquent. She never walked into town but she espied at least one cowboy, and always there were Indians and horses.

"I'll teach school in Flag and live there, if I can coax my mother to come," went on Sue. "My Daddy died years ago. There's nothing for Mother in Texas save memories. But I'll go back if I can't get her to come heah.... Shore, Flag isn't much of a town, but the people are nice, and there are such wonderful places to go; San Francisco

Mountains, the Cliff Dwellings, Oak Creek Canyon, Montezuma's Well, Sunset Peak—the mountain of volcanic cinders, the Painted Desert, and more places than I've time to tell about."

"I shall visit Flagstaff," declared Patricia smilingly.

"Oh, that'll shore be fine!" exclaimed the girl, radiant. "But I want it to be when I'm out of school."

"We'll plan my little visit when you come again."

"Heah are my folks looking for me. I reckon I'll have to go," said Sue regretfully.

"I've enjoyed talking with you more than I can say," returned Patricia, rising and holding out her hand to the flushed and smiling girl.

"Thank you," she said shyly. "Shore it has been a red-letter day for me. Adios, Miss Clay—till tomorrow."

During the half hour longer that Patricia lingered in the lobby, part of which she spent before the open fire, Miss Hilton approached her twice, first to inquire if the eastern girl wanted to hire one of the company's riding habits, and secondly, if she might be interested in the Indian dances at the Hopi house. It dawned on her that these were but pretexts. Either the woman was eager to be seen talking with her, or she was openly attracted or intensely curious. She conceived an instant dislike for the woman, for which she rather reproved herself as being unreasonable. But the feeling was intuitive. Miss Hilton had an ingratiating manner, a ready and agreeable tongue, and she was handsome in a full-blooded way. Patricia had unusually acute receptive faculties, and she felt that Miss Hilton was jealous, calculating, inquisitive. She had nothing of the wholesomeness which characterized a girl like Sue Warren. Wherefore Patricia was polite, but brief, and did not respond to the woman's advances.

That night Patricia had a strange and distressing dream in which Miss Hilton figured largely as a vengeful nemesis. But when morning came Patricia could not recall it. There remained in her consciousness, however, an unpleasant aftertaste. While getting into her riding clothes, Patricia mediated.

"If you can't escape from people, you're doomed to love some and hate others. A few love you and the most hate you. Ruskin was right when he wrote so many people are like thorns. They sting you. Others are like stones that weigh you down. Still others are weeds.... Oh, I wonder what I am going to be.... No thorn or log—or weed! That I swear.... But out here in the West human life must be wider, broader, freer. I suppose I'm bound to meet people like Miss Hilton, even out here in this land with its scanty population. For that matter, Sue Warren would make up for a thousand Miss Hiltons. I am going to love that frank, sweet girl.... I'm curious about her bad cowboy Nels.... And that deer stalker she admires so much. I wonder if there *are* men like that?"

At eight-thirty Patricia asked the clerk to direct her to where she could find the trail party she was to accompany. Outside the white sunlight dazzled her. Again the cold, pure, pine-scented air affected her like wine. It was only a short walk to the corral which was her destination.

Patricia espied two parties, one on each side of the corral. The more distant one, consisting of ten or twelve men and women, all mounted on sturdy mules, seemed about ready to start. They presented a ludicrous appearance. The riders were little and big, fat and lean, all garbed in a motley assortment of riding clothes.

Approaching the corral, Patricia, instead of entering the gate, went up to the fence and looked over the top bar at the second group of tourists. A few were already mounted, and they looked excited, self-conscious, and warm. Then she espied Sue, wearing flannel shirt, red scarf, fringed gauntlets, chaps, boots, and spurs—all of which had the look and the set of long service.

Sue stood beside her aunt, who sat, looking completely helpless, on a mule. A bowlegged cowboy, also in chaps, was endeavoring to shorten or lengthen the stirrups. A spirited argument was in progress. It was interrupted by the advent of another cowboy, a tall, slim, keen-faced young fellow, well-muscled, lean-cheeked, and square-jawed, with eyes of sleepy blue. He sauntered over, his big spurs jingling, and pushed a huge sombrero onto the back of his head.

"Tine, my outfit's rarin' to go, but I forgot my cigarettes," he said, in a slow, cool voice.

"Say, Nels, I'm plumb tired bein' your tobacco store," complained the other, his hands going to his breast pocket. He was ruddy-faced and painfully homely.

"You smoke too much, Tine," replied the cowboy with a grin. "Doc Miller told me so an' that I was savin' your life."

"Ahuh!" grunted Tine, fumbling in his pocket. He appeared full of protest and derision. Yet there was an unconscious loyal resignation in his glance.

"Thanks, cowboy," acknowledged the other, accepting the proffered package. Then he doffed his sombrero to Sue.

"Howdy, Texas," he drawled, his sleepy eyes on her pretty face.

"Good mawnin', Mr. Stackhouse," replied the girl. She tilted her chin ever so little and eyed him coolly. But when presently she turned her shoulder to him, Patricia espied a tinge of red through the golden tan of her cheeks. It suited the easterner then to step briskly to the corral gate and approach the young people. Sue stared an instant, and then her face grew bright.

"Shore I didn't know you," she burst out. "Good mawnin'. I was just going to run in to fetch you."

Patricia greeted her and the older woman, then looked from the cowboys to Sue and back again.

"Miss Clay, this is our guide, Tine Higgenbottom," announced Sue, "and this—Mr. Nelson Stackhouse."

The cowboys doffed their sombreros, not ungallantly, and mumbled their acknowledgments.

"Heah's your mount," interposed Sue, drawing Patricia away. "Joker's his name. He's a character. He gets that name from his habit of stopping along the trail, at the edge of the worst precipices, to look down. Tine swears the mule does it to scare tenderfoot tourists. He never plays his trick on expert riders."

"But, Sue, I'm a tenderfoot," rejoined Patricia dubiously. "I'm not so sure I want Joker."

"He's absolutely safe. Now get up and try your stirrups.—Funny aboot clothes, isn't it? Last night you looked so tall and slim. But in this riding outfit you do look like a movie star."

"Sue, I haven't anything on you," retorted Patricia, as she mounted to the saddle and smiled down into the glowing face of the girl. "In that riding rig you beat any cowgirl I ever saw at the rodeo. You look the real thing and I'll bet you are. So there!"

"Oh—Miss Clay—you shore embarrass me, but I'd be lying if I said I didn't like it. . . . Now stand in your stirrups."

"They feel just about right."

"Well, they're long. I'll take them up a hole."

Patricia slipped one foot out of a stirrup and bent to the opposite side of the saddle to ease the strain. And as she did so her sharp ear caught the whispering of the two cowboy guides who had drawn aside and had their backs turned.

"You see, Nels, I get trusted with the pretty western gurls, an' the swell peaches from Noo York. You're a handsome devil. I'm only a sawed-off, bowlegged, ugly cowpuncher."

"Tine, this ain't funny—yore ridin' off with Sue. I reckoned you was my pard. An' here you're double-crossin' me."

"Aw naw, Nels, you're loco."

"But couldn't you get sick or kicked or somethin'— so I could take this party and be with Sue? All the other guides are out. An' Sue's madder'n blazes at me."

"Huh! An' lose my job? Nels, you're not orful bright. It's better for you that I take Sue. 'Cause I'll fix it up for you. I got a hunch."

"You give me hunches before," complained Nels, "an' the last one near cost me my head."

"How come?"

"Didn't you say I ought to grab Sue up an' kiss her? Well, I did! She socked me one an' she's still sore at me."

"Nels, you didn't go at it right. Listen to this hunch. I'll talk this dame from Noo York into a trip over to the North Rim. She'll go. She's a thoroughbred, with money to burn. An' say, Nels, ain't she a lollapaloosa?"

"I'll say she is. Never saw such a looker like her in all my born life."

"Neither did I. An' what's better, she's nice an' sweet. Not stuck up like most of them eastern dudes.... Well, Nels, what you think of my idee?"

"Mighty fine. But there ain't no such luck. Why, cowboy, if you pulled that stunt for me I'd—I'd—"

"Good as done. Beat it! There's that fox Hilton lookin'. Meet you at the Gardens, mebbe. You work fast an' I'll work slow. So long."

The cowboys separated, Stackhouse striding to his mule and mounting with effortless ease and grace, while Higgenbottom advanced to meet newcomers joining his party. Patricia sat there, smiling to herself over the little plot she had unwittingly overheard. What boys they were! Already Patricia liked them. Should she reveal their plot to Sue or keep it secret and appear innocently to succumb to the machinations of these conspirators? Thought of a trip to the wild north rim certainly stirred Patricia; and if such trips were made by tourists, as the guides had implied, she would like to go. There had been longing in the voice of this boy Nels. But was he worthy of Sue? Patricia's first impression of Stackhouse had not been too favorable. Now she saw that she might have misjudged him. She decided to let the developments of the day guide her to a decision.

Suddenly she became aware that Sue was tugging at her arm.

"Whatever were you thinkin' aboot?" queried the girl gravely. Her big eyes, almost colorless except for the dark hazel centers, were uplifted to the light of the sun.

"Why?" she asked, smiling down.

"I spoke to you twice. You shore were far away."

"Pardon my abstraction. No, Sue, I was *not* far away. I was thinking of—of what happiness I might find in association with you."

"Me! Oh, how good of you!" exclaimed Sue, suddenly excited. "You mean comin' to see me in Flag?"

"Perhaps! But I shall not tell you now."

Sue gave her a steady gaze, thoughtful, wondering; and then replied, "Shore I could tell you somethin', too, only I won't now."

Higgenbottom placed Sue's aunt next to him in line, then Mrs. Price, then Sue and Patricia, and let the others fall in as they chose. They rode in single file down a road behind the hotel, across a wide flat past a rather picturesque building, that Sue said was the Bright Angel Inn, and so on to where the trail headed gradually down into the cedars.

Patricia saw where a great notch cut into the rim, and it was down the near side of this depression that the trail zigzagged. It was a wide, well-trodden trail, not at all steep at the start. Patricia failed to feel the trepidation she had expected: indeed she seemed quite gay, and she even found herself shouting bantering replies to some of the facetious remarks made by those behind her.

"Auntie, let your mule alone," protested Sue. "You don't have to turn his haid that way. He doesn't like it. What do you suppose he's learned, traveling up and down this trail a thousand times?"

"My dear, mules are like some people—they never learn anythin'," declared her aunt. "This one doesn't want to go anywhere but back."

The trail zigzagged down a pine-wooded slope that hid the canyon from sight. It began to grow steeper now. The yellow wall of rock on the other side of the notch loomed above them as the trail pitched ever downward. How scarred it was, and seamed! From above on the rim it had looked different; now, as she descended toward the river, far, far below, she began to appreciate the canyon's tremendous depth. Sue observed her craning her neck.

"That's what they call 'the Limestone'," she said. "Reckon it's aboot a thousand feet. Some cliff, don't you think?"

"It's amazing. Indeed, I'm glad I didn't try to form any positive conceptions of size and distance. I can see now, I'd have to change them."

"Shore. It'll be better for you to pay attention to the trail and things near at hand," advised Sue. "Then as you go down you meet places close up, and in the end you've passed from near to far."

Patricia thought it good advice. Besides she did not want a recurrence of her mood of yesterday. That was for lonely vigils. Today she would try to enter into the spirit of the trip as the other tourists were—as something of fun and adventure. They seemed impressed, naturally, by the majesty of the canyon walls and the color and beauty, but not in any sense overwhelmed.

"Sue, how often have you been down?" she inquired.

"Let's see, four—no, six times down Bright Angel, and two down Hermit trail. I've come with normal-school girls, as a sort of amateur guide."

"So many! And do you still find it thrilling?"

"I shore do. Reckon I love it more every trip. But I'm a little worried this time. That mule Auntie's on is going to balk with her shore as shootin'. If he does it in a bad place, she'll be scared."

The trail grew narrower, steeper, more crooked; it passed under beetling gray walls, and through cuts in the rocks so narrow that she bumped her knees, and around abrupt corners where she could not see anyone either ahead or behind. After that there was a level stretch where the narrow trail rounded a bold bluff, with a sheer, breathtaking drop to the left. Patricia did not look a second time. She heard Mrs. Price say she wished she had stayed on top; and behind, one of the women screamed.

"Let your mule have his own way," called the guide, with a reassuring grin on his ruddy face.

Patricia began to have some conception of how it must feel going down into a mine. Above, the great walls closed in, seemingly to blot out the sky. Below, the green and yellow slope apparently ended; she caught a glimpse of blue space, where there was nothing, and it looked as if she were riding to a point where further progress would be impossible. Yet the trail always found a way, mostly down, but often on a level and sometimes up-grade for a brief space.

Sue told her that they had descended from the Limestone to the Red Rock. The change was striking. The large pine trees gave way to cedars, then even the cedars became stunted, finally yielding to brush. Huge boulders alternated with rocks of every size and shape, many that evidently had rolled from the cracked walls above and seemed poised as if they might start rolling again at any moment. To ride beneath one of these great balancing rocks shook Patricia's nerve, but the trail wound past so many that she grew used to them. Wilder and more rugged became the slopes, steeper and darker of hue, with less and less green foliage to be seen. Suddenly they rounded a sharp turn and could see the trail zigzagging to a sheer, dizzy descent. The guide halted, looking nonchalantly back.

"Heavens!" ejaculated Mrs. Price. "Do we have to ride down there?"

"Jacob's Ladder. It ain't bad," replied Higgenbottom. "Wait till we hit the Devil's Corkscrew!"

"Well, this is devilish enough for me," declared Sue's aunt. "I'm goin' to walk."

"Auntie, don't pay any attention to Tine," advised Sue. "I told you he'd tease you. Nobody rides down heah. Everybody walks."

"Thank goodness!" declared Patricia as she dismounted behind Sue.

The trail here appeared slanted to an angle of forty-five degrees and would have presented a serious obstacle to most tourists if sapling poles had not been laid step after step down to where the descent became more gradual again. Patricia mounted her mule and once again rode along behind Sue. It was growing noticeably warmer in the canyon. The cleft down which they had descended grew wider as they approached what appeared to be a triangular-shaped plateau, spreading toward the black ragged line that Sue said marked the second or Marble Canyon. It did not seem possible to the New York girl that they would be able to get past a huge break in the wall below; but the trail took another unexpected turn to go around the narrow head of a gorge, and she could see it stretching level over red rock for a long distance ahead. Beyond that, it went down and down, crossing the bottom of the gorge and working its way onto another gigantic step-off. The abyss yawned again on Patricia's left; and when Sue called out warningly: "Keep your haid, heah!" the sensations of height and depth began to assume proportions that dwarfed any she had felt before. The trail was only a yard wide, with an overhanging cliff to the right and the bottomless pit on the left. Then it began to ascend. Patricia saw above her a corner of red wall. Here the trail seemed to disappear completely. Higgenbottom reached the point, and turned to call lazily: "Lover's Leap. Watch your step!" Sue let out a peal of silvery laughter. "Listen to that cowboy," she said to Patricia. "Don't you believe him. He's only kiddin' me. Nels and I once had a scrap right heah. Nels swore he'd jump off the corner there. And I dared him to. Shore it was a bluff."

Mrs. Price vanished around the corner; then Sue's

aunt, and then Sue. Patricia's mule reached it, but instead of turning close to the wall, as had the others, he deliberately walked out the few feet of that jutting point and stood on the very verge of a precipice that seemed to have no bottom. He looked down; he wagged his ears. Patricia was terrified, but she did not yield to a frantic desire to scream and jerk the mule back. One of the women in the line behind cried out. They all halted.

"Let him alone!" came Sue's clear warning voice. Then Patricia remembered that she was astride Joker, the wise old mule who played tricks on tenderfoot tourists. Presently he wagged his ears and stepped back, very carefully, foot by foot, until he bumped into the wall, whereupon he turned into the trail and went on. The New York girl's heart descended from her throat; and all of a sudden she was weak, cold perspiration breaking out on her face.

Sue was waiting ahead along the trail. Manifestly she was trying her best to look concerned when she wanted to give way to glee.

"That stubborn old mule tried it on you, didn't he?" she queried demurely.

"Sue Warren! You knew he would," cried Patricia accusingly.

"Why—Miss—Clay," said Sue haltingly. Then she ducked her telltale face, and her merry laugh rang out. The cowboy guide followed suit, and his "haw haw" came echoing back from the opposite cliff and bellowed down the gorge.

Patricia regretted she could not share the mirth of these young westerners. But considering that she was still trembling and her breast had not yet recovered from its caved-in sensation, she felt that she could not quite get their point of view. She had heard and read how westerners played tricks on easterners. It was not quite beyond her to think of one in retaliation. Yet, when composure had fully returned, she warmed to them only the more.

The descent varied and the trail still held curves and

grades that made Patricia's heart skip many a beat. There were no more stops, however, and at last the guide led them out of a narrow defile onto the apex of that triangular plateau which they had seen from above. From up there it had appeared level, but now they could see that it sloped downhill, rugged and rough for a considerable distance.

As Patricia approached the Indian Gardens, she found that what from the rim had appeared to be a green dot was in reality a beautiful oasis of cottonwoods and willows among which tents and cottages nestled. A stream of crystal water babbled between borders of bright green grass.

The guide led his party out across the plateau. Patricia saw the white trail winding across the undulating gray barren. Sue pointed out where it forked, one branch running down into a dark cleft and the other continuing out across the plateau.

"Some trail parties go on down to the Colorado and some out to the rim of Marble Canyon," explained Sue. "I chose this half-way trip for Auntie because it's not so hard. When I come over again we'll shore take the river trip."

Over this rolling wide plateau, Patricia was conscious of neither mule nor trail, but only of the majesty of the scenery all about her. Stupendous walls of red sheered up from the plateau, and above them, step by step, yellow and green slopes led aloft to the magnificent belt of limestone, and high over that towered the fringed rim, remote and far away. The gap by which they had descended seemed nothing but a tiny crack in the walls. Before her spread the plateau, miles across, and beyond it rose a succession of upflung pyramids, colossal at the base, and slanting to turrets, parapets, domes and peaks, pinnacles and crags, rising to the dignity of mountain summits. The golden, black-fringed belt of the North Rim, which she well remembered, was hidden from sight.

What a wild and naked world of rock, glaring under the noonday sun! It was unreal, ghastly, stark, yet of a noble austerity that exalted the soul. Patricia felt insulated, bound, shut off from the cool heights, lost in the depths of the rock-riven earth. Was it too vast, too huge for beauty—this varicolored canyon that was only a crack in the greater canyon?

She became aware, presently, that Sue had dismounted and was waiting.

"I've something for you," she said, "Take off your glove." And she raised her closed hand.

"No!" exclaimed Patricia.

"But it's very beautiful," protested Sue.

"I don't care if it is. I'll bet you've a bug or something horrid."

"Are you afraid, tenderfoot?" bantered Sue, yet with a challenge in her voice.

Patricia pulled off her glove and held out her hand. Sue put hers over it and left something warm and throbbing in her palm. Then the eastern girl's eyes fell upon a tiny horned toad, scalloped and ridged, softly red and gray and bronze, with eyes like jewels.

"There. That's the desert for you," declared Sue. "In the palm of your hand."

"It's beautiful—if that's what you want me to see," returned Patricia.

Sue took the toad and set it free upon the ground. "Run away and keep out of the trail. Some rider whose eyes are not so sharp as mine will let his horse step on you."

"That toad was the most perfect example of protective coloration I ever saw," remarked Patricia.

"Yes. I'd never seen him if he'd kept squatted down. But he ran."

The ride across the plateau ended all too soon for Patricia, though, as she dismounted on the rim of a black chasm, she forgot all the other spectacles she had already seen. Sue led her aside from the group.

"Marble Canyon," she said, standing beside her. "It's

as far down to the river as the distance we've already come down from the rim. There's the mouth of Bright Angel Canyon, on the other side. Rangers cross there in a cage, and sometimes tourists with guides. We hear a footbridge is to be built. And shore that would be fine."

Patricia had no words to describe what she saw. She gazed at a black V-shaped gap, vast as a valley between mountain ranges, somber and terrible, a grave it seemed for that dark red river. A sullen roar of chafing waters floated up, filling the desert silence. Patricia saw the winding river, frothy and turbulent between the constricting walls. This then was the secret of the Grand Canyon—that implacable, resistless river, flowing on forever, cutting, wearing, tearing.

The whole scene affected Patricia profoundly. Here it approached intimacy, whereas from the rim above, depths and distances were beyond human comprehension. Here the abysmal bowels of the earth, the travail of the ages lay naked under the eye.

This somber rent was neither beautiful nor glorious. It oppressed her, weighted her heart, tortured her mind. Dante's Inferno! If it was so sinister in the full light of the noonday sun, what would it be at twilight, at dusk, at midnight?

"Let us ride back to the Gardens," Patricia suddenly suggested to Sue.

The young girl pressed her arm understandingly and without speaking a word turned to help her mount and led the way back across the plateau.

It was very pleasant in the shade of the cottonwoods, eating lunch on the velvety green grass beside the murmuring brook. The air was drowsy, full of summer heat. Bees and flies buzzed around. Patricia noted with surprise the absence of birds. Through the foliage of the trees the red walls gleamed in vivid contrast.

Higgenbottom did not appear to be in any hurry to

start back; indeed none of his party seemed eager to begin the ascent.

"Three hours ridin'—an' walkin'," drawled the cowboy. "Get good an' rested here before we start."

Patricia saw that he was on the lookout for his friend, Nels Stackhouse. She herself was waiting and eager for the cowboy to begin his campaign. He chose a time, presently, when Patricia and Sue were alone. Then he seated himself on the grass, removed his big sombrero, wiped his wet brow, and then fired his first round.

"Miss Clay, you said you wasn't born on a hoss, like Sue hyar, but you sure beat any tenderfoot I ever saw. I wasn't worried none about you. Why, you could tackle real bad trails."

"Indeed? Thank you, Mr. Higgenbottom," replied Patricia, with gratitude that was not wholly pretense. Maybe the deceitful wretch's flattery concealed a grain of truth! Patricia found herself enjoying the situation.

"She's got nerve and sense, Tine," interposed Sue with asperity. "What'd you expect?"

"Say, Sue, don't I have tenderfoot women ridin' mules down this trail most every day?" he drawled good-naturedly.

"Shore. But not like Miss Clay."

"Wal, that's what I was tryin' to say. I'm sure appreciatin' her, an' you know, Sue, what a treat it is to have a girl like you on a trip. A guide has feelin's, though mebbe no one would suspect it. An' this job ain't no picnic.... Wal, Miss Clay, I was goin' to ask you how you like this little ride?"

"It has been a wonderful experience," replied Patricia sincerely.

"Wal, that's fine. Most ladies complain about somethin'. Now haven't you jest one kick comin'!"

"No, indeed. I'd be very ungracious to feel anything but delight and gratitude."

"But wouldn't this trail ridin' an' settin' in the shade

like this, an' lookin' at the walls, be a thousand times wonderfuller if, say, they was jest a few of us an' we was off the beaten track? Away from the tourists?"

How intelligently he had read her mind, and how subtly he had stated the truth! This cowboy was a past master in the art of salesmanship.

"Yes, I confess it would," returned Patricia frankly.

"Look heah, Tine," spoke up Sue with spirit, "stop beating aboot the bush."

"Sue, I ain't beatin' round nothin'," declared Tine vehemently, but with a grin on his ruddy face. "Can I help it if you're smart enough to read my mind?"

"Tine, I don't know what you're aimin' to do," replied Sue dubiously, shaking her blond head at him.

"Wal, I jest think Miss Clay would love a trip over on the North Rim. An' you'd love to go along. Now then!"

"Oh!" exclaimed Sue rapturously, disarmed of her suspicions by her enthusiasm over the prospect of a visit to the North Rim.

"Mr. Higgenbottom, it's kind of you to plan a trip for my benefit. Please tell me about this North Rim trip," Patricia said, making no effort to conceal her pleasure and completely forgetting that the guide had an ulterior motive.

The cowboy's response was something that almost broke Patricia's pretended reserve. He got up from his leisurely crouch, and the glance he bestowed upon Sue was one that carried a meaning which was beyond her. His air seemed one of supreme assurance and nonchalance.

"Wal, Miss Clay, this North Rim trip is no different from the Hermit trail trip or the Havasupi Canyon trip. You read about 'em in the booklet. The hotel company runs 'em. Girls, grandfathers, old women, an' kids can take 'em. But the North Rim trip is different. It's long, hard, an' expensive. It's seldom taken. We had only three parties all last summer and fall. . . . We take a pack-outfit an' a cook an' go down past here to the river. We cross in a cage swung on a steel cable, perfectly safe, but say, you'll get some kick out of that! Then we tackle the fifteen-mile trip up Bright Angel Canyon. It makes this trail look like Fifth Avenue. For miles your hoss—for you ride on a hoss this trip—has to wade the creek, an' right under beautiful waterfalls. If we're lucky we get up on top the same day, mebbe by sunset. An' say, sunset from the North Rim, lookin' down a hundred miles of canyon, is sure enough to make an angel out of a sinner. We camp on top in Buckskin Forest, the finest woods in the world. There'll be snow in shady places. An' that's good, 'cause we can camp anywhere. The North Rim is two thousand feet higher than the El Tovar. There's the silver spruce trees—an' if you love trees you must see them, an' the big black squirrels with white tails, an' the deer....Honest, Miss Clay, you'll see thousands of deer—born wild, an' yet as tame as calves in the pasture. The come right into camp, an' you can almost ketch the little fawns....You won't see a soul on the whole trip unless a ranger rides by. An' rangers are scarce an' Buckskin is big. It's wild, lonely, but somehow awful sweet over there. Makes me feel queer! An' sittin' on that North Rim, at sunrise an' sunset, by dark an' by moonlight, is jest about as grand, I reckon, as goin' to Heaven!"

"Very well, Mr. Higgenbottom. We shall go," replied Patricia simply.

The cowboy rose swiftly. He gave his chaps a hitch and put on his gauntlets. His face presented an interesting study. It glowed, yet the ruddy color was less evident. There was something about him then that thrilled Patricia and surprised her. It seemed to be an emotion the intensity of which there was no apparent call for. Then she remembered he was playing a deep game out of loyalty to his friend Nels. Patricia liked him all the better for it. He was acting a part, but at the same time it was plain to see that his feeling for the North Rim was sincere. A thrill of excitement stirred in Patricia's breast. The North Rim! She could scarcely wait to visit it.

"Miss Clay, I didn't make no mistake about you," said the cowboy quietly; and Patricia knew she had been paid a rare compliment. "When would you like to go? Reckon I'd like a little time, 'cause I want a special outfit an' hosses."

Patricia turned to Sue and was amazed and concerned to see that the girl's face had paled and her large eyes had darkened.

"When can you go, Sue?" asked Patricia.

"Are you—really going to take me?" returned Sue, almost breathlessly.

"I wouldn't go without you. Set a date. I'll hire a car and drive over to Flagstaff for you."

Sue was plainly laboring under a temptation too enchanting to resist. The color rushed back to her cheeks and the light into her eyes. If Patricia had wished for some expression of thanks she would have been more than satisfied.

"A week from Monday," replied Sue, almost in a whisper.

"Then it's settled," said Patricia trying to pretend she was making a matter-of-course arrangement, when in reality she was tingling all over with excitement and anticipation. "Mr. Higgenbottom, you be prepared to start with us early in the morning a week from Tuesday. Take supplies enough so we can stay as long as we like."

"All right—Miss—" he replied haltingly, as if divided between elation and an inhibiting emotion. He was gazing down into Sue's upturned face.

"Tine—you'll want *him*," she asserted rather than questioned.

"'Course I'll want Nels. He's the best packer an' hoss wrangler of the lot. An' he's a pretty good camp-rustler."

"You needn't enumerate Mr. Stackhouse's merits," replied Sue almost coldly. "But—to oblige me, won't you take someone else?"

"Sue, I reckon there's little I wouldn't do to oblige you. But I'd hate to go without Nels. Honest, it's not all because we're pards—"

"Be on the level, Tine," interrupted Sue.

The blood suffused the cowboy's face and he jerked up as if he had been stung.

"Sue Warren, I am on the level," he retorted hotly. "Mebbe more'n you'd ever believe. I'm standin' up for Nels, agin anybody, an' especially you."

"Then I beg your pardon, Tine," returned Sue. "I didn't mean to offend. I respect you for standing up for your friend, even if I do not admire your judgment."

Here the cowboy turned to Patricia, evidently in rather deep straits. Else he was a wonderful dissembler.

"Miss Clay, please excuse me for bein' sort of obstinate," he said. "You're hirin' me to take this trip an' you ought to know somethin' about Nels Stackhouse. You met him up in the corral. Wal, he's my pard. I'm bound to admit Nels has been a pretty tough hombre. But after he met Sue an' this here ranger Eburne, why he bucked up an' went straight. He hasn't had a drink or a fight since he started ridin' for this outfit. He's saved his money. What more could anybody ask of a cowboy?"

"I'm sure I don't know," replied Patricia, smiling up at him. "I couldn't, that's certain, but perhaps Sue is more exacting than I am. The matter rests entirely with her."

"Shore you both—make me ashamed," said Sue, averting her face. "I—I withdraw my objection."

"Wal, that's fine!" exploded Tine, turning away. Then he called out: "By golly, heah comes Nels now with his trail party. He sure must have rustled along....I'll fetch him over."

*T*HE COWBOY'S mode of locomotion, with his short bowlegs and wide batwing chaps, was amusing even when natural, but now, when he appeared to be trying to fly through the air, it was ludicrous. When he reached Stackhouse he exhibited other violent indications of thinking well of himself. He patted his back, threw out his chest, shook hands with himself. Nels broke out in a wide grin. Presently Tine led his friend toward the spot where Patricia and Sue were resting.

"Sue, if this boy is really objectionable to you, please be frank and tell me," said Patricia.

"Tine shore won't go with anybody else. I know these cowboys," replied Sue.

"Could we not engage others?"

"Yes-s, but—" admitted Sue inconsistently. "If only Tine wasn't lying aboot Nels!"

Patricia thought it best to let matters rest as they were. The cowboys approached rather slowly, and it was obvious from his gestures that Tine was now trying to make something convincing to Nels. At last they reached the brook and leaped it with jingling spurs. Tine's elation had suffered an eclipse. The other cowboy had lost the manner that had characterized him up on the rim. He removed his sombrero and bowed to Patricia, not ungracefully. The eastern girl thought she saw in this young cowboy what had attracted Sue and why Sue still loved him in spite of her better judgment.

"Miss Clay, are you really engagin' Higgenbottom to take the North Rim trip?" Stackhouse queried.

"Yes, indeed. It's all settled. He wants you to give him a hand," replied Patricia. "I'd certainly appreciate your services."

"I'm powerful pleased, Miss Clay," he said, "an' I'd be proud to go, but you'll excuse me, now, if I cain't, won't you?"

"Why, certainly," returned the New York girl, considerably surprised. She did not know what to make of this sudden change in the script. If the boy was not perfectly sincere, he surely was a wonderful actor. Then he turned to Sue.

"Miss Warren, I reckon you didn't tell Tine you'd be tickled to death to have me go?" he inquired.

"Well, Mr. Stackhouse, I don't remember using just exactly those words," returned Sue demurely. There seemed just a hint of sarcasm in her soft voice, but she dimpled as she spoke.

The cowboy turned to Tine. "There! She's made you out a liar for the nine hundredth time."

Tine's face grew ruddier. He threw up his hands. "That's the thanks I get. How can I remember everythin' perfickly? Talk to Sue yourself. Mebbe she'll tell you *jest* what she told me."

Whereupon Tine clapped on his huge sombrero and trudged away with head bowed, muttering to himself.

"You don't want me on that trip, Sue Warren. Let's have the truth! Do you?" demanded Nels, facing her again.

"What if I didn't?" retorted Sue pertly.

"Wal, there ain't enough mules in sight to drag me on it—if you didn't."

"What else did Tine tell you?" queried Sue with sudden curiosity.

"Never mind now. He must have been out of his haid. But he made me blamed sore ... I'm tellin' you truthful that up on the rim, this mornin', he said he would get Miss Clay to take the North Rim trip an' ring me in on it. I was sure tickled ... Now leavin' myself out, I think it's a wonderful time for you an' Miss Clay to go. I had a letter from my friend Eburne. You remember him. Wal, he wrote a lot about the deer. They've overmultiplied till there are thousands an' thousands more'n they ought to be. An' if somethin' cain't be done to save them they're goin' to starve."

"Oh, how dreadful!" ejaculated Sue.

"Indeed it is. What can be done?" added Patricia with quickening interest.

"Thad didn't say. He sure felt bad, an' I know he's doin' all that's possible ... So it'd be a great time to go an' see these deer. Mebbe the last chance! Anyway, I'm glad you're goin', an' I'm sorry I'll have to refuse."

"Have you refused?" asked Sue bluntly.

"Wal, I reckon—it amounts to that," he rejoined hesitatingly.

"Why?"

"I've a lot of reasons."

"But you're employed by the company. Miss Clay has engaged Tine. He needs you. Says you're the best packer and horse wrangler in the West. In fact he praised you so—especially your *present* virtues—that I feel you're a stranger ... How can you get out of going?"

"They can fire me if they want to. Fact is, I've a hankerin' for a real hoss an' ridin' the range. I've been offered a job as foreman on the Coffee Pot outfit. Looks good to me."

"They're a lot of tough cowboys," protested Sue.

"Sure . . . But this here's no way for us to talk before Miss Clay. An' it's time to hit the trail."

"What will Thad Eburne think of you if you leave the Canyon, where you're so well liked, and go back—to—to punching cattle?"

Nels dropped his head and turned his wide sombrero around and around in his hands. "Reckon he'd think me plain no good."

"What will *you* think?" she flashed, with color in her cheeks.

"Now, Miss Warren, you sure ain't carin' what I think about anythin' or anybody," replied Nels.

"Nelson, are you bluffing—or on the level?" she asked.

"Reckon we're wastin' time an' sure not thinkin' of Miss Clay," he said and half turned away.

"Then you won't go for Tine?"

"No!"

"All right, then, Nels . . . Will you go for me?" she asked softly.

"Now—Miss Warren, of course, if you put it that way, I'll be glad to oblige you," he replied blandly and, bowing to her and Patricia he leaped the brook and strode out into the sunlight.

"You shore can never tell about a cowboy," mused Sue, gazing after him.

"I'll tell you sometime, little girl," interposed Patricia gaily. "Cheer up. It's all settled. We're going to have an adventure."

"Shore, it might be more for me," sighed Sue and for a moment was lost in thought. Then Tine's call roused her to action. "Come on, let's get on and be going. They'll bunch the two parties on the way out. We want to be in front."

Back in the saddle once more, Patricia shaded her eyes and looked up toward the rim where they were returning. She gathered that the ascent would be harder work, but less wearing on the nerves. The more she gazed up that cleft in the perpendicular wall, the more she marveled that humans on muleback could ever climb it. Soon she was riding out of the sunlight into shadow. The great walls rose, dark bronze and dull red, vermilion, and then blazing gold, with a black fringe at the top. As she looked, the upper sunlit steps receded from her sight; the cavalcade left the plateau and began to ascend the first steep slope of the return trail.

As the sure-footed animals strung out, Patricia noticed that the party had grown silent and absorbed with their own thoughts. By the time the red rock had been surmounted, Patricia was pretty tired. How high the blue limestone loomed! And the rim, so far above, seemed unattainable.

The time came when Patricia no longer gazed upward; not even when Sue called back: "Hang on. We're almost up." The last zigzags, especially those that faced toward the canyon, were endurable because again Patricia saw the glamour of sunset on the upper slopes and walls. She was still climbing when the colors died, when the cold grays and purples predominated as dusk mantled the abyss. And it was nearly dark when Sue and her aunt and Mrs. Price dismounted before Bright Angel Inn.

"Shore it was dandy," said Sue. "Shall I say good night now, or come over to the El Tovar after dinner? You're mighty tired."

"Come to dinner, and bring your aunt and Mrs. Price," replied Patricia.

"Many thanks, Miss Clay," returned Sue's aunt, as she limped painfully up the steps. "I'm near dead an' I reckon Mrs. Price is too. But Sue can go...We had a fine ride. I wouldn't have missed it for worlds."

"I'll be right over," added Sue gladly.

Patricia was almost the last rider to dismount at the corral and creep with little stiff steps into the hotel. She found herself chafed, bruised, blistered, and full of pangs. No active pursuit in which she had ever engaged had cost her so much effort and endurance. Yet she had imagined herself as strong, tireless. It hurt her pride and vanity and stirred more resentment against the butterfly life she had led. Bathing and dressing alleviated her discomfort somewhat, but after sitting for a few moments in the chair by the window, she found it difficult to get on her feet. Her face was smarting with sunburn. Patricia stared at her reflection in the mirror and could not help feeling good in body and soul despite the stiffness in her muscles. All day out in the open! Already the West was having its healing effect upon her spirit. Suddenly she found herself thinking of the coming excursion to the North Rim, to the forest where the herds of deer were starving because nature let them be born and failed to supply the food necessary for their existence.

Sue was waiting for her in the lobby, and her devouring look did not need her accompanying words: "If I were a man it'd shore be all day with me!"

"Sue, I fear you are a sad little flatterer," smiled Patricia.

"Sad? I'm the happiest one you ever saw. Wait till I get so I'm not afraid to say what I feel!"

"Don't be afraid of me. I'll welcome your confidences—Come, let's go in to dinner. And afterward—shall I show you some of my dude finery, which you seem to admire so much, or will you take me to see the Hopis dance?"

"Let's do both," replied Sue shyly.

Later they went to the Hopi house, where Patricia found herself enchanted with the cavelike rooms, the colorful baskets and blankets, her first sight of real Indians, and the primitive dancing to the cadence of the drums, and above all the round-faced, brown-eyed Indian children. They looked so serious as they tried to imitate the motions of their elders. When they danced, Patricia could not refrain from laughter as she joined in the applause and the showering of pennies and nickels upon the floor. What fun to see the little rascals dart like mice and pounce upon the money. Indeed, they knew or had been taught what Uncle Sam's coins meant.

But Patricia's enjoyment was nothing compared to the delight Sue expressed when she saw some of Patricia's jewels and gowns and lingerie. Sue had the eternal feminine love of beautiful things; her heart, however, felt no trace of envy. At length she laid down the last shimmering fabric and said, "We western girls must shore seem to you to be campin' out in the woods."

"Sue, you are many times happier than I am, for all these possessions," replied Patricia earnestly. "I hope we become friends and that I may share some of your happiness."

"If that's what you hope, then we're friends right now," declared the girl, with her shining eyes on Patricia. "Things happen quick out west. You like people or you don't; there's no two-facedness, no kiddin' people along, that is, among my kind. The West is honest, open, big—raw I s'pose, to people when they first land heah. Somethin' like today! I saw how hard it was on you, and how crude my folks and the cowboys, and I too, must have seemed to you. But the way you stood the trip and us—why, shore that satisfied me that you are as game and fine as you are lovely."

Patricia put her arm round this gallant, outspoken young girl and did not trust herself to make any reply.

After Sue had gone, Patricia thoughtfully put her dresses away. She recalled the look of unconcealed admiration in the young Texas girl's eyes. There had been no trace of envy in them. She compared this unspoiled straightforward schoolgirl with the friends she had known in the East. She might do much for this little western girl, in the doing of which she would find forgetfulness of self and true happiness for the first time in her life. She divined that time would be generous with her, provided she avoided brooding introspection and idleness. One hard day in the open had given her a glimpse of the power of physical effort over self-pity. Within a span of twenty-four hours, tremendous and vital issues had dawned upon her; and she was humbly grateful for the new promise life held out to her. Just as the canyon had seemed to her last night to be a symbol of the chasm between the life she had known and the new life ahead, so this sweet, free-handed and free-hearted western girl was a symbol of her own new freedom from something evil that was gone from her life forever. In those old days Patricia would never have believed that she could have found so much in common with a normal-school girl so many years her junior.

Next morning she planned what to do with her time for the ensuing week. She would spend the morning hours walking and horseback riding to prepare herself for the hard trip to the North Rim with Sue Warren; each afternoon she would take one of the several bus drives along the rim; and in the evenings she would read books on the geological history of the Grand Canyon.

On her walks along the canyon rim, she met many tourists clicking cameras in each other's faces, usually with their backs to the awesome beauty of view, and she found it easy to be impatient with them at first. In the main they were all good-natured sight-seeing people, hail-fellow-well-met, ready to talk at the least encouraging look, and certainly she appreciated that they had as much as right to the canyon as she. But most of them were not serious, and as she was alone, and unfortunately one of those women, who attract, she met with many situations that she would rather have avoided. These, however, only occurred on the drives; when she walked or rode she seldom met anyone. People made fun of the canyon, indulged in jokes relative to its color, depth, width, and raved about it. But some were awed by its grandeur, and these individuals always got off by themselves.

Of all points on the rim that she saw, Patricia liked Desert View the best. It was over twenty miles by automobile from the hotel and overlooked the Painted Desert and the confluence of the Little Colorado Canyon with the Grand Canyon. Moreover, there was ample room to get off by herself. Here she could look across and up at Greenland Point, a great promontory that stood out over the vast red chasm in lonely magnificence. The thought that she was soon to camp on Greenland Point stirred her with impatience for the journey to come.

Only one incident marred the all-satisfying pleasure of these days, and that had to do with Miss Hilton. Patricia had to consult her about the hiring of saddle horses, and on one occasion, when no other person happened to be near, the agent looked at Patricia with curious bright eyes.

"Think I've seen your picture in some paper," she said.

"Indeed. Surely not a western paper," rejoined Patricia.

"No. It was in the Sunday supplement of some New York paper. An eastern tourist left it here. The picture favored you. But I'm sure the name wasn't Clay."

Patricia passed the matter off with some casual answer, but later she pondered over it. That perhaps had been the cause of this woman's rather inquisitive manner, probably augmented by the fact that the eastern girl had not responded to her first ingratiating advances. Patricia did not like Miss Hilton's reference to the picture because it recalled the past and, especially, the scandal in which her name had become involved. As a matter of fact, one of New York's scandal sheets had published a picture of Patricia, together with a story by a clever and unscrupulous reporter. That had been one of the things Patricia had endured for the sake of her friend.

"I wonder—could this Miss Hilton have seen that newspaper?" mused Patricia. "It's possible, but ... Well, it doesn't matter. What do I care what she thinks or knows?— But still, there's Sue—"

It occurred to Patricia that really annoying circumstances might grow out of such a possibility. A jealous, gossipy woman could make her visit at the El Tovar unpleasant and might curtail it. There were, too, other considerations. She had Sue Warren to think of. She did not want it to become known that Sue had taken a trip with a woman of questionable repute. Therefore she made it a point to match wits with Miss Hilton, with the result that she discovered the woman felt no certainty about the thing she had hinted. So, reassured, Patricia dismissed the incident and worry from her mind.

The morning arrived at last on which Patricia was to drive over to Flagstaff for Sue. She ate an early breakfast and started at once so that she could return that same night before dark.

The day had broken cool and rosy, like early spring in the East. She had engaged a touring-car and a driver well recommended by the hotel manager for the eighty-mile drive. Patricia was quite familiar now with the first fifteen miles of the road, which led through a magnificent pine forest. Beyond Grand View, the road turned away from the canyon and wound downgrade and soon left the pines for cedars. These failed, also, at length, and Patricia found the way proceeding between low gray hills.

Suddenly the car left the cedar forest and shot out into the open desert, dazzling in the sunlight, a vast sweeping floor that extended down and down, gray, drab, and white, to lead Patricia's fascinated gaze on to an upsweep of land, spotted and patched with green, which in turn rose to join the sweeping line of timbered mountains, rising black and ragged to sharp snow-capped peaks that split the blue sky. On the right, far distant, gray hills, marvelously symmetrical and bare, scalloped the horizon. To the left, the gray floor descended endlessly to vanish in purple haze and then rise again in brightly colored steps, surmounted by black buttes—the Painted Desert.

The driver drew Patricia's attention to Sunset Peak, explaining that its hues of red and gold and purple came from the fact that it was a mountain of volcanic cinders and, no matter what the time of day, it always shone with sunset colors. Far distant as it was, it loomed high, dome-shaped, and bright.

The scene changed with every mile. Patricia regretted the swift car and the way it swallowed up the long winding road. The air grew hot. She saw dust clouds down on the desert. It took an hour to traverse that vast shallow bowl of valley between the gray hills and the green cedars, yet for Patricia the time was all too short. Then soon again the cedars obstructed the distant view, and the car hummed on like the wind, up a winding grade, once more into a pine forest. She saw a signboard informing the traveler that it was twenty miles to Flagstaff. She could see nothing but trees, and the gray grassy slopes rising to either side and in front. There appeared to be a pass between two foothills, and when the car had wound up through the notch, the road pitched downward once more, winding through the forest for miles. It crossed a white-grassed park where cattle grazed, plunged into woods again, and passed a huge sawmill to run parallel with a railroad. Soon Patricia saw smoke, and then fences and ranch houses, and at last the outskirts of Flagstaff.

The town was ideally located in the pine belt that sloped down from the mountains. Patricia liked the broad main street, where autoists vied with Indian teamsters, and along which mounted cowboys loped with jingling spurs. Some of them waved as the car swept past, and she thought of Sue's friends Nels and Tine, and the canyon adventure so near at hand. Patricia discovered she was impatient to be off on that ride. Recalling Tine's moving description of the great forest and the vast herd of starving deer and the ranger who was in charge of them—she could not remember his name—she found herself strangely looking forward to the trip. She called at the hotel where Mrs. Price and Sue's aunt were staying, to find Sue with them, wistfully eager and glad, though changed somewhat to Patricia's remembering eye. Sue's cheeks were neither so full nor warm-tinted as they had been. The girl's face, when in repose, seemed somewhat sad.

The four had luncheon together, during which the amiable talk of the elder women added much to Patricia's knowledge of Sue's affairs. Later, when Patricia and Sue's aunt were alone for a moment, the older woman grew confidential.

"Sue's worked awful hard. An' she's been worried. Reckon you noticed that she looks fagged. Well, the fact is she's had bad news. Don't let on I told you. Sue has got to get right down to work, to care for her mother. They're poor an' it took all they had an' all I could afford to give Sue an education.... I'm glad you're takin' Sue on this wonderful trip. She loves this country. An' she needs a rest an' change. It'll buck her up. Reckon you're very kind to take such an interest in Sue."

"Thank you for confiding in me," replied Patricia. "I'm sorry about Sue. Perhaps I can cheer her up, at least make her forget her worries until we return. Then we'll see what's to be done."

Not long afterward, Patricia and Sue were speeding along the level road on the way back toward the green-forested mountains. The western girl took off her hat and leaned her blond head back against the cushion.

"Oh, shore it's too good to be true," she exulted. "I was so tired and—and...I'll forget it. Heah I am with you again! I was half afraid you might not come."

"I did, though," replied Patricia, laughing. "Tell me about your school work."

"It was hard and hateful. But I passed. I'm a full-fledged teacher," she returned. "Can you imagine me with a room full of boys and girls—especially boys? Oh, golly Ned!"

"Yes, I can imagine that, and I can see what a perfectly splendid little teacher you'll make."

"I shore hope you're right," replied Sue with a thoughtful look.

Patricia laid her hand upon Sue's. "Will you do something for me?" she asked earnestly.

"I shore will," answered Sue quickly, turning her face in eager surprise.

"Forget all the hard work you've had—and your present worries."

"Ab-so-lute-ly!" declared Sue. "I meant to, without your asking. Shore it's good of you.... Reckon my face gives me away. I look horrid."

"Oh, no—just a little weary," returned Patricia. "Now that's settled. You've forgotten.... We're going to have a wonderful time together. For me it will be an adventure like the fulfillment of a dream that dwelt unknown in my heart.... who knows, indeed, what may not come of it?"

"*Quien sabe?*" said Sue, with her sweet, soft, deep-toned laugh.

"You said a lot. And you were only thinking of us."

"Well, young lady, who else is there to think of?"

"I was just thinking of Nels Stackhouse, and that ranger friend of his. Nels will hunt him up."

"Suppose he does? It would be quite natural," replied Patricia slowly. "And I'm sure I'll be pleased to meet your deer stalker."

"Shore, but I was thinking of the hard luck it'll be for Nels and Thad," rejoined Sue with a merry laugh. She blushed slightly, and a roguish gleam twinkled in her eyes.

"Hard luck?" queried Patricia musingly. "I don't quite follow you, Sue."

"Listen. That North Rim is the widest, most beautiful and romantic place in the West. Now as far as I'm concerned, poor Nels is in a bad way already. Well, I'm not going to run from him, or be cross or nasty or distant, or anything but my best and happiest self. That's for you. I don't care a rap what it does to Nels. I've hunch, though, he'll be funny. Cowboys are all funny. They fall in love and out of it same as they fall off a horse. So much for Nels ... Now if Thad Eburne does turn up at our camp, which is a safe bet, he's shore going to see you, isn't he?"

"Why, of course. I'll not be invisible. But what of it?"

"Shore that lonely deer-loving ranger will be the same as struck by lightning," replied Sue soberly, as if she had just realized the possibility of a catastrophe for which she would be partially responsible.

"Child, you speak in riddles," said Patricia.

"I'm no child, Miss Clay," returned Sue. "I'm a western girl who knows the West and western men. Thad Eburne will fall in love with you. I'll bet he hasn't seen a half-dozen girls in a dozen years. You're so lovely—so different—so—oh, any many would! I'd not give two bits for one who wouldn't . . . Then Thad, poor devil, would have your face to haunt his lonely campfire!—Still, I don't know but what that'd be better for him."

Patricia found herself surprised, not at Sue's half playful, half serious words, but at their unaccountable effect. She discovered that she was looking forward to meeting this mysterious deer stalker, she who had been so sure that she never wanted to meet another man in her life.

"Sue Warren, I begin to sympathize with Nels," declared Patricia. "If I were he, or any young man, I'd—I'd—Well, no matter. Mr. Eburne will weather this crisis as he must have weathered many others. Meanwhile you're going to teach me about the West. I want to know everything about everything. Name the green things, the birds and animals and places, the stories, legends, gossip, facts—all about all that makes up the West."

"Shore I was trying to tell you about what a pretty dude should know about the West," replied Sue archly. "And I reckon to be on the safe side I'd better let you ask some questions."

*T*HAD EBURNE had not returned to V. T. Park from Kanab but had taken a middle course through Buckskin Forest, and on the evening of the fourth day he camped at a spring above the Saddle.

He had traveled leisurely, leading his pack-animal and taking pains to note everything possible in reference to the deer. He estimated that he must have passed more than five thousand of them, most of which were on the west side of the mountain, near the heads of ravines which ran down into the canyon. There was little grazing left for sheep and cattle, let alone deer. In another month, when the eastern committee of naturalists would arrive to study the condition of the deer and the preserve, there would be no grazing left, thanks to the unprecedented dry season. And it had followed years of comparatively little snow and rain.

Eburne's visit to Kanab had been productive of both gratification and dismay. He found the forest service officials there, most of whom were favorably disposed to

McKay's proposition to drive ten thousand deer across the canyon. They spoke of it as preposterous, yet undoubtedly were intrigued by the originality, the audacity of the idea. McKay was to be assured that it would receive careful consideration, with chances greatly in favor of its acceptance. Opposed to this was the no longer disputed fact that on the west side of the preserve there would be an open hunting season. Thad learned nothing about Dyott and Settlemire, but he did not push his casual questioning to the point of betraying what he knew. In fact, he believed he had more information than anyone in Kanab; however, the reticence and taciturnity of the Mormons was in no wise reassuring. What they knew they kept to themselves. Finally, Thad had been relieved to meet with no more open hostility from Cassell, or from anyone except Judson. Still, Cassell had appeared to be a much preoccupied official; he did not listen intently to Thad's detailed account of the deer-trapping and put the whole matter off until October.

Early next morning, Thad left his camp and rode over the rim on the Saddle trail that led down into the canyon to the river. He had never been at McKay's mining claim but had no doubt he could find it.

This trail down to the river was one of the wildest and most unfrequented along the whole two hundred miles of the canyon. Thad always walked and led his horse over bad places. He was glad to see clear and comparatively fresh tracks in the dust. No doubt McKay had made them recently.

The grandeur and solitude of the canyon were never lost on Eburne. He gathered the harvest of a faithful and ever-revering eye. The glory of the morning sun had just burst over the endless barren corrugated reaches of the Painted Desert. Away to the east, below the towering rampart of the Vermillion Cliffs, the canyon split the red walls and wound out upon the vast heave and bulge of the desert. It was a zigzag black line, exposed only here and there, strange even to a familiar gaze, and something beyond comprehension to a spectator who did not know what it was. But that line was the Grand Canyon. There, beyond Saddle Mountain, the mouth of the canyon of the Little Colorado came in, with its mile-high walls, and, far to the west, the great blue gaps below Grand View smoked in their slumbering shadows.

Thad walked and rode until he saw the vast fanlike and illusive shapes of the Mancoweeps lying beneath him. They were as strange as their name. Farther on and below him gleamed the Toyweeps, and below them the river wound, sand-bordered and rock-constricted. A solemn roar soared upward from the river. Often Eburne stopped to rest and listen and look. He never wearied of any canyon scene. He never felt alone. Years along the canyon rims had bred in him something of the Indian's spirit.

Some hours later, hot and dusty, Thad turned a corner in the wall at the bottom of the canyon and encountered the object of his search.

"Howdy, Mac," he called.

"Eburne! Wal, I'm a monkey's uncle!" shouted McKay, dropping his pick. "By gosh, I'd most give up seein' you."

He was a huge stalwart man, heavy of shoulder, body, and leg. His face was broad, dark, full of the deep wrinkles of toil and pain and years. McKay was sixty, yet not a gray hair showed on his tousled head. He had deep set black eyes, honest and bold, a nose like a Roman warrior, a determined full-lipped mouth, tobacco-stained and chapped by exposure, and a great square chin, craggy and hard as one of the rim promontories. His garb of blue jeans was ragged and earth-stained.

Eburne lost no time blurting out his good news. Mac's seamed face changed into a mass of lines, working, twisting, somehow expressing great gratification and joy.

"You don't say! Wal, aint thet jest too blamed good?" he exploded. "I was afeared they wouldn't even listen."

"I think it'll go over," replied Thad, "and here's why." Then he proceeded to tell about the failure to trap deer, the fact of the coming investigation, the drought and the growing scarcity of feed, and lastly, the probable antagonism of the State to the federal service, which were almost sure to result in an acceptance of McKay's proposition.

"They'll have a row," concluded Thad.

"Nothin' shorer in the world. But I believe the governor will be on my side. He'll shore be agin' the shootin' of deer. Mebbe I kin get the State game warden to back me up."

"You don't need them, and perhaps it'd be better if they'd openly oppose the drive, as we know they will the shooting."

"Wal, then, I'll go slow about askin' them."

"Mac, before you tell me your plan of the drive, I want to know how you're going to raise the money."

"I'll be hanged if I know," declared McKay, scratching his unkempt head. "Thet's been worryin' me some."

"It's the most important factor," declared Thad emphatically. "It's going to cost a lot of money."

"Now, I hadn't figgered it'd cost anythin' like what I'd make out of it. Fact is I was figgerin' on payin' the expense out of the earnin's."

"You can't do that. You'll need some ready cash, anyhow," protested Eburne, realizing at once the man's simplicity and lack of organizing capacity.

"Wal, I can raise some."

"How much?"

"Mebbe five hundred dollars."

"All right. I'll lend you a thousand. Then if you can raise some more by borrowing from people in Flag. . . . Say, Mac, there ought to be some moving picture outfit willing to pay something in advance. Because if you drive the deer it will make a grand picture."

"By gosh, Thad, I hadn't figgered on you lendin' me money, or raisin' any more thet way. It's mighty white of you. An' thet hunch just about settles the difficulty."

"No. It only helps. If you get a start you stand a chance of finishing. But you've got to start. That means money for outfit, supplies, for transportation, and all that sort of thing. Fifteen hundred dollars isn't enough."

"Wal, if it ain't, I'll get more," returned McKay offhand. His mind would not concentrate on figures, or evidently on small enterprises. He had always been mixed up in some large deal, more or less visionary, as his late boring for oil out in Utah, or his present delving for copper and gold here in the bottom of the Grand Canyon testified. Still, it was McKay's kind of imagination and enthusiasm that carried great projects to successful conclusion. McKay would hit the nail on the head sometime—find the treasure at the foot of the rainbow!

"Mac, just how do you plan to make this deer drive?" asked Eburne thoughtfully. "Jim Evers told me what you told him, but now, since I've ridden down that Saddle trail, somehow I'm not so sure."

"Simple as a, b, c," declared McKay, plumping his huge knee down on the sand. His large callused fingers picked up a fragment of stone. "Now, you look ahere." And he began to make marks on the smooth sand. "Here's the cedar slopes all along the east side of Buckskin, clear from the Cocks Combs along by Warm Springs to the Saddle. All the deer on the east side of the mountain go down when the first snow flies to winter on them sage an' cedar slopes. There's juniper an' buckbrush, which's what the deer will browse on this winter. Or starve! Wal, I'm gamblin' thet a big outfit of Indians on foot, ringin' cowbells, an' a lot of riders on each end of the Indian line can drive an' herd thousands of deer along them cedar slopes to the rim wall under the Saddle. There's one place I'll have to fence with wire."

McKay desisted in his talk and map-drawing long enough to bite off an enormous quid of tobacco, after which he resumed as volubly as before.

"I aim to drive the deer into thet big gap leadin' up to the Saddle. There they'll hit the trail down into the canyon. They can't go up, an' if they pile off the trail it'll only be down in the gulch. Thet leads into one canyon after another, all walled an' steep, an' they go clear to the river. Once through the gap, them deer have got to go down. We can fence breaks along the inside of the trail. Some wire with burlap or cheesecloth stickin' on it will turn deer back. Now, by fencin' a place at the river, we could head the deer right into the water. They'll swim across, hit Tanner's trail, which is the only place a rabbit could climb out, an' they'll go up on the big blue limestone bench.—Why, Thad, it's a cinch."

Eburne was won over, even against his better judgment. It was easy to take stock in something he wished for with all his heart. This idea was so incomparably better than that of shooting or trapping the deer.

"Mac, you've sold me on your drive," he declared. "Put it up that way to anyone who wants to save the deer and they'll fall for it too. My advice is for you to go to Flag at once and begin your preparations."

"But, Thad, there's no need rustlin'. I've work to finish up here, an' we can't start the drive till the snow flies," protested McKay.

"But, man, you can get ready," returned Eburne vehemently. "Don't you see the absolute necessity of that?"

"Reckon I don't, with all due respect to you," replied McKay bluntly.

"There are many reasons," went on Thad, striving to maintain his patience. "You must begin to raise money while getting your drive approved by the service. You might lose because of lack of preparation or by putting the drive off until winter sets in. November would be ideal, if snow came. But usually snow doesn't come to stay before early December. That's pretty late, unless you're ready to drive when the first snow sends the deer down. You'd be taking fearful chances to begin after that."

"Aw, the weather keeps good on them cedar slopes till Christmas," declared McKay. "No, Thad, nothin' is goin' to fuss me 'cept thet order from the forest supervisors. Gimme thet an' the deer's as good as drove."

"Mac, I told you it was pretty sure. I know these men. There's only one thing likely to kill it."

"An' what's thet?"

"Jealousy. The fact that the plan did not originate in the minds of the supervisors."

"Ahuh! I get you. An' thet's a stumper. Howsomever, if the service people really want to save the deer, my idee will stick in their craws."

"Yes, I'm banking on that myself. I know personally how proud all the forest service are of the deer herd. I'm bound to confess it."

"Wal, I've a hunch they'll be so tickled with my drive thet they'll have me make one every year. An' I'll clean up some big money, beside doin' the country good. . . . When'll I see you again, Thad?"

"Not soon, unless you come up to Big Spruce. I'll be there alone for a few weeks. Then I'll be one of the guides with the deer investigating committee. After that I'll probably go across the canyon to Bright Angel. When the shooting season opens I'll be back riding the forest. That is going to be some job. Last, when the snow flies I hope to be with you on the big drive."

"Mebbe I'll ride up to see you when I'm through here. It wouldn't be a bad idee for me to have another look at the trail. Every time I go over it I change my mind. Funny! But them Mancoweeps are sure the foolinest places in this here canyon. . . . Thad, I near forgot to tell you I seen a lot of fresh hoss tracks round the lower slope of Toyweeps. Shod hosses, too. I hadn't time to trail them far. Lost them anyhow. But I figgered it was queer an' might have somethin' to do with Bing Dyott ridin' Buckskin again."

"Mac, what do you make of him?"

"I don't make nothin' of Dyott. I *know* him. Twenty

years ago I knowed him. Bing hasn't changed none. But times have. When I was drillin' for oil up in Utah, he was pullin' off some two-bit rustler deals. They don't pay, an' he can't risk the old-time stuff. Now I figger this way. Dyott's bein' on Buckskin this summer has got somethin' to do with your deer herd. What else is there on the mountain? No wild hosses. An' he sure wouldn't do real work, such as this here diggin'."

"I agree with you," replied Thad soberly. "But *what* is his game?"

"Wal, have you any idee he means good by the deer herd?" queried McKay with something of sarcasm.

"Good? No, I haven't. But neither can I see Dyott and his gang constituting any evil. That is, to an appreciable extent. He'll kill deer for meat. Maybe he's so hard up that he'll try to make a little stake this fall by killing and selling deer. I did have another suspicion, which concerned Dyott's possible relation to certain cattle interests. But I hesitate to—"

"Wal, thet's a pretty good idee," interrupted McKay. "Hesitatin' is good sense. I've knowed the cattle business in this country for over forty years. No easterner can ever savvy it."

Eburne reflected upon the peculiar import in this old Arizonian's speech. Manifestly his point of view, whatever it was, differed markedly from his own or that of Jim Evers or Blakener. Cattle and sheep meant little or nothing to newcomers to Arizona. But the old stock—how the very fiber of their lives seemed woven in with brands and wool and the long-established customs of early days!

Eburne left his friend early and addressed himself industriously to the long ascent, well satisfied with his visit on all scores except that allusion of McKay's to Bing Dyott. It was open to much interpretation. As far as the ex-rustler was concerned, the plot thickened.

Sunset found Thad back in camp, wholesomely tired and glad his outside tasks were, for the present, done. He would leisurely travel back to V. T. Park to see Blakener and get fresh supplies, then go to his summer camp at Big Spruce Spring, there to await the coming of the appointed committee. He would be glad for a rest and freedom from the perplexing problems and strifes which, after all, had so little to do with his real purpose there in the forest. These were outside duties that had been imposed upon him and had little to do with the warm, intimate kinship he felt for the woods and its wild denizens.

CHAPTER
8

PATRICIA and Sue had a late dinner, owing to a delay in getting back to the El Tovar.

"I promised our duffel bags for tonight," said Patricia. "Tine is to call for them. It appears Nels and the cook are to leave with pack-animals at daybreak. We're to follow with Tine and catch up with them on the trail."

They found the guide waiting for them in the lobby. "Like to have your bags," he requested, after greeting them.

"Mine's all ready, Tine," replied Sue.

"I can finish packing in a few minutes," added Patricia.

"Then I'll take Sue's along with me an' come back to fetch yours," returned the guide.

Patricia noted with dismay the small size and light weight of Sue's bag. "Oh, I am a tenderfoot," she exclaimed, pointing to a large bag she had packed and a small one not quite ready. "I didn't know what to take and what to leave out."

"Shore that's all right. Pack what you want," reassured Sue smilingly. "I'd have brought more things, only I didn't own any more."

"You relieve me, Sue. I always was a great person to carry so much more than I needed. I'll be glad to share with you."

"I wonder why I'm such a lucky girl?" queried Sue, gravely gazing up at her new friend.

"How are you lucky?"

"To meet you and go with you."

"If you call that lucky and want to know why, I can surely enlighten you."

"I shore want to know."

"It's because you're frank and lovable," replied Patricia, pausing in her work. "Indeed, I've come to sympathize greatly with Nels Stackhouse. I think I know what ails him."

Sue blushed scarlet and actually covered her face with her hands. "Oh, I—you—you spoiled such a sweet compliment," she exclaimed in confusion.

"Sue, I took the trouble to make inquiries about Nelson, just to satisfy myself," said Patricia seriously. "He has a fine record here. Straight, sober, industrious, gentlemanly, they say. He is very well liked. Now, whatever he has been in the past, this change ought to weigh with you. It's what a man *is* that counts. I believe I'd rather have a man that had once been bad and turned over a new leaf than one who'd always been good."

"But don't you see—it—it only makes me—him—oh, everything all the worse?" burst out Sue, almost piteously. Tears were on the verge of welling up in her eyes.

"No, Sue, I don't see," returned Patricia gravely.

They were interrupted by a knock on the door. Tine had come for the rest of the baggage.

"Miss Clay, I near forgot somethin'," he announced. "Nels wants to know if he's to pack two bed rolls."

"What are they?" inquired Patricia dubiously.

"A bed roll is a bunch of blankets rolled up in a tarp," replied Tine with droll dry gravity. "An' a tarp is a big piece of heavy canvas. Both together they make a bed. An' a bed is somethin'—"

"Thank you, Tine," interrupted Patricia. "I hope your idea of a tenderfoot isn't something as elemental.... You said Nels wanted to know if he is to pack two of these bed rolls. I'm sure I don't know."

"Cowboys and packers always travel as light as possible," explained Sue. "What Nels means is, will one bed be enough for you and me."

"Oh!... What do you think?"

"Shore it would—for me. I'm used to sleeping double. It's great fun when you're camping. But you must consider your own comfort."

"I should think you'd be a comfort," responded Patricia, "especially out in the dark, lonely woods where there are wild beasts and creeping things.—Tine, you're to pack only one bed roll for us."

"All right," said Tine, shouldering the bags. "Seven o'clock tomorrow. I'll be waitin'."

That night, long after Sue had fallen asleep, with her curly head nestled low on the pillow, Patricia lay wide awake, thinking, listening to the strange sough of the wind in the pines.

In the semi-darkness, for moonlight was shining in the window, the New York girl could see Sue's little head and sweet face; and if she had yielded to her yearning, she would have slipped closer and drawn the girl into her arms. Patricia knew she was going to love this western girl, if she did not already do so. And the knowledge hurt. Love had cost her a great deal. But she found she was neither bitter nor cynical any more. She had discovered the uplifting, all-satisfying, mellowing power of love. Yet she did not yield to it easily. Sue was shy with her, a little afraid of her. And Patricia's long habit of restraint made it hard for her to unbend.

But she knew that this acquaintance, so casually begun, would grow into a lasting friendship. Patricia experienced real happiness in dreaming of what she would like to do for Sue. It had been her good or bad fortune to have more money than she knew what to do with. She gave herself credit for having always been charitable. Yet if she had ever done any good in the past, it had not brought happiness to her such as the thought of helping Sue now brought her. But Sue Warren did not want charity. She needed work, independence, freedom from worry, and a home. The New York girl began to formulate plans to achieve these for the Texan without hurting her independent spirit. If Sue really loved this keen-eyed cowboy Nels, which was something Patricia had begun to suspect, and if Nels turned out to be a man!— "I'd buy a ranch and have Nels manage it," mused Patricia, and was charmed with the thought.

The trip to the North Rim would decide a great deal for this western girl and her cowboy; and Patricia had a premonition that it would be well for them. Then she wondered what the trip might decide for Patricia Edgerton. Almost mockingly she recalled Sue's playful words about the deer stalker. But in the silence of the night, with the sleeping girl so close and warm beside her, Patricia could not think long of self. She found it now for the first time in her life easier to think of giving instead of getting. And she found it pleasant.

Shadows of branches moved across the moonlit bed. The moan of the wind was sad, but it did not fill her with loneliness. The unknown future called out of the sound of the wind in the forest. It began there in that silent room— her future—and it stretched across the canyon, and then wherever she might go. But she could not evade it, and for the first time in years she did not want to. In fact, she was eager now to hurry toward it and meet it!

"Good mawnin'," the soft southern voice penetrated Patricia's dreams. She stirred; she awoke. Sue was standing beside her, gently shaking her. "Shore thought you'd never wake. It's six o'clock. And the boys will be rarin' to go."

Not since girlhood had Patricia awakened with the

zest and thrill that stirred in her this morning. As she took her bath she wondered when she would again be able to enjoy the luxury of a warm bath. Bath tubs were apt to be rare on the Northern Rim! They hurried down to breakfast, and at the appointed hour were at the head of the trail. Tine awaited them with small, staunch, gentle horses saddled and a cheerful grin on his face.

The sun was tipping the long cedared escarpment to the east of El Tovar. Golden bars and shafts, yellow fan shapes of light streamed slantingly down into the canyon. Through these streaked veils, transparent as amber, slumbered the chasm, purple in hue, mystic in line, deceptive in depth.

Patricia rode down the trail, under the golden rays, into the shade beyond, with the beauty of the morning stirring her heart.

The horses Tine had selected were fast-gaited and sure-footed. They were at home on the steep trails. Patricia, after her ten days of training, could ride with ease and pleasure. Only once did she dismount on the way down to the plateau. By the end of two hours they had passed Indian Gardens and had reached the fork of the trail, where the way on the right led down to the river.

The new trail seemed to plunge headlong into a rugged bronze-hued crack. It wound, wove, zigzagged down, down into narrow gorges, vastly different from the open country above. All was iron-bound rock, dull, dark, burned by some mighty cataclysm of fire in ages past. The air grew hot and oppressive. Tine lost no time on this descent, and Sue kept close to him, and Patricia a dozen yards behind. This lower trail was a surprise. It followed narrow passages that certainly were canyons, yet none such as she had seen before. The trail was steeper, more difficult, more restricted as to view, and it curled under cliffs that reached to the heavens. Patricia gazed aloft to see a narrow winding stream of blue which was the sky.

At last the canyon opened, so that she could view

looming walls, bottomless depths. Patricia saw Sue dismount at what appeared the end of an iron-red ridge.

"Devil's Corkscrew!" she called. "Get down and walk."

Patricia was glad to comply. When she reached the point, it was well indeed she stood on her feet. The descent from that ridge dropped almost perpendicularly. Far below she could make out a narrow winding sandy floor, with a stream of water in the middle. She let her horse go ahead.

That corkscrew descent dropped a thousand feet, it seemed to the New York girl, and when she reached the bottom and gazed back upward, she marveled at its apparently unscalable height.

Mounting again she spurred her horse forward in order that she would not get too far behind the others. Though cottonwood trees and willows, exquisitely green, and long grasses and ferns and flowers relieved the stark barrenness of that canyon, Patricia felt imprisoned.

The stream bed was sandy, gravelly, and the water ran over it clear and shallow, welcome to eye and ear. For a brief moment Patricia felt the hot summer sun on her back. As the canyon wound on, stretches of dark shade alternated with the sunlit ones.

Then, suddenly, she became conscious of a deep, low roar. It swelled in her ears. Soon she recognized it as the sound of a swift-running river. A moment later the trail turned sharply left, and Patricia saw that she was riding into the black Y-shaped chasm she had seen from above—the Marble Canyon of the Colorado.

Tine and Sue dismounted on a sand bar, and while Sue waited, the cowboy gathered up her bridle and turned to meet Patricia.

"Get down an' come in," he drawled, with his ruddy smile. "You're at the foot of Bright Angel, an' there's the river."

Patricia saw it, sullen, dark red in color, gliding, hurrying, leaping, chafing its black, ragged shores, roaring around a bend in the canyon beyond her sight. She gazed up. The black, scarred slope led her bewildered gaze to far-towering sun-tinted peaks and crags and spires and walls. She could not speak. Sue met her and led her across the sand bar and onto the edge of the black shore, beyond which the reddish water swirled greedily.

"Here's your black archaic Rock," said Sue, pointing to the marble under their feet. "And there, my lady from New York, is our cage—our bus line across the river, our automobile by cable."

It was then that Patricia saw a dark cable sagging across the river, quite high up, and a boxlike cage of slabs slung on wires and pulleys. She also espied Nelson Stackhouse sitting on a stone, his sombrero in his hands, with a grin on his tanned face for the approaching Tine.

"Yes. I see Nels, too," replied Patricia, suddenly remembering the rest of their party.

"Why, shore. So do I, now," drawled Sue, with her low, lazy laugh, tantalizing and sweet. "Come on, lady, heah's where you take your medicine."

"Oh, Sue, you mean I'll need chloroform," cried the eastern girl, viewing rather doubtfully that apparently flimsy vehicle in which she was supposed to cross.

"Mawnin', folks," was Nels's greeting. "Reckon you made fast time. Only eleven o'clock! That's sure fine, 'cause if we're lucky we'll get on top before dark."

"Where do we eat?" queried Sue jokingly.

"Over there. Nice shady, sandy place. Reckon we can spare an hour for rest an' lunch.... Climb up to the cage an' I'll shoot you across."

It was quite a little step up to the place where the cage rested, one edge tilted on the rock. Patricia entered first, aware of Sue and Tine bantering about something behind her. But what it was she did not hear. Perhaps the roar of the river deadened their voices. Sue stepped in beside her and took hold of her with firm hands.

"Hang on to the pommel. Shore she may pitch with us," cried Sue gaily.

Nels closed the gate and took his position above her. "Shove her off," he yelled.

"Adios!" shouted Tine with a look of glee at Patricia.

There was a lurch. Then the cage shot away from the shore. It swayed from side to side, creaking, groaning. Patricia shut her eyes in instinctive terror. She clung to Sue. Wind and motion and the roar of the river quite robbed her of her sense of bearing. Then she grew aware of a lessening speed and sway, but the frightful river underneath still roared on. Thus she stood for what seemed endless moments, which at last were broken by a violent bump.

"Change for the North Rim," cheerily called Nels.

Patricia opened her eyes, to see rather dimly that they were across and that Sue was leading her out onto the sand.

"Whew! If that wasn't the limit, Nels Stackhouse," declared Sue indignantly. "Why didn't you—you prepare us?"

"I—I'm all right," spoke up Patricia. "Just surprised—and scared."

"Reckoned you'd both get an awful kick out of that," said Nels disappointedly.

"You reckoned correctly, Mr. Stackhouse," returned Patricia.

"Now, Sue, didn't you get one too?" queried Nels.

Sue vouchsafed him no answer and led the New York girl into a shady spot where clean red sand invited rest.

"Did it make you sick?" asked Sue solicitously, bending over her.

"Yes, a little."

"It did me, too. But I'm about over it. I've heard of Bass's cage, down the river twenty-five miles. They say that it's hundreds of feet above the river and the cable sags far down. It must be awful to cross there. We got off easy."

Patricia soon recovered from the momentary nausea and dizziness, but her heart did not at once recover its normal beat. She watched the cowboys cross with the horses, one at a time.

"I wonder why those boys didn't let us come last," she murmured. "If I had seen the horses cross first, I'm sure I wouldn't have minded it—so much."

"Shore, I don't wonder," retorted Sue, "but I suspect that Nels Stackhouse did it on purpose."

"Well, evidently he thinks I want thrills and you need them," laughed Patricia. "Don't be angry, Sue. We'll think up a trick to play on them."

"That should be easy," agreed Sue.

They did not have long to enjoy the spot they had selected, for the cowboys soon had their horses in motion and led them into a side canyon, high-walled and sheer which widened presently and merged into an intersecting canyon. Here the deep roar of the Colorado River was replaced by the shallow rush of a brook over stones. Patricia cried out with pleasure when she espied a green-white, swift stream tearing and foaming down along a deep-cut channel. A halt was made in another shady place, where the sand was white and clean and warm.

Then Patricia became aware of several pack-mules and the last addition to their party, a fat, jocund-looking individual, who obviously was the cook. When presently he spread a piece of clean canvas upon the sand and deftly heaped a generous lunch thereon, the New York girl was willing to concede that he was a welcome member of the party.

"Ladies, this here is Bill Little, who come all the way from Winslow to cook for us," introduced Tine grandiloquently. "Reckon he has only one fault. His grub tastes so good you never eat enough an' jest naturoolly get gastromeetis."

Tine's speech struck a gay keynote for the meal, and it turned out to be a merry occasion. Sue was on her good behavior. She did not address Nels with any of her bantering remarks, though her big eyes, excited and dark, often

flashed over him. Nels appeared quiet and somehow sub-
dued. The good fortune of being on the trip with the little
Texas girl seemed to leave the cowboy tongue-tied. Tine,
however, made up for his quiet friend. All too soon this
pleasant interlude ended.

"Reckon we got to rustle," warned Tine, consulting
his watch. "Half after twelve. I'll say we're a swift outfit.
But it's step out pert now, folks, an' no laggin'. An' ladies,
don't fuss if you get your feet wet."

"Do we ford that stream?"

"Miss, that's Bright Angel Creek, an' we ford it, swim
it, ride in it jest nine hundred an' forty-six times."

"You're not serious?" queried Patricia, smiling.

"Most as serious as Nels, if you've noticed him. Jest
you count the times we pile into that creek."

Bill and his pack-mules headed the advance up the
canyon. Patricia failed to see any trail such as had made
travel easy on the other side of the river. When she rode
up ahead beside Sue, she saw that the cook was driving
his mules across the creek. With their heavy packs they
had no easy job of it. The water looked deep and swift.

"Reckon it's lower than I ever saw it at this time of
year," observed Nels. "Not much snow last winter. We're
pretty lucky."

Tine beckoned to Patricia. "Pile in after me, an' keep
on comin'. If your hoss slips, yell to me. Better shake loose
from your stirrups when the water's deep."

Single file they rode into the foaming water, Nels leading, with Sue close behind, then Tine and Patricia. The
horses splashed in as if they enjoyed it. Patricia felt cold,
sweet water on her hot face. The sensations that followed
were not as pleasant. She had to lift her boots high to keep
them dry. The hoofs of the horses clattered upon the sub-
merged rocks. The green-white water swirled up to the
breast of her mount, but sturdily he stemmed the current
and crossed without so much as a slip. Patricia gathered
courage, and when she faced the next ford, she essayed it

with less trepidation. The time came when she thrilled at the many crossings, unmindful of rush and roar, welcoming the splashing.

The canyon opened wider, allowing the afternoon sun to pour its warmth down upon the riders. The sand and stone and walls of rock reflected the heat. Sue's tanned cheeks took on a tinge of red. Patricia felt the burn on her own face and through her blouse. They rode on and on, winding, climbing, fording, never far from the creek, always working back to it, and sometimes riding straight up the channel.

Patricia found that every rider had to far for himself. Tine, observing how well she got along, paid her the compliment of letting her alone, though at bad places he always had an eye on her. Nels rode ahead of Sue; and they all kept yards apart, seldom speaking, each absorbed in the business of the moment.

The wild, ragged, iron-red canyon gradually became for Patricia a stubborn obstacle to be overcome. By mid-afternoon the creek had become a torrent pouring in tiny cascades down the steep gorge. Now and then a waterfall with rainbows of mist and golden veils, like gilded cobweb lace, blocked their way, and they had to climb around it. The trail zigzagged more, bit deeper into the red earth, grew steeper and steeper; and the dim, lofty parapets began to look less unattainable.

As the afternoon wore on, Patricia grew tired. She kept the others in sight, though how she accomplished it was a puzzle to her. She became less and less interested in the scenery. The trail climbed steadily upward. Fording the stream no longer intrigued her. And late in the afternoon, when she wearily rode out of a notch in the gray limestone to join her waiting companions at the edge of a forest, it was none too soon for her. Evidently, Bright Angel Canyon cut far into the rim, for the main canyon seemed a smoky void far back toward the south.

"Now to find a snowbank where we can camp," remarked Nels, leading the way into the forest.

"Looks awful dry to me, cowboy," rejoined Tine.

They entered a magnificent forest of majestic pines and stately spear-pointed spruces with spreading silvery branches. As Patricia rode over the pine needles that deadened the hoofbeats of the horses, she soon recovered her enthusiasm and, weary though she was, realized with a thrill that this dark forest was the black band she had seen from the canyon rim days before.

"Buckskin Forest," called Sue, "and heah's your deer!"

Sleek, graceful gray forms appeared ahead, some standing quietly with ears alert, others bounding away with their white flags raised. A whole troop of wild deer! Little spotted fawns, slender does, sturdy bucks trotted to one side of the glade and stood motionless.

The sun was westering, almost ready to sink, and shadows were creeping along the forest floor. Nels peered intently on both sides of the trail, manifestly searching for a snowbank on some sheltered north side of a ravine. Finally Nels and Tine separated, the better to search. Bill appeared to be having trouble with the pack-train. The mules seemed uneasy in this deer country. Suddenly Patricia heard a crashing of brush. She wheeled in time to see a big buck leap out of a thicket right in front of the mules. They broke into a run, turning back on their trail, and quickly disappeared, with Bill galloping behind them.

Some moments passed before the cowboys rode back, attracted by the noise. Nels spurred his horse and sped away through the forest.

"Think of that!" ejaculated Tine. "Them mules stampeded. I jest knowed Bill couldn't drive them."

"They shore bolted," declared Sue seriously.

"Reckon they'll run clear back to the canyon an' down, by gosh, if they get there first! But mebbe Nels will head them."

"Tine, you'd better help Nels," suggested Sue. "It's after sundown, and if we're going to make camp before dark there'll have to be some rustling. We'll get off and tie our horses heah."

Tine rode off at a swinging gallop.

"You look worried," remarked Patricia, glancing at Sue.

"Shore. I feel that way," replied Sue as she dismounted. "Things happen, and sometimes they're not any fun. The boys may have trouble finding those mules. It's pretty late to see far in the woods. Well, we've got to make the best of it. Tie your horse and we'll walk around a bit."

Some little way from the spruce thicket where they tethered their horses, a long beautiful glade opened in the forest. The gray forms of deer kept crossing it, adding a singular effect of wildness to the woodland scene.

"Shore you're walking Spanish," laughed Sue as she espied Patricia's cramped little steps.

"It was a long ride," answered Patricia ruefully.

"Well, pupil, another ride like that will graduate you out of the tenderfoot class," declared Sue. "You shore did fine. Tine thinks you're great—Say, isn't that a cabin down there at the end of this open stretch?"

"It surely is," replied Patricia, espying a long gray log structure just at the edge of the forest.

"Looks old—deserted," said Sue. "Let's go down there. We might find water."

"Who ever could have built a cabin in these lonely woods?" queried Patricia.

"Rangers or wild horse hunters, most likely."

They soon reached the cabin, to find it an old but well-preserved place. Patricia experienced a little chill as she peered in through the open doorway. The big room was empty except for a bench before a rude stone fireplace. A ladder close to the right of the door led up to a loft that extended over half the room.

"Wonder if the boys knew of this cabin," said Sue. "It'd not be a bad place to camp, especially if they get back late. I'm shore glad—"

Sue broke off abruptly and bent her head. "I hear horses," she added quickly.

Patricia could not hear anything but the soft rustle of pine boughs against the roof.

"Listen. Off heah," said Sue, pointing. "Wrong direction for the boys to come back.... Now, I don't like this."

Patricia became conscious of a tremor running over her frame. She listened and soon heard the faint sound of horses' hoofs on the forest floor.

"I see a bunch of riders," Sue whispered, and clutching Patricia's arm, she dragged her quickly inside the cabin. Then she peered out from behind the half-open door.

Patricia did likewise, disturbed by Sue's agitation and her sudden action. But she could not see any riders, though the muffled thud of hoofs seemed louder. The sun had gone down, and among the huge trees of the forest, gray gloom was spreading. But in the glade daylight still lingered.

"If there were any cattle up heah I'd say that was a bunch of cowboys," muttered Sue, talking to herself. "Four riders, with pack-horses.... No, there's not a cowboy in that outfit."

"What are they?" whispered Patricia, beginning to be alarmed.

"Men. And tough-lookin' hombres at that," replied Sue swiftly. "Looks like they'd pass close."

"Suppose they do?" queried Patricia.

"Shore it'll be all right if they do....! They're haided right for the cabin. I don't like this a little bit."

"Sue! You frighten me."

"Miss Clay, we're alone. We haven't even got a gun. There are two desperados in that bunch, and the fellow ridin' ahaid is no ranger, or cowman, or rancher."

"You mean—they might be desperate characters?" faltered Patricia.

"I shore do. It's not impossible to meet bad men on this side of the canyon.... Oh, don't look like that. It's all right. It just worries me. Shore they won't harm us. But—they're comin' right to the cabin....hide up in the loft!"

Patricia felt again that strong clutch on her arm, and she was dragged to the foot of the ladder. Sue climbed up like a squirrel. "Hurry," she whispered down. "Don't make a noise."

Patricia climbed awkwardly, with unsure hands and feet, but she reached the loft, where Sue drew her back from the edge and whispered, "Lie down flat and be quiet!"

The intense silence of the next moment was broken by hoarse voices.

CHAPTER

9

THE THUD of hoofs slowing to a stop, the jingle of spurs, the creak of saddles attested to the fact that riders had halted to dismount before the cabin.

"Reckon this hyar shack's the place," spoke a husky voice, deep and thick, suggesting a matured man. "I ain't never been hyar."

"Wal, Bing, it can't be no other place," replied another voice, high-pitched and nasal. "Pedro herded sheep on this end of Buckskin. We're about a quarter mile from the road, straight up from the swale you said was where we turned off. Sure this is Long Park."

"Boss, air we throwin' the packs?" asked a third man.

"Jake, I ain't sartin what we'll do yet," returned the leader. "But if there's water I reckon we might as well camp heah. Pedro, how far is Long Park from thet ranger Eburne's cabin?"

"Aboot three mile," came the reply.

"Too close for comfort. Wal, we'll see. Suppose you all scatter out an' look fer water."

"Bing, I hear a car hummin' up the road," said the man with the high-pitched voice.

Silence ensued, into which presently crept the low, melodious murmur of an automobile.

"Ha! That's my men. They're on time. Now you all clear out an' come back when I whistle. Find some water or snow."

"Bing, wouldn't it be sense to let me hang around?"

"Yes, it would, Dave," replied the other. "But he said for me to be hyar alone, at dark. He wouldn't talk else I did. It's a queer deal, Dave. I'm skatin' on thin ice, savvy? Take the hosses in the woods an' wait."

The voices ceased, and there were more thuds of hoofs, creaks of leather, and metallic jingles. These grew softer, gradually died away.

Sue placed her lips to Patricia's ear and whispered, "We've shore happened on somethin'. Don't make a noise."

Patricia had been clamped as in a vise, palpitating, yet thrilling with intense excitement. She relaxed her rigid muscles and sank on the dusty floor of the loft. In the dim light she saw Sue raise her head to peep down into the cabin. At the same moment she heard the man outside grunt as he sat down in the doorway. Then followed the scratch of a match, a flickering light that died, and the sound of slow puffs. Silently Sue lowered head and shoulders.

Patricia strove to hold in mind the thought that there was no real danger, that these strange men would soon leave or the cowboys would return. But the idea wavered. Sue had said there were bad men on this side of the river. These probably were the very ones she had had in mind.

The odor of tobacco smoke floated up to the loft. The man below puffed heavily. Patricia heard the chirp of insects, the sound of faintly rising wind, the distant yelp of some wild creature. Sue's persuasive and cautioning hand found her arm and clasped it. Twilight had fallen, and inside the cabin was dark. Then rapid footsteps sounded outside.

"That you, Dyott?" queried a low, sharp voice.

"Reckon so," replied the man in the doorway.

"Are you alone?"

"My outfit's off in the woods."

Patricia heard these quick queries and replies with tingling ears.

"Wal, all right, walk around the cabin if you want," growled the man in the doorway, whose name seemed to be Dyott.

She heard the rapid footsteps pass around the cabin. Dyott's boots scraped on the doorstep. He had risen. Then he knocked something on wood—his pipe.

"Get inside," said the man with the sharp voice. "Talk in whispers. Walls have ears. And be quick."

Dyott cursed under his breath. Then his heavy boots stamped on the cabin floor, to be followed by the quick light ones of his visitor. They went to the far end of the cabin, and there began a colloquy of whispers— the husky, impatient, reluctant whispers of one, and the guarded, decisive, imperative whispers of the other. Patricia could not distinguish a single word. But then her ears were full of throbbing and beating. She felt the racing of her blood, a constriction in her throat.

Soon the colloquy ended. The man with the quick steps and sharp voice left the cabin as silently and mysteriously as he had come. Dyott's heavy feet appeared to drag across the floor, and he was breathing hard.

"Holy Moses!" he ejaculated hoarsely. "I'll end by pluggin' thet fellar."

Then he whistled and strode from the doorway, out into the open, where the girls could hear him pacing up and down.

Patricia leaned noiselessly over to Sue and whispered, "Who are they? What does it mean? Are you afraid of— of anything?"

"Shore stumps me," replied Sue. "But I'm not afraid— yet. Reckon worse's to come."

"Oh—what—how?"

"That outfit's going to camp heah, and we're likely to be discovered before the boys get back."

Patricia's answer was checked by Sue's hand softly covering her mouth, and an excited whisper: "Keep still. They're coming."

Again the sound of hoofs and hoarse voices could be heard coming from the woods. What was going to happen? Surely she and Sue would be found hiding up here. And if they were discovered, what then?

"Find any water?" called Dyott.

"That's a snowbank handy," came the reply.

"Fetch the packs in, an' rustle firewood. We'll camp hyar."

Patricia was certain that she felt Sue's hand tremble in its contact with her arm. As for herself, the cold chills were chasing hot flushes over her body. She tried to make herself believe that the cowboys would return soon. Meanwhile her ears were filled with the hard words and coarse laughter of these men, of the pound of hoofs and thud of packs, the shuffling scrape of boots accompanied by the musical clink of spurs. A man entered the cabin, and there followed the sound of brush being dumped on the floor. Again Patricia heard the scratch of a match and saw a faint light gleam. It grew. The roof became distinguishable. Sue's form took shape. Then the crackling of sticks and the spluttering of flames told that a fire had been kindled. Other men entered to throw packs thudding on the floor, and following that came the clatter of pots and pans, the clink of metal.

It relieved Patricia to see that the space above Sue and her was obscured in black darkness, for the floor of the loft obstructed direct light from the fire. If they could only keep still! Patricia could conceive of no reason why the men should want to explore the loft, unless something made them suspicious. Yet the strain of guarding against making the slightest sound, of sneezing or coughing, was unbearable. That whispered colloquy in the darkness of the cabin between the man Dyott and his visitor did not have an honest look. Even a tenderfoot could discern that. And if Dyott discovered there had been listeners in the cabin at the time of his meeting with the stranger, he might be ugly.

"Bing, how'd you make out?" queried one of the men when evidently he and the leader were alone.

"Wal, Dave, not to please me particular," was the response. "Settled fer thet Utah deal. But this hyar new idee of mine didn't jibe. You know he's really agin Settlemire, though he pretends to be fer him, an' thet's why he won't trust me. It's do his way or nuthin'. An' I had to take him up."

"Makes a lot of work fer us—when our plan'd be easy," complained Jake.

"Wal, I'd a hunch thet after this he wouldn't be able to hold a Mormon jail over my head," replied Dyott gruffly, as if to excuse his weakness in giving in to the stranger.

"Ahuh! Mebbe you was—" The entrance of others interrupted Dave's response, and he lapsed into silence.

Patricia moved her head carefully to find an easier position, and she rested it upon her arm. She was lying prone, facedown, the same as Sue, who was, however, a foot closer to the edge of the loft floor. Patricia caught a faint ray of light penetrating the floor, very close to her. It appeared to come through a long crack. By moving slightly, she could see down into the room below. The fire was bright; pots were steaming at its edge; an iron kettle sat right in the flames, and a little grizzled man appeared to be wiping it out with a rag. She saw one other man, who sat within range of her vision. He had a thin face, dark, smooth, with sloe-black, glittering eyes. He held a cigarette between his fingers, daintily, and now and then he put it to his lips. Surely he must be one of the desperados Sue had mentioned. This position grew uncomfortable, cramping her neck. She resumed the former one, at the same time reaching cautiously to find Sue's hand. She appeared to be calmer now. There was absolutely no doubt in her mind that very soon one of the cowboys, or all, would enter the cabin. They would return to where they had left her and Sue, find them gone and the horses tied, and at once begin a search, which would lead to the cabin. But suddenly the thought occurred to Patricia that when they did come the situation might be worse rather than better. Those cowboys might put up a fight! But then how were they to know Sue and she were hidden up here, unless they revealed themselves.

Sue's thoughts must have been following the same line, for just then she whispered in Patricia's ear, "When Nels and Tine come we'd better keep mum until we see how this Dyott acts."

"I was thinking the same thing," returned Patricia. "But how will they find out we're up here?"

"That Nels is sharp. If he walks in this cabin he'll shore know I'm up heah."

Sue's reply was illuminating in a way she had not intended it to be.

She had scarcely concluded when a rapid and rhythmic beat of hoofs came to the ears of the girls on the loft floor. Sue gave her hand a quick squeeze, then let go.

"Bing, thar's someone comin'," spoke up one of the men.

"Heard him myself. Reckon it's that thar ranger Eburne," growled Dyott.

"Nope. Thet's a cowboy, or I don't know nuthin'."

Outside, spurs jingled, boots thudded. A quick step sounded at the door. The men below were silent.

"Howdy, men," drawled a cool, slow voice Patricia easily recognized as belonging to Nels.

Sue raised herself on her hands to peep over the edge of the loft floor. Patricia, as curious as she was agitated, bent over to put an eye to the crack in the floor. She saw

Nels saunter into the line of her sight and up to the bright fire.

"Who'n thunderation air you?" demanded Dyott.

"I was just goin' to ask you that same. More civil like, though," returned Nels.

"Wal, we're a hoss outfit from Utah, lookin' for strays."

"I'm Nels Stackhouse from Flag. Me an' my pard Higgenbottom come over to see the deer herd."

"Ahuh! Wal, fetch him in an' eat with us."

"Thanks, reckon we don't care if we do," drawled Nels.

Patricia could not see Dyott, but she had a fairly good view of Nels. He surely was a capital actor. He seemed casual, indifferent, lazy, with no particular interest in these men. Yet the covert roving gleam, of his eyes revealed much to the New York girl. Suddenly his gaze swept the loft, glinted, and dropped blankly. An instant later she felt Sue leaning over her, scarcely breathing.

"Nels saw me," she whispered tensely.

More of the jingling spurs and lazy steps gave Patricia the idea Nels was leaving.

"Me an' my pard aimed to camp here tonight. Any objections?" he said.

"None a-tall," rejoined Dyott. "More the merrier."

They heard Nels walk out, mount his horse, and ride away.

"Nice set-up young cowpuncher," remarked one of the men. "Funny how you can allus tell thet brand."

"Wal, I was thinkin' it wouldn't be a bad idee to git some outside news," rejoined Dyott thoughtfully. "So I was sociable."

This last remark of Dyott's had subtle power to ease the tension of Patricia's nerves. Sue very cautiously edged closer to her until their shoulders touched. In the pale gloom of the loft she could just make out the girl's face. Her fingers, too, as they closed in Patricia's, had less of that steel-like grasp. Sue, too, was feeling relieved that Nels and Tine were close at hand.

"If they find us heah there'll be a fight, shore," she whispered. "Nels has a name for bein' a bad hombre. But I begin to feel we'll escape."

"Why a fight—if they discover us?" whispered Patricia in Sue's ear.

"Because Nels won't stand much. And this Dyott will get ugly if he finds out we were heah when he met that man. He wasn't very anxious to have any witnesses to that meetin'."

"Did you hear anything they said?"

"After they began whisperin' I couldn't catch a single word. But Dyott would never believe it."

Down below, the men were moving about and there was a clatter of cooking utensils. Under cover of the noise, the girls held a whispered conversation without risk of detection. It helped Patricia toward a recovery of her composure.

"There, the boys are heah. Hear them?" whispered Sue.

Somebody below was also aware of the arrival of the cowboys. Heavy steps approached the door.

"Grub's ready, boys," called Dyott.

But Nels and Tine, though answering, did not at once come in. Presently the sound of hoofs ceased, to be followed by clinking footsteps outside, on the step, and then in the cabin. Heavy thuds on the floor marked the dropping of bed rolls.

"This here's my ridin' mate," said Nels, as obviously he and Tine were walking toward the fire.

"What's your handle, son?" queried Dyott.

"Higgenbottom. Tine Higgenbottom," replied the cowboy.

"What a handle! Thet's orful."

"What might your name be, Mister?" asked Tine coolly.

"Wal, it might be Abe Lincoln, only it ain't," replied Dyott.

"Haw! Haw! Haw!" roared one of Dyott's men.

"Reckon who I am won't interest you boys much," said Dyott, "an' if you ain't got any fine hosses you won't be sorry you met me."

"My pard said you was a wild hoss hunter, not buyer."

"Wal, reckon I'm both."

"It ain't worryin' me none, 'cause I'm ridin' a plug."

"Come an' git it before I throw it out," yelled the cook.

The call to supper roused loud acclaims, stirrings about, clankings of tin pans, pouring of hot coffee, and sundry other sounds incident to a group of hungry men crowding around for food. Then things quieted down, while the men were busy eating. Patricia became aware of a pleasant permeating fragrance of coffee. It made her realize that it was a long time since she had eaten. Sue whispered in her ear, "Of all the hard luck! I'm starved. And they shore got a cook."

"Jevver hear of Oliver Twist?" queried Tine.

"Nope. Whar does he ride?"

"He was a boy who asked for more grub. Mister Lincoln, I'll say you have some cook."

"Help yourself, lad," replied the cook, speaking for himself. "Plenty meat an' beans."

"Wal, tell us what's going on in Flag an' all over," demanded Dyott presently, raising from his seat.

"Lots of news," drawled Nels, and he began to talk as if that were his forte. "There's a lot of fellars dyin' from drinkin' bootleg whiskey. Tur'ble stuff that is. An' there's more fightin' in Noo York between bootleggers an' officers than there was in the war. The Japs are buildin' a million flyin' ships to fly over the U.S. an' blow it off the map."

From that introduction Nels skipped blandly to Flagstuff and discoursed on local politics, business, cattle, sheep, lumber, the dry season, motion pictures, railroad wrecks, and what not.

"Wal, boy, you're a regular encyclopeder," replied Dyott.

"Bing, we're shore livin' in a cave holed up at each end," said the man Dave significantly.

"Seems like," returned Dyott. "Say boys, air thar any talk about the starvin' deer on Buckskin?"

"Some," replied Nels reflectively. "I read in the paper about it. Not much talk yet, though."

"Wal, it's a fact. Reckon most the herd'll starve this fall an' winter. Twenty or thirty thousand, anyway. They're eatin' bark now."

"Too bad," said Nels. "That was one thing me an' Tine wanted to find out. If there was such a big bunch of deer in the first place, an' if they was starvin' in the second."

"They're starvin' every place. Haw! Haw!" replied Dyott. "Wal, men, seein' we have to wrangle hosses at daylight an' git started early, we'd better turn in."

Somebody kicked the dying fire and threw on a stick of wood. Then followed shuffling of feet, sliding of packs.

Patricia heard boots on the ladder. Sue's hand pressed down on her hand, as if to compel silence. But Patricia could neither have screamed nor moved just then. Someone was climbing to the loft. Her blood froze. She held her breath.

"Tine, throw my bed roll up. I'll bunk in the loft," called Nels.

Sue let out a little gasp. Patricia for a moment lay rigid; then her body went slack. She opened her eyes to see Nels's head and shoulders above the floor of the loft. He sat on the edge and leaned to catch his bed.

"Tine, reckon you stuffed too much good grub," drawled Nels. "You're plumb weak. Heave her, now—"

There followed a grunt, a deep breath, a wrestling sound, then hand slapping hard on canvas, and a dull thud.

"You didn't have to stand under it when you pitched it. Tine, your mind ain't operatin'. Try again."

Nels caught his bed roll and heaved it up on the loft floor and rolled it over between the ladder and where the girls lay. He was on his knees whistling, not very distinct in the gloom. Then he stretched out and put a reassuring hand on Sue's shoulder and after that on Patricia's. It had a warning yet hopeful pressure. But he did not bend nearer. Unrolling his pack, he pulled out blankets and tossed one to Sue and one to Patricia, all the time humming tunelessly.

"Nels, shall I bunk up there too?" queried Tine.

"It ain't particular level up here, Tine," responded Nels, "but now I got my roll open I reckon I'll stay. You sleep right under the edge, so when I fall off I'll light on somethin' soft."

Nels did not get into his bed but reclined upon it, with his hand toward the girls, and only a few feet away. Sue had quietly spread her blanket and rolled upon it, a task Patricia finally had courage to essay. It took her a long time to accomplish it noiselessly. The blanket mitigated some of her discomfort.

After a few moments, Nels's dark form began to worm silently closer, until his head was right at Sue's. He whispered, but Patricia could not catch what he was saying. After he had moved back to his former position, Sue leaned over toward Patricia.

"Nels says when they're all asleep we'll slip out," she whispered.

That was welcome news to Patricia. And she relaxed into a less strained position. Possibly the distant day might come when she could recall this adventure with a pleasurable thrill.

Gradually the men below quieted down, and deep breathing and snores took the place of voices. The fire burned to a ruddy glow of coals and soon pitch-darkness enveloped the loft. Mice began to squeak and patter somewhere under the roof; the wind outside had a strange mournful sound; she heard the sharp bark of a forest animal. It began to be a difficult matter to keep her eyes open. She could not see anything, but when she shut them, a drowsiness stole over her. That she might go to sleep was amazing. Still, the day had been one of long and toiling hours, and she now felt unutterably weary. She fought sleep. Then, when she was about to succumb to it, she felt Sue's hands.

"Come, we're going," Sue whispered. "Crawl close to me. Careful. No noise!"

Sue's voice, with its purport, caused Patricia's muscles to shake so that she could scarcely get to her hands and knees. Inch by inch Sue crawled. And Patricia, guided by Sue's boots, kept close behind. But she could not crawl without rustling, scraping sounds. When Sue reached back to give her a sharp tug, she knew what it meant, and that made her only worse. How black the darkness! The cabin was like a cave underneath the ground. Patricia nerved herself to the utmost in anticipation of descending that ladder silently. This was he first real experience with actual physical fear. There were other emotions, too, but fear predominated. While she found to her surprise that her spirit rose rather than sank under it, she had no control of her muscles, and inevitably she made a noise.

"Hey cowboy, what you fussin' about up thar?" came a gruff query from Dyott.

After a moment, Nels replied, "Huh? What? It's me. Aw, reckon I had a nightmare."

"Wal, I most forgot you was up thar," said Dyott. "Had an idee a wildcat was prowlin' around. Come near takin' a shot at you."

Then silence ensued, fraught with a terrible suspense. Nels did not answer or move. Sue did not move. Patricia had to stay there on hands and knees, absolutely motionless, for so long that she grew numb. At last Sue turned and crawled back beside her to whisper so softly that Patricia could scarcely get her meaning:

"Nels says too big risk. Must wait till mawnin'."

Sue's message brought immense relief to Patricia. At the same time she realized that it was her fault that Nels's plans had to be changed. Anything but that infinitely slow, silent crawl toward the ladder in the darkness! Somehow she got back to the blanket and sank upon it utterly spent. She had been shivering and now she was burning. She had no fear now of falling asleep! The long hours seemed to drag, but for all she knew they might have been moments. Sue neither moved nor whispered again. The time came when Patricia had to stretch forth a hand to assure herself that Sue was really there. Her hand was trembling. Instantly Sue seized it and held it tightly for a moment.

Waiting and listening, with mind crowded by thoughts and feelings, Patricia lay there in the pitch-black night so long that it seemed as though she could no longer endure the motionless position, the lonely moan of wind outside, the constant proximity to these ruffians below. Then, suddenly, she made the discovery that the blackness of the loft was changing to gray. Dawn would be coming soon, and with it some decisive change for better or worse in their present predicament.

Someone below rolled over, yawned heavily, and sat up, evidently to pull on his boots.

"Pedro, you an' Mex crawl out an' wrangle the hosses—you hear me?"

It was Dyott's voice giving these orders. Other orders followed, and they were carried out with alacrity. In a very few moments all his crew were up, and a fire was crackling.

"Nels," called Higgenbottom, "are you dead?"

"Say, is it time to get up?" called Nels sleepily.

"It's time for a lot," replied Tine in an ambiguous tone. He might have meant anything.

Presently Patricia and Sue were left alone in the loft, gazing at each other in the growing light. Below them a considerable bustle attested to the hurried preparations of Dyott's men for an early departure. Patricia heard the voices of Nels and Tine mingled with the others. Time passed, and daylight appeared to have arrived. If anything untoward was to happen, it would not be long now. Again Patricia felt the mounting of suspense. But daylight seemed to lend her more reason and control, if not actual courage.

Sue was growing impatient and curious; she crawled forward a little, dared to raise her head to peep. When Patricia heard the thud of many hoofs and realized horses were being brought in, she applied her eye to the crack in the floor, and by pressing her face down to the board, she managed to see part of the cabin room below, the doorway, and the ground outside. It was broad daylight now.

She saw a big man pause before the doorstep, stoop, and pick up something. Nothing less than her beaded and fringed buckskin gloves! Patricia suffered a violent shock, then a bursting sensation of ice suddenly congealing all along her veins.

"Dyott, come out hyar," called the man sharply.

Another burly man entered the range of Patricia's vision, blocked the doorway, then stepped outside. At the same instant, Nels appeared a little farther out; and in a flash his tanned face turned pale. His eyes, sharp between narrowed eyelids, were fixed on the gloves the man was holding out to Dyott.

"Found them right thar," he said, pointing to the ground beside the step.

"Wal!" ejaculated Dyott.

Nels stepped forward to confront the leader.

"Reckon I dropped them," he said.

"Orful pretty gauntlets," dryly remarked Dyott's comrade.

"Dave, them's a gurl's," declared Dyott, holding one of them out and letting it hang.

"I knowed thet as soon as I seen them," replied Dave, with a huge dirty paw stroking his bearded chin.

Nels reached a lean hand, like a claw, to take the gloves, but Dyott pulled them away. He glared at Nels and then at Tine, who had come close.

"Say man, they're mine," said Nels testily. "Bought them at El Tovar for my girl. Reckon I dropped them out of my pocket last evenin'."

"Pocket, nothin'!" burst out Dyott. "They look like

thet, don't they? Flat like you set on them in the saddle, huh? I don't think! Them gloves have still got the shape of hands to 'em."

Dyott thrust them to the man Dave and then swiftly he drew a gun on Nels.

"An' you too," he said, hard and grim, indicating Higgenbottom by a wave of the gun. "Line up together, an' be orful careful."

"Is this a holdup?" queried Nels sharply.

"Dave, hyar's my gun. Jest keep these gennelmen covered. I've a hunch."

Patricia shrank back from the crack and looked at Sue. She was crouched, as if ready to spring erect. Below, the excitement had extended to the rest of Dyott's men.

"Ahuh! Look at thet," spoke up the leader harshly. "Little boot track, made last night. Hyar's more, an' a little one. . . . Git back out of the door, you fellars."

Dyott stamped inside and plumped down on his knees at the foot of the ladder. There followed a moment of silence, in which Patricia thought she was going to faint. Suddenly she heard Dyott's boots crunch on the floor and then thud on the rungs of the ladder. Sue swung erect to her knees, rigid, instinct with fright. Patricia was at last terrified.

A big-headed, burly-shouldered man appeared above the level of the loft floor, wheeled on the ladder to see the girls.

"Wal!" he shouted. "Reckon I had it figgered . . . Come down out of hyar!"

That broke up the inaction below; the men crowded forward, exclaiming.

"Who's up thar, Bing?" queried one ringingly.

"What'd you think? A couple of gurls!"

"Ben up thar all night?"

"Wal, I should smile, an' thet's what's eatin' me," replied Dyott. "Who air you, anyway?"

"None of your business," retorted Sue.

"Is thet so? Wal, pile down out of hyar pronto. I want a look at you gurls."

Sue made no move to comply, and Patricia felt clamped in cold lead. She saw the man lurch up higher, thrust a huge knee over on the loft floor, and glare at Sue.

"Air you comin' down? If have to git up hyar—" he said roughly, snatching at Sue and almost reaching her.

"Don't you—touch me," cried Sue, her voice breaking in fear and rage. "Get back down the ladder. I'll come—we'll both come."

Dyott backed down out of sight and jumped heavily to the floor.

"Bing, what's the deal?" demanded the man with the sharp voice.

"Great Scott, men, thar's two gurls up thar," answered Dyott.

"Then they was thar last night when you come in hyar with your man."

"Thet's jest what we're up against," said Dyott sullenly. "Hey you up thar. Hurry down."

Sue must have had a thought of how terrible this must be for Patricia, for she helped her to her feet and to the ladder. Then Sue descended first. Patricia found strength to grasp the upper rung, step down, and slowly descend to face the four most villainous-looking men she had ever seen. The biggest of them, bearded, gleaming-eyed, fiercely ugly, deliberately thrust her and Sue out of the door. The eastern girl nearly fell. She caught herself and staggered back against the log cabin. The fifth ruffian still had Nels and Tine covered with a gun.

"Let's hev a look at you," began Dyott. "Ahuh! Two pretty gurls, one little an' one big. Both wearin' men's pants! Wal, reckon you can be handled like men."

"Dyott, you'll get yours if you touch those girls," burst out Nels, white and glazing-eyed.

"Come hyar, you yellow-haired kitten," growled Dyott, suddenly grasping Sue by the front of her blouse. It ripped.

He swung her clear off her feet and, drawing her close, bent his huge head until it was almost parallel with her face. "You was up thar last night when we rode in hyar, wasn't you?"

"Yes—we were," panted Sue. "Let go—you brute!"

"Stop squirmin' an' squallin' or I'll tear your shirt off," he bawled. "Listen hyar. You was up thar by accident? Seen us comin' an' hid, huh?"

"Yes," answered Sue, ceasing her struggles. Her face was now white except for red spots in her cheeks, and her eyes burned with a wonderful fire.

"You heard me come in with thet man an' what he said?" he queried furiously.

"I heard every word," declared Sue.

He flung her back against the wall beside Patricia, and as he faced his men, he actually threw up his hands.

"Well, he was right. The walls did hev ears. Now what'n earth's to come off?"

None of his men appeared able to help him out of his dilemma. Dyott glared at them, then at Dave and the cowboys.

"Reckon I can tell you what you'd better do," spoke up Nels.

"Shet up, you loose-jawed gab flinger, or I'll mash you one," returned Dyott fiercely. Then he wheeled to Sue. "Who're you?"

"My name is Sue Warren. I'm from Flagstaff," replied the girl. "My friend heah is a tourist from New York. We crossed the canyon with the cowboys as guides. Our pack outfit stampeded, and while they chased off we happened on this cabin. We saw you ridin' up and we hid in the loft."

"Ahuh! I figgered somethin' like," returned Dyott darkly. "Wal, it'd been better fer you if you'd not hid up thar."

Dyott turned to the tall sallow-faced, drooping-mustached member of his gang.

"Reckon we gotta tie up this oufit. I'll take them down in the brakes an' hold them prisoners till—"

"Bing, I'm advisin' agin thet," interrupted the man. "It's bad enough to throw a gun on cowboys, let alone kidnap two girls. Well, man, we ain't back in the old Hash Knife days."

"I've a chance to clean up an' I'm takin' it," responded Dyott grimly.

"Wal, I'm passin' the buck. I'll stand fer the deal we're on, 'cause there're men in sympathy with it. But this hyar stunt is a fool stunt."

"Say, you'd let this sassy little cat go blab all she's heerd?" demanded Dyott incredulously.

"Sure I would," replied the other bluntly. "Thet'd be better than makin' it wuss. Mebbe she's bluffin, anyhow. She looks equal to it."

"Wal, I can't afford the risk. Even if she never heerd a word, she could queer my deal . . . Tie them cowboys up."

Two of the men advanced, one to take a lariat from a saddled horse, and the other to walk back of Nels and pinion his arms behind.

"Bing Dyott, you'll pay dear for this," muttered Nels, his lean face corded and drawn.

"*Look out! Grab her!*" yelled the tall man.

The sharp command roused Patricia out of her trance. Sue had darted by the men. She was as quick as a fleet-footed boy. Leaping upon one of the horses, she screamed and kicked. It reared with a snort, plunged down, and broke into headlong flight across the glade. Dyott and his men stood petrified. In a moment Sue had entered the forest; in another she was out of sight. Nels let out a cowboy yell. It was a shout of relief and admiration of the Texas girl's courage.

"Chase her," harshly ordered Dyott, frantic with rage. "Pedro! Mex! Run her down!"

E *BURNE* left his cabin at Big Spruce and rode down toward V. T. Park, which was distant by a day's slow horseback ride. At a point where the trail crossed the new road, he espied fresh motorcar tracks.

"Way up here," he muttered in surprise. "First wheel track I've seen up here this summer, or for that matter the first I *ever* saw. They would have to build this new road."

He got off to make sure just how fresh the tracks were. "Made this morning maybe. Last night sure." Mounting again, he turned down the road, for no particular reason that he could account for except that the impulse was strong.

The morning was beautiful, one of the first without frost, and all about him birds, deer, squirrels, and grouse seemed to be participating in the joy of life. Eburne would have had that forest as the Indian would—without roads, cars, white men, cattle. Let nature take care of the deer! But this was impossible because government appeared to be made up of the same kind of men as those who lived off the range. They wanted to run things to suit themselves, and each set of men, the same as new ranchers, cattlemen, prospectors, hunters, changed these things according to their idiosyncrasies or personal desires.

Presently the ranger's keen nose detected smoke, and soon, at a turn of the road, he espied an automobile camp near the edge of a grass park. He rode up at a brisk pace to confront three men eating breakfast around a campfire. Two of them he recognized as Settlemire and Judson, but the third man he had never seen before. Eburne was fairly familiar with his type, which appeared anything but that of a tourist. He had the sharp, pale face of a man of affairs from Chicago or Los Angeles, looking for some business deal in oil or lumber or cattle.

"Hello, Settlemire. What you doing way up here in the woods?" he inquired with cool curiosity. He did not greet Judson. They had clashed more than once. Upon the third member of the trio Eburne bent speculative eyes.

"Hello, Eburne. If it's any of your business, I'm up here for my health," retorted Settlemire with ill-concealed chagrin and hostility.

"I'm an honest-to-goodness forest ranger. Do you get that?" replied Eburne.

"Yes, I suppose I do. But it doesn't matter particularly to me what you are."

"Well, it explains *my* business here," Eburne returned.

Settlemire recovered himself somewhat and began to talk about his cattle, complaining of the lack of grass and asserting that if the government did not order ten thousand deer killed on the preserve he would remove his cattle to Utah.

"What difference would that make to the government?" queried Thad curtly. "Besides you've already had the government orders to move your cattle off the preserve. *And* you haven't done it!"

"I have, too—thousands of cattle," declared Settlemire.

"You've still four thousand head over on the west side," rejoined Eburne coolly.

"Is that so? You know more about it than I do, I suppose. But you don't know that the government is one thing and the forest service another."

"Yes, I know that, too."

Settlemire spoke of the overmultiplication of deer, that owing to this and a dry year, his cattle and those belonging to other ranchers were starving for grass and water. "I had a chance to sell out," he concluded, waving a nervous hand at the third man. "But he won't buy because of this deer problem."

"Settlemire, don't you realize you're dealing with United States property?" asked Eburne, amazed.

"My cattle belong to me," returned Settlemire.

"Your cattle, yes. But not this range. That belongs to the United States government, and right now you are using it against the law."

"Yes, and I'm going to get the government to permit the killing of ten thousand deer."

"Where?" demanded Eburne hotly.

"Right here in your Buckskin."

"You can't do it," replied the ranger with passion. "I can't conceive of the government permitting a horde of pot-hunters and amateur sportsmen and automobilists to come in here. They'd murder these tame deer and cripple twice as many as they killed. Great Scott, *what* kind of hunters would shoot these tame, half-starved animals?"

"Thought you was a vegetarian, Eburne," returned Settlemire with sarcasm. "No doubt you've helped the deer graze off the range."

Judson and the stranger haw-hawed at this as if it was a huge joke. Eburne passed the insult by, though it made his blood boil.

"Ten or twenty thousand of these deer have got to be killed," added Settlemire with finality.

"Settlemire, if the federal government permits the killing of deer, the State government will oppose it," returned Eburne with equal finality.

"You're for McKay's plan, hey?" queried Settlemire jeeringly.

"I sure am. The right and humane thing to do in this case is to save the deer. Not to kill them or try to trap them alive. They should be driven from Buckskin into other parts of Arizona where deer are scarce and feed abundant."

"You're a ranger, a deer stalker, they call you, and yet you've faith in that wild plan to drive ten thousand deer across the Grand Canyon?" queried Settlemire derisively.

"It *might* be done," answered Thad.

Here Judson intervened by rising to kick a billet of wood upon the fire and to speak with deliberation: "Settlemire, you know Eburne's great at chasing deer across the canyon. But you spell it d—e—a—r!"

Loud guffaws greeted this sally.

Without more ado, Thad slipped off his horse and, leisurely stepping up to Judson, he swung his fist hard on Judson's jaw, knocking him over the improvised camp table, flat to the ground.

"That'll do from you," said Thad without any rancor, but his tone was menacing.

Judson was not quick in getting to his feet. Livid, with a hand at his bleeding mouth, he glared at Eburne.

"You fellows want to be careful how you talk to me— personally," went on Thad. "And as far as other things are concerned, for instance deer and cattle and campfires, don't forget I'm still an officer in the forest service. And I've not only the power but *cause* to arrest you."

"You're locoed, Eburne," harshly retorted Settlemire, but his face lost some of its heat. "If you did take me to Kanab on some framed-up case, all that'd happen would be you losing your job."

"Not quite all," returned Thad coolly. "I might be able to show the *state* government, anyhow, that you'd benefit by the killing of ten thousand deer....And that it's not beyond the bounds of possibility for you to help do it."

"Help do it! How, Mister Ranger?" inquired the cattleman.

"Why, shoot them yourself," rejoined Thad contemptuously.

"Bah!" ejaculated Settlemire, and it was an expression of relief.

"Your meeting Big Dyott up here in the woods looks queer," flashed Eburne.

"Who says that? I never did," blustered the cattleman.

"You're a liar. Blakener *saw* you, and he'd swear to it."

"Dyott was foreman of my Sevier River ranch. I could talk to him if I met him, couldn't I?"

"Yes, he *was* your foreman. And he also was one of the Hash Knife gang. Settlemire, you can't bluff me. You big cattlemen pull political strings, you make friends, you run the little cattlemen off the range, you steal each other's water and calves. And you call it business. I've got another name for it. You all evade the law, or get around it, or keep within it, technically. But watch your step. I'm on your trail, Settlemire. No doubt you can get me fired. But you can't keep me out of these woods.... That's all. Good day."

As Eburne mounted and turned his horse back down the road, there was a blank silence. Suddenly it was broken by the sharp high-pitched voice of the third man. He was talking fast, and his tone was angry. Thad could not distinguish what he said. "Wonder who he is," soliloquized Thad. "Some outsider like Settlemire. A sucker, maybe. But he didn't look it. He'll be one, though, if he buys Settlemire out or any of these big cow outfits." Thad rode on, soon getting out of earshot of the men. He felt a deep inward satisfaction at having expressed his feelings. What the result would be was of small moment. He loved the great deer herd, but he did not care much any longer for this thankless job. All he hoped for was that he would not get the inevitable discharge before McKay's deer drive. Still, that need not prevent his helping.

Preoccupied in mind, he rode back, and passed where the trail crossed, and for a considerable distance before he was aware of it. When about to turn, he heard the swift rhythmic beat of galloping hoofs.

"Shod horse, whoever's riding him," muttered Thad. "And he's sure running!"

Reining in, Thad gazed down the road to a thickly wooded bend. Soon a big bay horse shot into sight. His rider was a bare-headed girl whose golden hair streamed in the wind.

"A girl! I'll be hanged," ejaculated Eburne. "Something wrong.... Say, but she can ride!"

At second glance, the ranger thought the horse was running away. But as he came gliding on smoothly, evenly, fleet as a deer, Thad felt assured the rider was making him run. The stirrups were flying out, dangling. She did not have her feet in them, which fact further attested to her horsemanship. She could not have avoided seeing Thad, for he stood right in the middle of the road. The rhythm of the clattering hoofbeats broke. Then Thad saw that the rider was pulling up her horse. But she was able to break only his gait. She appeared to be a mere slip of a girl, certainly not strong enough to check that powerful steed. Suddenly she leaned far back in the saddle and dragged with all her might. The horse slowed, plunged with thudding hoofs, reared aloft, mouth open flecked with froth, eyes wild, and then came crashing down to skid along the woods road.

"Stop, you big—" panted the girl, straining at the bridle. Her white face seemed distorted. She pulled the horse to a stop in front of Thad.

"*Thad Eburne!*" screamed, and that tense, drawn face changed as if by magic.

"Sue Warren!" exclaimed Thad in amazement. "For Heaven's sake, what does this mean?"

"They're—after—me," she cried. "Come off—the road."

With that she urged the horse at a gallop into the woods. Thad followed, gazing back along the road. But no riders appeared, and soon the road disappeared from sight. He tried to catch up with the girl, but her horse got down to running again and he was very fast. He ran away from the ranger's horse. Then, at a good safe distance from the road, the girl halted him and waited for Thad. He soon reached her side.

"Oh—what luck—to meet you!" she panted, reaching for his outstretched hand. "I'm so—out of breath. It shore—tore me to pieces—ridin' this horse."

"Sue, who's after you?" demanded Thad sharply, his keen eyes on her pale, drawn face.

"Bing Dyott's men," replied Sue. "Some of them—anyhow.... Listen. We've got—to be—quick." She put a hand on her heaving breast and tried to get a deep, full breath. "I'm over heah—with a Miss—Patricia Clay. We met at the El Tovar. She wanted to see—the North Rim. Nels Stackhouse and Tine Higgenbottom brought us over. Last night, just after we got on top, the pack-mules bolted. The boys went back. Miss Clay and I walked around. We found a cabin over heah at the end of a long, narrow park. Then we saw a bunch of riders. I shore didn't like their looks. We went into the cabin, hopin' they'd pass by. But they didn't. Then we hid in the loft. I heard Dyott send his gang out into the woods. He was waiting for a man who was to meet him there. It got dark. The man came. He had a sharp, high voice. They went into the cabin and whispered. It shore was a secret deal of some kind. Then the man left quick as he'd come. Dyott's gang came in, made a fire, started supper. Pretty soon Nels arrived. He was suspicious. He shore had a hunch we were up in that loft. But he jollied Dyott. Lied like a trooper. Then I moved so Nels could see me. He left then, to come back with Tine. They ate with the gang. Nels came up in the loft and fixed his bed up there. We tried to slip out, but Dyott heard somethin'. He was suspicious. We didn't dare. We stayed there all night. Not a wink!...Day came. Nels went down. Dyott's man found Miss Clay's gloves. That let the cat out of the bag. Dyott threw a gun on Nels and Tine and then forced us to come down. He was furious. He was afraid we'd heard the whispered secret with the strange visitor. I lied. I said I'd heard every word. That was a mistake, for if I hadn't we might have got off. Dyott threatened to keep us all prisoners. One of his gang opposed this. But Dyott was scared and mad. He ordered them to tie up Nels and Tine. Then I jumped on this horse, got away. Shore haven't ridden more than three or four miles. Didn't see anyone chasin' me, but they must be, for I heard Dyott yell."

"I know the place," replied Thad tersely. "We'll ride around and come up back of the cabin."

Eburne's first thought, as he wheeled his horse away, was of the bravery of the little western girl. She had talked as fast as she had ridden, but she hadn't shown any hint of fright. Then the significance of her words dawned upon him. Dyott had a rendezvous with some man he did not want his gang to see or hear! That man was the stranger with Settlemire. Eburne remembered the sharp, high-pitched voice. The plot was thickening, if it was a plot; or else it was just a miserable little deal between Dyott and these cattlemen. Eburne recalled many such. This reaction of Dyott's, however, was serious, whether or not he had good cause. It was not an absolutely rare thing for a gun to be drawn along that border between Arizona and Utah, even in these modern days, but the mistreatment and threatening of women tourists with guides was something unusual and desperate. This was going too far. Eburne's anger rose as he led the way back to the road.

He rode at a swinging gallop through the woods, every glade and ravine of which he knew, until he reached a thickly wooded swale. Here he dismounted, and tying his horse, jerked his rifle from its saddle sheath.

"Shore I'm goin' with you," declared Sue resolutely, leaping off her big mount.

"All right. But stay behind me, and do what I tell you," said Eburne.

He hurried with rapid stride through the forest, never slackening his pace until he caught sight of a sunlit open park ahead. He had struck it at about the middle. The cabin, he knew, was situated at the east end, at the edge of thick timber. Altering his course a little, he went on and soon made out the dark blot of the cabin against the light of the clearing. Luckily the timber all around was thick. Eburne turned to find Sue right at his heels, keen as a whip. He did not need to tell her anything.

When he got within a hundred yards of the cabin, he saw a couple of saddled horses nibbling at the grass just inside the clearing. He heard a loud voice, but the owner of it was out of sight behind the cabin. Eburne paused. There was a thick clump of brush and saplings at the right of the cabin. For this shelter he headed, half running. He heard Sue's soft footsteps close behind. In a few moments he reached the covert and again halted a moment to catch his breath. His straining ears caught the sound of angry words: "...I'll tell you thet you're dead wrong."

"Dave, if you're scared, beat it back to Utah," answered a harsh voice that Eburne took to be Dyott's.

Then the ranger, slipping between the brush and the cabin, reached the corner and looked around. He saw a man, back to him, sitting on a log. Nearby lay the two cowboys, Nels and Tine, bound hand and foot.

Eburne leaned forward for a better look around the notched logs. Suddenly his gaze encountered a woman's face. He saw her form, too, but only vaguely. The face was the most beautiful he had ever beheld. It was white as snow, with great dark, frightened eyes fixed in loathing upon someone not visible to Eburne. Her lips were parted and trembling. Then he saw that she was leaning against a sapling—that her arms were tied behind her.

A fury, desperately hard to resist, rose in Eburne, but he had control enough to wait. Dyott was not in sight. It would not be wise to rush out there and risk a shot from him from inside the cabin. At that moment Eburne heard his heavy footfalls on the floor, then on the doorstep. A burly man in shirt sleeves, with lowered bushy head, heaved within range of Eburne's sight.

"Air you goin' to tell me?" he demanded impatiently of the trembling woman.

"I can't tell you what I never heard," she replied.

"You lie! Thet yellow-headed little cat heerd. She spit it at me. You're lyin' to me. If you don't tell it'll be the wuss for you."

"I didn't—hear," she faltered.

The other man spoke up. "Bing, I reckon she ain't lyin'. Thar ain't any reason why she wouldn't say so if she heerd yore precious secret."

"Shet up!" yelled Dyott.

Then he took a long step that brought him within reach of the woman. She shrank as his big dirty hand neared her breast and she struggled to free herself from the tree to which her hands were bound behind her.

Eburne leaped from his shelter and discharged his rifle over Dyott's head. Then, working the lever, he ran to the cabin doorway, from where he could command the situation.

"Don't move, you on the log," he called.

"I ain't movin' an I ain't goin' to," replied the man.

The girl in dungerees ceased struggling with her bonds as her eyes became fixed upon the ranger. Her tormentor had stopped in his tracks.

"Dyott, I'll not miss next shot," said Eburne. "Turn around."

The burly form moved around as on a pivot, to disclose a livid visage, pallid under beard and dirt. It had deep-set, smoldering eyes, a big nose, and a loose mouth.

"Eburne, the deer stalker?" he muttered in surprise.

"Yes, you—you skunk! I've a mind to kill you."

Swiftly, then, Eburne reversed the rifle and swung it. Dyott tried to jerk his head back, but the stock struck him behind his left ear, felling him like a bullock before the ax. Then, as Eburne wheeled to face a possible move from the other man, Sue rushed past him to the assistance of her friend.

"Oh, Patricia, everythin's all right," she cried. "Brace up. Shore it's Thad Eburne come to rescue you."

"Say, Eburne, reckon you needn't point thet cocked rifle so close to me," declared the man on the log, querulously. "It makes me nervous. An' I haven't done nuthin'."

"That's so, Thad," spoke up Nels. "He tried to make Dyott see sense."

Whereupon Eburne, still keeping one eye on the man in question, took out his knife and cut the ropes that bound Nels, and then those on Tine. Both cowboys got up, red in the face, stretching themselves and rubbing out the kinks in sundry places.

"Thad, you sure cracked Dyott one on his thick nut," declared Nels with satisfaction as he viewed the prostrate form. Then he walked over for a closer look. Dyott was not unconscious, though he appeared stunned.

Tine came over to have his say, which was not over-elegant in form or content. Meanwhile Sue had freed Patricia from her bonds and led the bewildered girl to the doorstep and seated her there.

Eburne handed his rifle to Nels. "Keep an eye on these men till I see what's best to do," he said. Then, with a quickening of his pulse, he strode over to the doorstep.

"Are you—all right?" he asked haltingly, under the restraint of an unfamiliar emotion. Patricia's head with its dark, rippling masses of hair, somewhat disheveled, lay against Sue's shoulder. Faint blue veins quivered under the clear whiteness of her skin; her eyes were a singularly dark hazel as they looked up into the face of the tall ranger.

"Yes, thank you," she replied.

"Patricia, this is Thad Eburne, the ranger I told you about," said Sue. "Thad, this's Miss Clay from New York."

"Mr. Eburne, it's no exaggeration to say I was happy to meet you—a moment ago," murmured Patricia, suddenly smiling.

"I'm happy to meet you, Miss Clay, but I am sorry you have had such a rough time of it over here on our side of the river. Still, I suspect men like Dyott can be found most anyplace." He found her grave, penetrating gaze most unaccountably hard to meet.

"Thad, hadn't we better get away from heah before the others come back?" queried Sue. "They must have chased me."

"Indeed, yes," declared Eburne quickly. "You girls have had more than enough. Do you feel up to a short ride, Miss Clay?" he asked.

Patricia rose rather unsteadily to her feet, with Sue helping.

"I'm fine," she replied frankly. "Let's go where I never have to set eyes on that vile ruffian again."

"Thad, you shore gave him a wallop," said Sue, and with a grimace she took a quick glance at Dyott. "Reckon he's got a haid of wood."

"Nels, where's your outfit?" queried Eburne, turning to the cowboys.

"Over here a ways in the woods," replied Nels, handing back the rifle. "I left our cook with the grub an' pack-mules. Tine an' me fetched out beds over."

"Get them and come along," said Thad, and then turned to the man on the man on the log. "You tell Dyott if I run into him again on this preserve I'll arrest him and put him in jail. Not in Utah, but in Flagstaff! One of these girls has several influential friends down there."

"Sure will, Eburne. An' if you want to know, I'm trailin' back across the line."

Sue was leading Patricia out into the park, and Thad joined them.

"Patricia, it was *bad*," Sue was saying, talking fast and cheerfully. "But it might have been worse. Suppose I hadn't run into Thad! That brute was mad clear through.... Well, anyway, it's over. And after a few days, when you forget it, you'll have just as wonderful a time as we expected. I shore think you were a thoroughbred not to go down and out completely. Heah with those men, and the cowboys hawg-tied! Oh, but Nels is mad. He'll shore kill that Dyott if he ever meets him alone."

Sue glanced nervously back over her shoulder. Thad turned to see Tine staggering across the park with his bed roll on his shoulder and Nels coming out of the cabin.

"They're both coming," said Thad.

"Sue, it took four of those men to tie up your friend," remarked Patricia.

"Which one?" asked Sue.

"Why, Nels. Dyott pointed a big revolver at both boys. Tine kept quiet, but Nels fought. They had all they could do to conquer him."

"Nels shore used to fight for fun and for exercise when he was in a good humor. And when he was drinking—oh, he was terrible."

Thad stole a sidelong glance at Miss Clay. Yes, she was quite tall, her head coming above his shoulder. A slight color was flushing her white cheeks. What long, dark eyelashes! From this side view her eyes appeared almost purple.

"Look at my wrists, where he tied me," she said suddenly, extending her hands. There were red and blue marks around the slender white wrists. "Oh, I forgot my gloves. He has them."

"Who? Dyott? I'll go back and get them," returned Thad.

"Don't, I beg of you," she cried, turning to him. "I have others, I couldn't wear those again."

"I'll go anyhow," said Thad and, wheeling, he strode back across the park. He passed Tine, but Nels threw down his bed roll and joined him.

"Reckon I want to be in on anythin' now I'm not hawg-tied," he explained.

Dyott was sitting up while his ally tried to stanch the blood from a wound in his scalp.

"Dyott, I want the gloves that belong to the young lady," demanded Thad.

"They're stickin' in my coat pocket, over thar," returned Dyott, pointing. And after Thad had secured the gloves, he added, "Eburne, I'm goin' to carry your mark. So I won't forget you."

"Is that a threat, Dyott?" queried Thad.

"Take it any way you like."

Thad glanced down at the brutal blood-stained face and thought better of the remark that was about to pass his lips.

"Dyott, take a hunch from me. Don't let these selfish cattlemen force or bribe you into deals they'd never have to suffer for if you got caught."

With that, Thad dragged the aggressive Nels away.

"Say, Thad, you're a queer cuss," drawled the cowboy. "Bust a man's head an' then talk kind to him!"

"Nels, I sort of got an idea that old rustler was being imposed upon and I felt sorry for him. Sure he ought to have been shot for mistreating the young ladies. But such men in these days don't always get their just deserts. If it's found out I cracked his head, I'll have trouble."

"Wal, it's a cinch Dyott won't blab."

They caught up with Tine and then joined the girls. Thad tendered the gloves to their owner, who received them with reluctant thanks. Presently Thad espied the El Tovar horses and mules some distance away in the pine woods. Beyond, a film of blue smoke hung against the green foliage. The cowboys' camp appeared to be in charge of a very badly worried cook.

"Little, shake with Thad Eburne, ranger," said Nels. "An' then rustle some grub. If I'm near starved, what must Miss Clay an' Sue be? They haven't had a bite since yesterday noon."

"Patricia, you sit right heah," Sue was saying. "I'll fetch some water and a towel. I'll bathe your face and brush your hair. Then, with a bite to eat and a few hours sleep—"

"Excuse me, Sue," interrupted Thad. "Suppose we get farther away from Dyott and his gang. I don't trust them."

"Shore I never thought of that," replied Sue. "We'd be nervous heah."

"Miss Clay, do you think you can stand another short stretch in the saddle?" inquired Thad.

"I think so," she replied, smiling at him. "I'd certainly rather make the effort than stay here."

"Well, we'll go then, as soon as you've had a little rest and something to eat," replied Thad. "Meanwhile I'll get my horse and return the one Sue rode. Then we'll ride over to my cabin. It's isolated and not far from the rim. I'm sure you'll enjoy camping there a while."

IT SEEMED to Patricia that the ranger's "short stretch" to his cabin was very long indeed. Yet, despite the fact that she swayed in her saddle, she felt a strange pleasure in the ride. Already the terror she had experienced during the past few hours had passed completely from her mind. A sense of peace and confidence filled her spirit. How much the magnificent figure of the ranger, tall, lithe, with his keen, dark, lean face, up there as the head of the party, had to do with her feeling of well-being she did not know. Now and then he looked back at her with solicitude in his gaze.

Eburne and Tine were riding in front with Little and the pack-mules. Sue rode beside Patricia, keeping close watch on her, with a hand ever ready. Nels acted in a way rather unusual for him. Patricia became aware that the cowboy could not keep away from Sue. He watched her all the time with faithful doglike eyes of devotion. It was impossible that Sue did not notice this, yet she gave not the slightest sign. She kept on trying to amuse and interest

Patricia, doing everything she could to keep the eastern girl's mind off the distressing experience she had just gone through.

"Sue, I'm all right," said Patricia at length. "I'm not worrying and I shall not fall off my horse. You ride ahead with Nels. You make me feel so—so helpless."

"But you're so pale, Miss Clay. I'm afraid you had more of a shock than you think. Anyway, Thad told me to stick close to you," Sue replied, "and I'm obeying orders."

"Never mind what he said. And don't call me Miss Clay. You've called me Patricia several times. I liked it."

"That will be dandy," said Sue shyly. "This mawnin' I do feel as if I've known you a long time. When people get out this way in the open they soon grow close together or far apart. Shore there's nothing like a hard camping trip to show what's in a person. And I feel about you just like Thad Eburne does."

"How is that?" asked Patricia, with a curiosity she could not disguise.

"He said, 'Sue, she's shore game and sweet. It was a rotten deal for a girl new to the West. This experience has taken more out of her than she realizes. You keep close watch over her. It'd only embarrass her if I did.' "

"That was nice of him," murmured Patricia, flushing. "But I don't think very highly of myself. Last night if I had not been clumsy and confused we'd have escaped. That would have been just fun for a western girl like you. And this morning I was terribly frightened."

"Maybe you'll not believe it, but I was too," admitted Sue. "You see, how could I tell what had happened to you? When we saw Dyott going for you, and you tied helpless to that tree, you were enough to scare anyone. I've never seen Thad so mad."

"How did I look?" queried Patricia.

"Shore if I'd been a man it'd have been all day with me," drawled Sue.

"You've said something like that before. I gather you

mean to be flattering. But you're not too explicit. How did I look? Sue, please allow for a little natural vanity."

"Oh, so that's it," laughed Sue, "Well, if you'd try for a million years you shore couldn't make yourself look more appealing. Patricia, you were white as death. Your eyes were something to see: proud, defiant, and despairing. You'd have fallen but for that sapling where you were tied. And your body quivered all over. Reckon Thad was looking for Dyott and missed all I saw. But if he *did* see you I'll bet his heart is plumb gone forever."

"Sue Warren, I did not ask for quite so much—information or deduction," replied Patricia confusedly. "I begin to fear you are a little—well, a confirmed scallawag if not a tease. No wonder poor Nels lives in perpetual torment."

"Patricia, I'd love to tease you if I dared," said Sue with sweet earnestness. "I'm western, you know, and blunt, and perhaps I seem crude to you. But I don't lie and I do hit things plumb on the haid."

"You may tease me all you like," returned Patricia. "But I'm not teasing when I say that you are the bravest girl I've ever known. I wish I could ever be half as game. Now go ride with Nels. Let me try to take care of myself."

"That cowboy is shore queer this morning," declared Sue dubiously as she gazed ahead at the rider, usually so easy and graceful in the saddle, but who now kept turning sidewise to look at Sue.

"Sue, I can hit things on the head, too," said Patricia. "I'd say that our experience has humiliated and awakened him. He must feel to blame. He must be furious with himself because he did not prevent the incident or rescue us from it. That was just bad luck. And then when you defied the men and rode off for help—he'll never get over that."

"Why not, Patricia?" inquired Sue with slow-dawning smile.

"He liked you before, but now he adores you," replied Patricia quickly.

"You like Nels, don't you, and you're on his side?"

said Sue soberly, her eyes glinting with fun. "Reckon that is going to be bad for me. Shore I'll find it hard to hold out against you both."

"Sue, why not consider the possibility of *not* holding out?" asked Patricia. "I've known many men and have met hundreds more. This boy seems to be true-blue."

"Shore he is, right now," cried Sue bitterly. "But will it last?"

"I'm sure it will, if you make it last."

Now there were tears in Sue's eyes and she seemed to be fighting hard to control herself. Patricia divined that the girl wanted and needed sympathy, yet could not bring herself to the point of confession. Despite the unusual situation and the dawning of what portended to be a lasting friendship, the time had been too short for a real exchange of their innermost thoughts.

"Sue, come to me when you're ready. Now go give Nels a chance to excuse himself for what he feels to be his shortcomings in regard to last night's adventure."

She saw Sue spur her horse up beside Nels's. Soon they were talking earnestly. Then Sue laughed, and Nels looked glumly at his hands. The Texas girl wasn't giving her admirer too easy a time of relieving what was weighing on his conscience.

But Patricia's mind soon drifted from them to the grandeur of the scenery through which they were passing. Her tired body did not prevent her from delighting in the wildness and beauty of the forest. They were riding gradually upgrade, through a sunlit, golden-rayed, shadow-barred woodland, inhabited by herds of grazing deer. Most of the graceful creatures stood and watched the cavalcade. Others bounded away or slipped into green thickets. It was no longer a lonely forest. The pines and spruces towered magnificently, spreading gnarled brown branches and spear-pointed silver tips to mingle with each other high above the trail. White banks of snow gleamed in the thick coverts. The air was cool, yet the sun shone hot. And everywhere the perfume of the forest, thick, piny, sweet, and dry, hung like incense between earth and sky.

It was noon when the party arrived at the ranger's cabin, a small one-room structure of logs, picturesquely located at the foot of a sunny slope above which the great monarchs of the forest towered.

"May I help you off?" asked Eburne, who was at her side before Patricia could swing a leg out of her stirrup. He led the two girls up onto the porch and into the cabin. It was lighted by a door and two windows and it was clean and neat, with red-blanketed bed built of stout aspen poles, a big stone fireplace, rude and smoke-blackened, and a comfortable home-made chair. The peeled log walls were adorned with bleached antlers and some of the biggest pine cones Patricia had ever seen.

"Well, Thad Eburne," burst out Sue, "you shameless old bachelor housekeeper! How dare you keep a place as spick-and-span, as nice and cosy as this? Shore you defy woman! Beware! Some girl will rope you in and revenge our sex by messing up this dandy place."

"No such luck for me, Sue," laughed Eburne, evidently pleased with her compliment. Yet there was a touch of seriousness in his voice. "You and Miss Clay take this cabin. We men will live outdoors. I think it would be a good idea if you young ladies would lie down and sleep for an hour or two."

"We shore will. I'm daid on my feet," rejoined Sue heartily.

Eburne went out, saying he would unpack and bring in their bags.

"Patricia, what do you think of this little old cabin in the woods?" asked Sue.

"It's a revelation to me," sighed Patricia as she sank on the bed and gazed around the room.

"Me too. But don't get the impression that all western cabins are alike, or ever were like this one. I was born in one, Patricia! I've been in many pioneer cabins. You could live in them, eat and sleep, keep warm and dry. But this one is shore different. Why, heah's a lamp. Books! Magazines! Maps!"

"Sue, your deer stalker does not need a wife," murmured Patricia with a smile, as she gratefully laid her head back upon the red coverlet.

"Looks that way," replied Sue meditatively. "But there's shore many a woman who needs a man like him. Patricia, I'm going to pull off your boots and cover you with a blanket. Then I'll crawl in beside you."

To Patricia, Sue's last words seemed to come from far away. She was sinking into sweet rest when heavy steps roused her. It was the ranger entering to deposit the bags. She tried to open her eyes, but the lids were too heavy. She heard him whisper and Sue's whispered answer. Then again she drifted away, relaxing in oblivion.

Days had passed, how many Patricia never knew or cared. They flowed by like so many endless, dreamy, golden eons, filled with many activities, many excursions into the purple depths of the canyon, many hours of sitting thoughtfully looking out upon a beautiful world from some point of vantage. A sweet lassitude seemed to fill her spirit. Never, since childhood, had life seemed so uncomplicated, so enchanting. Day after day the sun rose in a cloudless sky and went down in golden and mauve sunsets.

She and Sue with Eburne and the cowboys had roamed the forest and ridden the rim, descended and climbed and explored, watched the troops of deer and listened to the barking squirrels.

The adventures shared and the unplanned freedom of those days meant much to her, but even more precious were the many lonely walks and vigils with the ranger, sometimes through the forest in the rich, thick golden light of morning, but mostly along the wild craggy rim, in the solemn hours of noonday or when the afternoon began to wane, at sunset and dusk, or in the black night before the white moon soared overhead, blanching the canyon into silver mist; and in the dim gray dawn when all that world was saddest and loneliest, or when the sun rose, bursting red, blazing fire, heralding the day and the world and life and love.

One afternoon, when the shadows were beginning to lengthen and turn to somber black under the eastern faces of cliffs, Patricia and Eburne sat on the rim in a favorite spot, where a lone giant pine rose from its fragrant mat of fallen needles on the very edge of the chasm. They crouched like eagles upon a mountain crag. The canyon view here was limited to its upper strata of blue limestone and red rock. The wild ruggedness of the North Rim was here at its grandest, a wilderness of timber, of blue cliffs or yellow crags and red slopes, spread out in an utter solitude and dominated by an everchanging beauty.

Before Patricia had absorbed the canyon or had been absorbed by it she had found conversation impossible. But now she could watch and listen and feel in silence for hours, or she could express herself as never before in her life.

At the ranger's cabin, in the forest, among the deer, the New York girl had been insatiably thirsty for knowledge. She knew now all about the tragedy of the deer herd, the history of Buckskin Forest, the conflict between the various types and classes of men who lived off the range. Moreover, she had gotten from Eburne the story of his life there in the lonely woods, and she had divined the ideal that kept him there. The two young people, he lonely for contact with someone who would understand him, she lonely in a new world she had never known to exist, gravitated toward each other as two lonely planets.

For a long time they sat there under the ancient pine tree in silence, then suddenly he spoke.

"You have been here ten days," said Eburne, his fine eyes upon her thoughtful face.

"So long? Oh, impossible," she exclaimed.

"It doesn't seem so long. I was surprised when Nels spoke of your supplies getting low. Of course you're welcome to mine. But they are coarse and not too fresh."

"How hungry I've been! I never knew how good plain food could taste. But I could go without or certainly eat your food to stay a little longer in this blessed place."

"But you must go presently?" he queried gently.

"Please do not make me think of it," she entreated, with almost a note of impatience in her voice.

"It is something to be faced," he said softly. "But before the time comes I hope to know more about you—Patricia."

She seemed not to notice the ranger's use of her given name.

"Does that matter, Mr. Eburne?" she asked wistfully.

"No, come to think of it," he returned thoughtfully. "You came, you will leave. My life will go on here, I suppose, or anywhere else that I may drift. Yet because of these days nothing can ever be the same again."

"We all change. People have incalculable influence upon each other," she spoke rather hurriedly, as though to evade her own rushing thoughts. "I have utterly changed in these few days. I owe so much to little Sue, and the canyon—and to you."

"Me? Indeed you owe me nothing, except what I did in the line of duty. I wish I could have done more."

"We do not agree on what I owe you. I'll not argue, but even the minor things which you call 'in the line of duty' have meant so much to me. The forest and the deer! I have seen them through your eyes. There are many things, Mr. Eburne."

"Will you forgive me if I persist in being inquisitive? When you leave the canyon where will you go?"

"Flagstaff, I think, for a little while. I want to see all those wonderful desert places. And if Nels and Sue come to some understanding for the future, I want to help her."

"They will. He's a fine, spirited boy, with lots of good in him. She cares, but she's afraid. She needn't be, for Nels will go straight. He'll not be a trail guide very long. That boy is bright. He has a future."

"You are encouraging me in a secret little plan of my own."

"Won't you tell me?" he asked. "I've had some little interest in Nels. I got him to come to the Canyon."

"Sue told me of your kindness to Nels. It was splendid of you.... Now please keep my little secret. If Sue really loves Nels I would like to buy a ranch somewhere around Flagstaff and have him manage it."

"You are—generous indeed," he replied slowly. "I'm very happy to hear that.... Then, in such case, you would come to Flagstaff occasionally."

"I shore would, as Sue says," answered Patricia happily.

"That'll be good to know. You'll be back in the West sometimes.... You see, Miss Clay—Patricia—I fell in love with you at first sight. It's a terrible fact for me, yet somehow it'll be may salvation. I want you to know—if I wasn't a poor ranger, I mean—if I had a future worthy of such a woman as you, I'd ask you to marry me."

"Mr. Eburne...You shouldn't...I mean...you don't know..." murmured Patricia, closing her eyes as they suddenly filled with tears. She could not face him after that simple statement, nor the dreaming canyon below, nor the tumult of uncertainty and panic his confession had aroused. Her ears seemed full of the thrumming beats of her heart. Suddenly she longed to be alone. She had somehow felt that Eburne loved her; but to hear him avow it, with simple strong words, in unconscious pathos, unnerved her completely. She found herself trembling. She could not speak.

"After Flagstaff, you'll go to California, I suppose, then back east?" he was asking. His eyes were on the far-distant rim of the canyon. Suddenly she found her voice. But it was high-pitched, quavery, unsure.

"California, perhaps, but not east, unless for a brief business trip, and that not for a long time. I'm not sure. I have no plans. I can't go back . . . I can't go back to so many things in my life. . . ." The tears were welling up again. He did not appear to notice her emotion.

"But Sue told me New York was your home," he asserted in surprise.

"Yes, it was. But I gave up my home, and I shall never go back."

"Miss Clay! Your family?"

"There was only my father. He did not want me or need me."

"Wasn't there someone you—you—loved?" he went on tensely.

"Yes."

"Was it a husband?"

"No. I have never married."

"Someone—someone who died in the war—?"

"No. It was only a girl friend."

Patricia knew that the time had come. She forced herself to tell him all of the truth that was possible for her to confess, and she did it out of respect and sorrow for him, and the longing to appear as nearly as possible in his eyes as she knew herself to be. She had dismissed the past. Recalling it did not hurt, she found to her amazement, but the yoke of that past, the unalterable fact of the dishonor which she had accepted, now suddenly appeared in a different light.

"I've been out of the world," Eburne broke in, "but I'm not quite a recluse. My mother and sister write me often, send me papers, books, and magazines. So while living alone with the deer and the forest, I've still kept up pretty well with the times. I know what life is like back there, Patricia, that you're not at all like the young women I read about and whose pictures I see."

"You mean I don't bob my hair, pluck my eyebrows,

paint my face, smoke, and all that sort of thing so prevalent in this so-called modern age."

Eburne laughed. "Well, I hadn't figured it all out yet as concisely as that, but I suppose it's what I meant."

"It's a queer age, Mr. Eburne, and hard to understand." She seemed suddenly eager to talk of something other than herself. "I'm for the modern woman, but there are extremes I don't care to take. Yet you'd find many sensible girls back there, and I'm sure your sister is one."

"Well, she seemed sensible enough," he said thoughtfully. "She was twelve when I left home." Eburne lapsed into silence.

After a time he spoke again. "I'm grateful to you, Miss Clay," he said, "for what you've told me of your life back where you came from. I'm grateful to you, too, for not laughing when I tried to tell you how I feel toward you. You think now that you can't go back to your old life. But you couldn't live the life that we live, that Sue lives out here. And knowing that, I had no right to tell you of my love for you. I ask you now to forget what I said. You say these days on the North Rim have meant much to you. I would never forgive myself if I spoiled the rest of your stay here in the deer forest." Now he was smiling. "I'm ranger Eburne," he said, jumping to his feet and holding out his hands to help Patricia up. "This is the tourist season, and please call on me to do all I can—within the line of duty."

The sun was setting as they started back to camp. There were so many things she had wanted to say, to deny, but the words had not come. Now it was too late.

CHAPTER
12

*T*HERE came a summer storm—great white and black columnar clouds rolling over the chasm, blinding zigzag streaks of lightning, palls of gray rain, and thunderous crack and bellow, and reverberating, endless echoes that confounded the ears and froze the heart.

Patricia and Sue had watched from the rim while the grand pageant swept down upon them out of the west; and, riveted to the spot, they had been caught in the flood of rain. They were drenched to the skin and arrived at the cabin bedraggled and disheveled, but as gay as two schoolgirls returning from a picnic.

A change to warm, dry garments, a good supper, and afterward some blazing sticks and red embers in the fireplace tended to keep up their high spirits. This day marked their friendship as a settled fact. It had been a climax to many all-satisfying days. Even the Dyott incident, harrowing as it had been, had contributed its share to the close bond which had grown between the two girls.

When night set in and the rain ceased, the air grew chill, and the wind roared and rushed through the forest. The gale shook the sturdy cabin and at first was disturbing to Patricia, who feared one of the giant pines might come crashing down on the roof. It was no wonder, the eastern girl thought, that Sue crept close to her. She welcomed her, and then they lay there in the impenetrable darkness, with the roar of the gale enveloping the cabin.

"Shore this'd be great—if only I—I wasn't unhappy," said Sue, close to Patricia's ear.

"What are you unhappy over?" asked Patricia.

"Two reasons. First, this can't last forever. I'll be losing you soon."

"Sue, you'll never lose me, if you want me near you. I can't begin to tell you how much I—I care for you, how good you are for me."

Sue kissed her warmly on the cheek.

"But you'll go away?"

"Not very soon. And when I do, I'll come back. What's the other that makes you unhappy?"

Patricia felt the girl's reluctance to tell what was troubling her, and at the same time her ardent yearning to confide in her.

"Nels."

"Sue, you love him?"

This was harder to confess, but Patricia felt it coming like the irresistible tide of pent-up water after a dam has burst. Sue hugged her close and shook as if she had a chill.

"*Yes!*"

"Oh, I'm glad, Sue. But that should make you happy."

"Patricia, I'm not unhappy because I love him. It's the worry, over everything."

"Sue, are you afraid Nels will go back to drinking and that hard life he used to lead? If so, I think you're mistaken. Thad Eburne says Nels is pretty much of a man now. Why, Sue, he was only a reckless boy. Hope of winning you has steadied him, made him older. You must consider that, Sue."

"Shore it's not that I don't trust Nels now and that I don't believe he has turned over a new leaf for good. I do. To be honest, he has shore made me proud of him."

"Well, then, what in the world is the matter?" queried Patricia.

"Nels wants me to be engaged to him. He swears he'll not nag me to marry him until he's saved a lot of money and got a bigger job. His dream is to own a ranch. Well, shore he'll never get one unless he goes out heah and homesteads a hundred and sixty acres of Uncle Sam's wild land. And there's the rub. I don't want Nels to live on some lonely homestead without me. I wouldn't mind the hardship of homesteading, and believe me, it's shore pioneer life. But I *can't* go. I've got my mother to take care of. She's not strong and she'd die out in some log cabin, without comfort or a doctor handy. I couldn't do my best by Mother in that way. I'll have to teach school, wherever I can get the most money....And that's what's worrying me."

"Sue, that's nothing to worry about," returned Patricia. "You have a fine young man to love. You have him and your mother to make a home for. Sue, I would gladly change places with you."

"What!" cried the girl, amazed, and then dropped her head back on the pillow. "Maybe I am a selfish little beast. I thought I had a terrible problem. It was been killing me."

"Sue, dear, I don't underestimate your trouble," replied Patricia seriously. "It *is* a problem. But it has not worried me, because I have solved it for you."

"You!" cried Sue, starting up.

"Yes, I," returned Patricia. "Now Sue, please listen. The immediate present is very easy to dispose of. I want to make my headquarters at the El Tovar for this summer. I am eager to see all these wonderful places you've talked about: Rainbow Bridge, Natural Bridge, Monument Valley, Montezuma's Well, Keetsill and Betatakin, Painted Desert, Petrified Forest, and, in fact, every beautiful and interesting place you know of. I want to hire Nels to arrange these trips for me, buy our own horses, and outfits, as you call them, and get the men or guides necessary. I want you for a companion, or secretary, or chaperon, whatever you want to call it. We'll certainly take in this deer drive Thad Eburne talks so much about. Then, at some opportune time between two of these trips, I'll buy a ranch and ask Nels to run it for me, on salary or shares, or both, whatever is fairest to him. You can marry Nels, then, have your mother come to you—and live happily ever afterward.— Now what have you to say?"

"Oh! Oh! Oh!" screamed Sue wildly above the roar of the wind outside. "What a horrible temptation to spring on a poor little weak-minded girl! No! No! Patricia, I can't— I can't accept that. Oh, thank you for all you are offering me—us—but we can't accept your charity, even though I know it comes from the heart."

"Sue, don't be hasty. This is a reasonable proposition I am making you."

"Shore I can't see that. You've been carried away by this canyon. You feel sorry for Nels and me. You want to do some generous thing for us. It's wonderfully good of you, but I won't stand for it."

"Of course there is sentiment about it," rejoined Patricia persuasively. "But it is business, too. I will have to hire someone to do these things for me. I have indeed been overcome by this canyon. I want to own a place near it where I can come and have my own things. I am sure Nels will consider it a good business proposition."

"Patricia, have you said anything to that cowboy?" demanded Sue sharply.

"Not a word. Not a hint. I did tell Thad Eburne something of my plans and asked him to regard it as confidential."

"Aw!" breathed Sue, sinking back. "Shore, I was afraid that accounted for Nels's being out of his haid lately."

"How so?"

"Oh, he's been wanting to kiss me, and everything."

"Naturally. And of course you let him?"

"I did *not*."

"Well! Then I propose that you tell Nels of my plan and then kiss him. That'll mean acceptance, engagement, marriage, home, future. All in one fell swoop!"

"You torture me," wailed Sue. "I can't think. You've knocked my legs out from under me.... It all sifts down to money, and I never had any. I don't know how to figure, to judge what is right. Shore this plan of yours would cost a lot. Such a risk you'd run. Ranching is uncertain unless you can hold on."

"Sue, I have more money than I know what to do with," replied Patricia. "It's all I do have!—Surely you can see how right and good it is for me to help make two fine young people happy, and by doing it find happiness myself! Is there any doubt of that logic?"

Sue fell upon Patricia's neck and, burying her face, she began to sob, "Oh! I—love you.... It's too—much—for me!" She was convinced. The New York girl held her closely and felt the slow tears well from her own eyes and wet her cheeks. In this winning of Sue's consent to her plan she had won something precious for herself as well. The girl wept as if a long pent-up flood of worry and responsibility had been swept away. But gradually the storm subsided and at length ceased.

"Shore I am a—baby still," she murmured, with a tremulous little laugh and a catch in her voice. "Something broke in heah," and she pressed Patricia's hand to her breast.

"Sue, won't it be fun telling Nels?" asked Patricia, taking the young girl's hand.

"That'll shore be the grandest hour of my life," burst out Sue. "I'll begin by being terribly serious. I'll tell him I've at last been persuaded to consider his proposal of marriage.... Oh, gosh! Then I'll paint in vivid colors my poverty, that he'll have Mother on his hands and a lot of relatives and we'll have to live in a homestead cabin. Shore he'll be game and swallow the whole outfit. But he'll sort of sink down in his boots. When he gets way down I'll say, 'Nelson Stackhouse, do you realize you're going to marry a fortune?' I'll be proud and mysterious. Then, when he's about out of his haid, I'll spring my secret on him.... Oh, it's sweet, it's beautiful.... And you're so wonderful to me, Patricia!"

And as outside the storm raged, they talked and planned. Patricia found it romantic to picture in her mind's eye a great timbered and grazing stretch of ranch land and a rambling, picturesque ranch house, built after ideas of her own. In spite of herself, there appeared in the picture the tall, dark figure of a forest ranger.

"Shore, then you'll come often," cried Sue happily.

"It might become a home," breathed Patricia, almost to herself.

"Patricia, you *must* have a home. Why, even the birds have nests and the beasts have holes. You'll love Arizona. You *must* have a home—and a man, too."

"The first, perhaps, but hardly the other."

"Isn't there someone back East?" whispered Sue. "Someone you care for?"

"No."

"Then shore there *was*."

"Not if you mean a man."

Sue nestled close to Patricia and took a long, hesitating moment before whispering, "Then, isn't there a wee little bit of a chance for Thad Eburne?"

The whisper, loving, insidious, tender, brought before her eyes again the scene at sunset beneath the ancient pine on the canyon's rim when a man had humbly told her of his love, and when she, knowing of her own unworthiness, had listened to his avowal in silence. And now the young girl beside her, in her happiness wishing those she loved to be happy too, was asking if there was no chance for Thad Eburne. But Patricia had no power to answer.

"Thad Eburne loves you," went on the temptress softly. "I said when he saw you it'd be all day with him. Well, it shore was.... Patricia, he's an easterner, he's educated, he comes from a good family. He's a poor ranger, I know, but what would that matter to you? He's fine, clean, strong. I wouldn't say he is wasting his life in this forest stalking deer, because he loves the woods and wild creatures. And he does good. But all the same he has no future heah. *You* could advance him, perhaps put him at the haid of the forest service. Or better, help him devote his life to conservation, independent of any petty little authorities. If Thad had the means to travel and study, in foreign countries as well as ours, he would do something big. All over the West the timber, the water, the game, are being stolen and destroyed by greedy men. It shore will take *big* men, not selfish ones, to save the West for our children. There's a future for Thad. And a wonderful one for you. Aren't you the least bit interested in that, Patricia?"

"You eloquent little matchmaker," exclaimed Patricia, trying to laugh. "You'd turn the tables on me, wouldn't you? Throw me at your ranger friend!"

"No, Patricia, I'm talking sense," declared Sue spiritedly. "Didn't I weaken when you talked sense to me? Am I not the happiest girl in the world?"

"Yes, it seems so," murmured Patricia, more afraid of Sue's logic than she dared to confess. This girl rang true. She had no false sophistication; she saw things clearly.

"You've told me a little about yourself," went on Sue. "I don't want to pry or to hurt you, but please tell me one thing. Are you free to marry?"

"Certainly I'm free. That is if not being married or engaged or promised to any man means free."

"That's enough confidence for me, Patricia," continued Sue in relieved earnestness. "Western folks are not curious. You stand or fall by what you say and do. The whole West is full of people who have come from east, south, north. Nobody out heah cares a whoop what they

were back there where they came from. It's what they are
heah....Well, I've been close to you, and in spite of the
democratic spirit I just bragged about—in westerners—
I've thought and figured over your case. You've had trouble. It's in your eyes. You've the sweetest, saddest mouth
I ever saw on a woman....Listen to this. One day Thad,
when I asked him if he'd noticed how sad your mouth was,
jerked up and said: 'Great Scott! Yes. I've had the longing
to kiss it once and jump into the canyon.' So you can see
Thad's no mollycoddle, and he knows you've suffered....
Patricia, I never asked Thad, but I'll bet he figures as I do
that something terrible has happened in your life, but it's
not your fault. No one can tell me otherwise. If it's misfortune or disgrace—or—or dishonor, it's not from any
sin in you. I *know*. Any woman would know if she could
live with you a while. Well, you're young, beautiful, rich.
What difference does it make *what* has happened? You're
alive and your heart is not broken. If there's any chance
of your caring for this ranger, tell him what your trouble
was, then forget it and let yourself go. That is what I'd do,
or what any western girl would do."

"But suppose to tell would violate my deepest sense
of honor—my conviction of what I believe myself to be?"
whispered Patricia.

"That wouldn't happen if you loved Thad," replied the
girl simply. "Patricia, I always had a hunch that the shadow
in your eyes came from some great sacrifice. Share your
secret with Thad. Then it'll be as if it had never been."

"Oh, Sue, disgrace has a long arm," cried Patricia, torn
by conflicting emotions. "A ruined woman, whether by sin
or misfortune or—or sacrifice, can never change the mind
or memory of the world. If I married Thad or any man,
sooner or later the story would trail me down."

"Shore, that wouldn't make any difference if it did,"
returned Sue bluntly. "If you confided in the man you loved
and he knew and understood what you'd been through,
then nothing would matter. Western people would take

you as Thad took you. It's a new country, Patricia, memories of the past seem to fade out heah. We do not ponder and weigh. Shore we get out and do things. With our hands! We don't have time for much social life. People are scarce and live far apart. If some woman would come to me, like that Hilton woman did, and try to gossip about you, I'd tell her to keep her nose to herself. If some man would speak ill of you to Thad or in his presence, he would knock him down. Shore. That's the West, Patricia."

Long after Sue had fallen asleep, the older girl lay there in the blackness of the cabin, wide-eyed and thoughtful. The storm had passed away with its roar and crash in the pines, and now only the usual gentle soughing of the wind broke the forest silence. There seemed to be no end to this rending of her spirit, the tearing away of old beliefs, fears, doubts. How ineradicable and monstrous the past had seemed! Yet this clear-eyed, clear-souled western girl had shaken the very foundations of her sense of values, of her perception of things, of her ideas of truth.

What had seemed crude in Sue Warren was only simplicity, a straightforward outlook upon life, an honesty of soul. Patricia faced the truth that if she could hold to the illuminating flashes of light which Sue had shed upon her morbid mood they would lead her to happiness. But life was not as simple as this western girl had stated it. One's old life could not be shucked off as easily, even in the West.

Hours passed. The moan of the night wind and the rustle of branches died away. When the first gray of dawn showed at the window, Patricia still lay awake. The long night beside the sleeping Sue had brought no relief for the strife in her soul. The long hours of probing and analyzing had only added to her confusion of mind. For in her heart she realized now that she could not have prayed for any greater happiness than to live here in this little cabin as the beloved and honored wife of Thad Eburne.

*   *   *

Next day, Sue seemed to have been reborn. She was the incarnation of joy, radiant where she had been only smiling, and where she had been but pretty she was now beautiful. She was haughty and coy to Nels by turns, gentle and indifferent, angry and pleased. The poor fellow was in a daze, for the instant he realized and accepted a certain mood, then, in a flash, she had changed to another.

Patricia stood it as long as she could and then she declared, "You tease, you roguish little gal. Tell him or I shall!"

"Tonight, I promise," pleaded Sue.

At suppertime Tine Higgenbottom manifested a sudden keen interest in Sue. He watched her dubiously; he shook his head; he nodded it with profundity. Then suddenly he attacked a high pile of firewood that Nels had stacked. He kicked it down and sent the billets flying. Nels burst out in a most unusual fit of temper.

"Say, you pie-faced, lantern-jawed, bowlegged cowpuncher, what you mean by that?" he demanded.

"Nels, there's something screwy going on here," Tine roared. "I don't get you, pard," rejoined Nels resignedly, but he straightway became thoughtful.

Patricia took the opportunity to tell Sue that Tine had come pretty close to guessing something of the truth and advised against letting the cowboys be alone together. Several times Tine tried unobtrusively to get Nels away from the campfire circle, but all of these attempts Sue frustrated. In desperation, Tine deliberately attempted to drag Nels away.

"Where you goin', Nels?" asked Sue, with her sweetest voice and smile.

Nels became as immovable as one of the giant pines. "I reckon I'll be goin' crazy pretty soon."

"I'm not flattered. Are you forgettin' tonight is full moon and you have a date with me to see it rise over the canyon?" returned Sue.

Patricia knew from Nels's face that there had been no

arrangement of the kind and that he was struggling with a complexity beyond him, and a possibility of bliss too good to be true.

"I—we—you—'course I didn't forget," he floundered, valiantly trying to rise to the occasion, "but I thought you had."

"Get my heavy coat, please. We'll go now," she answered calmly.

As they walked away together toward the rim, Tine Higgenbottom gazed after them with an expression upon his homely face that Patricia found utterly indescribable. She burst into a peal of laughter.

"Hang it all!" he muttered under his breath. "Gurls are wild cattle."

Patricia and Eburne also took the trail for the rim, and reached the canyon at dusk. The chasm was filled with shadow; the ragged line of timber showed black above the pale gleam of cliff; the sky was dull blue, except where a silvery brightening along the horizon heralded the advent of the moon.

They walked to a promontory, upon the point of which, indistinct in the gloom, Sue and Nels sat close together. Eburne appeared unusually quiet, even for him, and Patricia had no desire to talk. The canyon air seemed laden with its old fragrance, its mingled aroma rising from dry pine-needled capes and grassy, flower-dotted slopes.

The bright glow above the black fringe of forest lifted and spread. Soon a radiant disk of silver slipped out of the dark. It moved, it rose, it slid up into the blue—a blazing silver moon, grandly soaring, transforming that vague forest and dim canyon into beautiful realities.

Suddenly Patricia's absorbed attention was rudely broken by sounds of a scuffle, a scream from Sue, and a wild whoop from Nels. In the clear moonlight the cowboy could be seen enveloping Sue in a bearish embrace.

Then, to Patricia's amazement, Nels came bounding back over the promontory, straight toward her and Eburne.

He took great, long leaps. Bearing down upon Patricia, he seized her, gave her a mighty hug, and followed it with a hearty smacking kiss on the cheek. Then, quickly as he had grasped her, he released her and made for Eburne.

"You big deer chaser!" he shouted, pounding the ranger on the back. "You Indian! You biscuit slinger! You sad old bachelor! Listen. I gotta beat you up. I owe you somethin'. A million dollars! This canyon chuck full of gold! You first, an' then this Patrescia!"

Eburne at last managed to get away from this onslaught.

"Nels, I gather that you are to be congratulated," he said, his voice rich with emotion.

"You said it, pard. Shake," returned Nels, and he wrung the ranger's hand. Then turning to Patricia, with less of violence and more of dignity, he continued, "Miss Patrescia, it's somethin' grand for a man to be loved by a girl like Sue an' trusted by friends like you an' Thad. So help me God, I will never fail none of you. An' the blessedest good I could hope for you both is that you could feel what I feel now."

Another morning dawned, the last for Patricia on the North Rim. The food supplies were exhausted, the grain for horses was gone, the snowbanks had melted away.

"Wal," drawled Tine, "you all may live on love, but me an' the cook an' the horses have to have a little more sustenance. We're breakin' camp. Reckon my work's done, an' it was a very good job, if I do say it myself."

The summer morning was balmy, sweet-scented, and the rosy sunlight tinted the silver spruces. Deer and squirrels and birds appeared in unusual numbers in the surrounding forest.

Patricia avoided gazing directly at Eburne, lest she betray what she had reserved for the very last moment. He rode beside her through the forest to the head of Bright Angel trail, a goodly distance from his cabin, and not once did he break the silence. They reached the rim. Tine and the cook drove the pack train down the trail, whistling and singing. Nels and Sue bade the ranger good-by.

Patricia gazed into the canyon. For the thousandth time the stupendous yawn of it, the black and blue and gold and red, the glory and might of it, seemed flung into her face. If she watched and listened there forever, it would be always to see more of the beauty and mystery of nature, to hear more silent voices in the rushing of the winds, to feel more of the meaning of life.

"You must not get far behind Nels," said Eburne. "The trail is bad—and it's time to say good-by."

"Not really good-by," she returned, gazing straight into his eyes. If he could but know it now, her heart was in her eyes. She sat tense and quiet upon her horse. Her face was very pale. "You will come to see me at the El Tovar when next month's work is done?"

He stared up at her, his lean dark face slowly turning white.

"Patricia, I will come, if you ask me," he said huskily.

"I do ask you," she replied.

Then she urged her horse into the trail and down. She slackened the bridle to let the horse pick his way, and for the same reason she did not look back. It would have been of no use, for she was suddenly blinded by tears.

*L*ATE one afternoon, Patricia returned to the hotel after a long ride along the rim. The mail clerk handed her a bulky envelope addressed to her in a bold handwriting. The postmark was dim and obscured, and the envelope was wrinkled and badly soiled, as though it had been carried in a man's pocket for some time. Wonderingly the girl removed her glove and opened the envelope. The letter was written on report sheets of the forestry service. Patricia's heart began to beat more quickly as she read:

Dear Miss Clay:

I had a chance to send this out by a tourist, and I don't know when it will reach you or in what condition, but I want to explain why you have not seen me on your side of the rim, especially after the gracious invitation you extended to me the day you left the North Rim with Sue and the boys.

The following week a message was brought in

from the committee on wild life conservation informing me that I had been delegated to guide the group
in their tour of the Buckskin Preserve. Since you
seemed to be keenly interested in the problem of what
is to be done with the great deer herd when you were
camping in my cabin at Big Spruce in the early summer, I thought you might like to hear what progress
is being made.

I met the commission (at the last moment my
friend Blakener came down with a touch of fever and
could not accompany me) on the evening of the six-
teenth at the Big Springs range station, below the
northwestern rim of the Kaibob Plateau. There were
twenty-some men in the party, and I am glad to say
that nearly all of them were serious-minded, com-
petent, and practical men. A few of them were the
usual visionary type, but as a group they were hon-
estly prepared to get at the true conditions in the
preserve and to report them as they saw them to the
U.S. Department of Agriculture. I don't think they realized how much ground we were to cover in ten days'
time nor what a rough trip it was going to be.

That evening we were briefed as to exactly what
information the report to Washington was to contain.

(1) We were to arrive at a more accurate estimate
than that contained in the old Biological Survey, of
more than a year ago, of the number of deer com-
prising the Kaibob or Buckskin Mountain herd.

(2) We were to determine just how big a herd
can be maintained in a thrifty condition in view of the
available forage and taking into consideration the local physical conditions and the frequent occurrence
of seasons of limited rainfall.

(3) We were to try to find out whether the government would be justified in reducing the number of
domestic livestock grazing in the preserve to assure
the safety of the deer.

(4) We were to give our recommendation, if we were convinced that a reduction in the size of the deer herd was inevitable, as to just how that reduction most effectively could be made.

As you will recall, Miss Clay, from our talks this summer, all of the answers to these problems are pretty obvious. Even a tourist driving through the preserve knows that the herd has increased at least 50 per cent, due to a number of reasons, that there is only enough forage for about half the present deer population, that livestock grazing already had been limited if the service would enforce the restrictions, and that the only sure way to prevent the deer on the preserve from starving is by mass migration of half the herd to some other range, where grazing and browsing is plentiful.

But mine was not to reason why. Orders are orders. And I was expected to guide the expedition, twenty-some strong on horseback, with a pack train and camp supplies, from Big Springs to Indian Hollow to Quaking Asp Canyon, through the Big and Little Saddle regions, up Parishawampitts Canyon, and out on Greenland Plateau. We were to stop at Little Park, V. T. Park, Pleasant Valley, Jacob's Lake, Powell's Plateau, the Cocks Combs, Houserock Valley, and North Canyon.

On the twenty-fifth there is to be a hearing at the Rust Hotel in V. T. Park, where I hope there will be a showdown.

We have had some adventures. Some day I hope to tell you of them. Most of the men are enjoying the outdoor life and seem appreciative of our efforts to make them comfortable. I think that some of the commission were surprised to learn that grass is a very secondary source of deer food. They were under the impression that deer grazed just as horses and cattle do. But, as you know, deer are largely browsers. Their natural diet is composed of the leaves, twigs, and tender shoots of trees and shrubs. The only grazing they will do when their normal food supply is abundant is limited to certain tender weeds and grasses in the spring and a few of the more palatable plants like clover.

Well, the members of the commission are having a thorough look-see, too thoroughly, I'm afraid, for some of them, who have been more accustomed to office chairs than saddles. One thing that impressed them was something you observed this summer—that there are no running streams in any part of this territory. The only source of water for the herd is from twenty widely scattered springs and a few tanks or pools which hold stagnant and often polluted rain water (when there is rain).

As I read over what I have written, it all sounds terribly dry and uninspired. I have a horrible feeling that it must have sounded the same way this summer when you listened so sweetly and so patiently to my long harangues on the subject of deer and their habitat. Beware of a man with a single-track mind. I hope that you may be able to read between the lines of this letter the things that I really want to say—the things which perhaps I have no right to say.

I have thought often, often of that day we sat on the rim under the old pine when I rushed in with what was in my heart for you, when I first should have sent a scouting party of angels in to see whether the ground was all right for treading.

As soon as the hearing is over and the commission files its report, I shall avail myself of the invitation which I have been cherishing in my heart all these long days to visit you at El Tovar. While you spoke no words to give me too much hope in regard to your feelings for me, there was a look in your dear eyes when you said you would be glad to see

me again that has sustained me during all these
weary miles.

Sincerely,

Thad Eburne

As Patricia finished reading Thad's long letter there
was a mist in her eyes which made the last paragraph almost illegible. It brought back in a sweet flood of memories those weeks in the forest. How strange that her
recollections of that fearful day when she had been
Dyott's captive had almost faded from her mind! In their
place were those long walks and talks with the deer
stalker, his loyal championship of the cause of the pres-
ervation of the herd of deer, his fierce scorn of the bun-
gling bureaucrats and the selfish cattle interests and the
cold-blooded slaughterers with hunting licenses, his genuine sorrow that one by one the last lonely fastnesses of
the Buckskin Preserve were being thrown open to the
careless tourist.

For a long time she sat in a chair in her room with
the pages of Eburne's letter held idly in her hand. The
sun sank lower and dusk began to fall. Still she sat there
thinking. At last there had come into her life a real man,
one she could love and honor and respect. Here was a
man who never questioned or doubted. Why could she
not be equally straightforward and sure and candid with
herself?

On a sudden impulse the eastern girl left her room
and walked slowly downstairs. Through the hotel lobby
she went as in a daze, out the door and down the steps.
Now she was standing on the canyon rim, her eyes seek-
ing to penetrate the darkness that she knew to be the
forest beyond the Northern Rim.

*T*HERE was a chill in the air that indicated the approach of fall. A fire roared and crackled on the hearth of the ranger cabin at V. T. Park. Before it lounged Thad Eburne and his friend of many years in the service, Blakener. They had been discussing the hearing held late in August at the Rust Hotel by the committee on wild life conservation, following the committee's tour of the Buckskin Preserve. The memories of that hearing still rankled, and Thad was in a discouraged mood. Blakener, who had had to miss the tour of the commission through the deer range, did his best to cheer up his downcast fellow ranger.

"It don't do no good worryin'," he said. "You done all you could for the herd. You told them the truth. A man can't do no more."

"What hurts," replied Eburne, "is that our own service testified against us. Judson and Cassell gave all the answers they thought the commission wanted, and they are the answers that will get into the report and to the ears of the

Secretary of Agriculture." He stared moodily into the fire.

"Did they give you a chance to have your say?" asked Blakener.

"Yes, in spite of Cassell, who tried his best to discredit me," replied Thad. "I told them that there had been a great herd of mule deer here even back in the days before the Indians used Buckskin Mountain as their hunting ground. And even back in those early days when predatory animals roamed the mountain, there was unequal distribution of the deer. You see, some of the committee couldn't understand why in some parts of the range where the forage was ample they saw only a few deer. You know—the Greenland Plateau."

Blakener nodded.

"Then they couldn't understand why there should be so many deer in the scrub oak belt and in the neighborhood of the open grassy parks, where the forage is all used up. I told them that they would find the same cockeyed distribution of the deer on their winter range. Even humans can starve in a land of plenty. Why, over in Europe right now foodstuffs are rotting in some places that could prevent people only a few miles away from starvation. Deer don't seek the best forage the way water seeks its level."

"Didn't you tell them how the snowfall limits the winter range of a big part of the herd to the sheltered slopes of the plateau?" asked Blakener.

"I certainly did," replied Eburne. "I told them something about cover, too, how deer normally lie up during the day, and so naturally the amount of cover available in any particular section tends to affect their distribution. Neither can you overlook the fact that natural barriers, such as steep rock walls and box canyons, limit the animals' freedom of movement and affect their distribution on a given range."

Blakener grunted. "That shore is the answer to the question why they's so blame few animals up on Greenland Plateau," he said. "Why, that plateau must be twelve miles long if it's an inch, an' it's connected to the main land only by a narrow neck, a mile wide, an'some steep rock walls."

"And don't forget," added Thad, "that Greenland Plateau projects far to the south of the general east and west direction of the drift of the deer. I showed them on my map how the drift would leave the plateau to the south and that would explain the relatively few deer there in spite of the good forage."

"What did they have to say to that?" Blakener wanted to know.

"They seemed a little skeptical about this drift I had mentioned. But I had a chance to tell 'em about that later," said Eburne with considerable satisfaction. "I wanted to finish up with the point I was trying to make about why the deer are so badly distributed over the preserve. Deer are controlled by habit pretty much as other animals are— even humans. Take their breeding habits. You know and I know, Blakener, that deer are gregarious and tend to remain together and stay in a given locality unless compelled by natural or artificial causes to move elsewhere. Let's say that the does returning to their summer range don't get beyond the central forest before they drop their young. The inability of the young fawns to travel results in holding the herd to that region. When the fawns grow up, habit tends to keep the mature animals in the locality of their birth, or, if there is a seasonal migration, it is habit which leads them back to the same haunts and causes them to remain there throughout the season."

"Wal, you don't need to argue with me, Thad," exploded Blakener. "O' course I know habit holds deer to certain localities even when the feedin' gets slim. What happened next, Thad?"

"We had dinner," Eburne replied. "And when we got back from the dining room, the chairman of the inquest seemed to take a different tack. He got up and said something like this: 'The number of the deer in the Buckskin Mountain National Game Preserve and the methods and means of preserving a permanent herd in a thrifty condition has been made the principal consideration of this investigation; but the committee believes that the danger now threatening the range conditions is at least equal to, and just as alarming as, the danger threatening the existence or welfare of the deer herd.'"

"Man," interrupted Blakener in open-mouthed admiration, "them perfessor fellars can't seem to talk English, can they? But I bet that was the chance the cattlemen wanted!"

"As a matter of fact, they didn't rise to the bait just then," continued Eburne. "We got onto the subject of drift. They had me on the grill all afternoon. I told them that out here we used drift, as applied to the herd, in two ways. There is the seasonal drift of the deer from the winter to the summer range or the other way round."

"Everybody knows that the heavy snow—"

"Exactly," replied Thad. "I told them that deer naturally prefer the higher altitudes and would most probably remain on the Kaibob Plateau proper all through the year if it weren't for the heavy winter snows. The map you and I made shows that the summer range of our herd is roughly an oval-shaped area with its long axis north and south. Then I showed them how the summer range area is surrounded by a belt of lower ground which is the winter range."

Blakener again interrupted. "Did you point out to them dudes that the winter belt is a great deal wider on the sides, the western, specially, than on the north an' south?"

Eburne got up from his chair and placed another log on the fire and stretched his arms above his head before he sat down again.

"Of course I did," he said. "And I showed them that when the deer are forced off the high plateau when the snows come, only a few can move to the narrow strips of winter range on the north and south. So the direction of their seasonal drift has to be from east to west." The ranger paused.

"But I could see," he continued, "that the commission was more interested in the longer meaning of drift. What they were looking for was the evidence of a permanent movement or migration off our range to some other range. They wanted to know whether there was any possibility of creating or accelerating an overflow of the surplus deer from Buckskin Forest to the surrounding country which might need restocking with deer. I had to spoil their little pipe dream there by telling them that no permanent drift exists because of the natural barriers, such as the desert on the north and the canyon on the south."

Blakener yawned. Eburne got up from his chair. "I guess you've heard enough for one night, old-timer," he said. "Let's hit the hay."

"Sit down, Eburne," ordered Blakener, "you can't stop now. Besides, we can sleep in the mornin'. No orders have come through whether we're to go on trappin' them poor critters or not."

"Well, all right, partner, if you fall asleep it's your own funeral," said Thad with a laugh. "One of the Utah people took exception to my claim that there was no exit from Buckskin. 'Aren't you forgetting?' he asked, 'that low ridge connecting the slopes below the northeast corner of the plateau with the higher country across the valley? Why couldn't some follow this timbered ridge to the Red Bluff Mountains in Utah?"

"'And get shot!' I answered him. 'That's where your Mormon friends graze their sheep. And a deer has about as much chance of crossing into Utah alive as he has of reaching the North Pole!'

"Well, that ended that," continued Thad. "But right here, I thought, was a good spot to put in a plug for McKay's plan to drive a big herd south across the canyon onto the Coconino Plateau."

"What did they say to that?" asked Blakener eagerly.

"The plan seemed pretty well known," said Eburne. "The Utah people tried to make out that McKay was a crazy man and that such a wild scheme could never succeed. The Arizona delegates, however, were all for the drive. Quite a bit of heat was generated from the debate, and the chairman had to rule that a deposition would be taken from McKay and included in the report.

"Then one of the commission who had been one of my party read a paper on 'The Condition and Number of the Deer in Buckskin Mountain Preserve.' He said he had counted 1,028 deer in a drive of one hour and ten minutes along the highway between the rim and the lower end of V. T. Park. But he said the animals were in poor condition. At a time of year when they should have been in the pink of condition, he found them, even including most of the large bucks, extremely thin. In many cases hollows along the flanks and above the hip joints were very noticeable. He had found some dead deer. He spoke of the severe drought but refused to believe that the drought could account for the scarcity of forage on the preserve. To prove his point, he called attention to the Dixie National Forest and the Fishlake National Forest, which he had visited, and where, he said, the dry spell had been equally severe, but that food there was abundant for deer. It was his opinion that the number of deer on a range should be limited to the number the range could maintain in a thrifty condition on the amount of forage and browse the range afforded—"

"Wal, now what do you think of that?" roared Blakener, slapping his knees. "That fellar is a deep one! How many deer did he figger are in the preserve right now?"

Thad laughed shortly. "He had it all worked out on a slide rule—the annual fawn crop less the number which fail to survive plus the number of twins plus the number that survive as a result of the extermination of predatory animals minus the number killed illegally by hunters equals twenty-six thousand."

Blakener roared. "Thad, you know and I know that there are more'n fifty-thousand deer up here on Buckskin!"

"That's the number that went into the report," replied the deer stalker with grim satisfaction.

Both men sat in silence for a long time, staring into the fire. Finally Eburne spoke. "Blake, do you recall telling me about seeing Judson and Dyott together in a confab, and then later the time in the summer when Dyott went almost completely loco, when he tied up Miss Clay because he thought she had overheard him conferring with that dude in the high-pitched voice?"

The older man nodded.

"Well, Settlemire finally showed his hand at the hearing. He and his Los Angeles dude were both there. They made a great show of being patriotic citizens by insisting that their herds had been removed from the Buckskin Preserve, even though they could prove conclusively that cattle were grazers and mule deer were browsers and that cattle and deer could subsist on the same range without affecting the supply of food available to the deer. Their smooth talk might have gone over with the commission if it hadn't been for some photographs we took on the tour.

"When feed is scarce, cattle will browse too, and it is easy to distinguish their browsing from the work of the deer. They chew off and break off much larger twigs and branches than deer. When I showed Settlemire our photographs and asked him whether they showing the effect of the browsing of deer or of cattle, he said he wasn't a detective. When I flashed a photograph in which a steer had been caught in the act of pulling down a big branch of an aspen, he said, 'that doesn't prove a thing.' Then, when he saw one of his own brands on the steer's flank, he shut up mighty quick."

"What's the commission recommendin'?" asked Blakener.

"Removal of all livestock for such a period as the complete recuperation of the range may require AND the reduction of the deer herd to 50 per cent of its present numbers."

"Well, I guess that fixes Settlemire's wagon," said Blakener.

"Except that they left the usual loophole. The Grand Canyon Cattle Company, that's Settlemire, has to move out, BUT the stock belonging to local settlers may stay. All that this is going to mean is that Settlemire's stock will now be registered in southern Utah as owned by the Mormon settlers, and they'll stay on the range. The cattle will stay, but twenty-five thousand deer will have to vamoose!"

"They goin' to have the forest service carry 'em out piggy-back?" asked Blakener in disgust.

Eburne groaned. "In spite of all my reports on how impossible it was to capture deer, even little fawns, in traps, to be shipped alive to other localities, Cassell stood up there and said it could be done. He admitted that the first experiments weren't too conclusive, but with the right men in charge—and he gave me a dirty look—it would be a comparatively easy matter to trap deer in considerable numbers, crate them, and ship them to other forests, preserves, parks, or private estates for restocking purposes, and that it was his recommendation that the forest service do it free of charge except for the cost of the crates and the freight."

The older man spat disgustedly into the fire. "Judas H. Priest," he groaned. "We spent a week catchin' an' tamin' two fawns an' killed a dozen does and yearlin's in doin' so! An' these young sprouts think they can trap twenty-five thousand wild deer an' mail 'em out to their friends like Christmas postcards! Why do they need deer stalkers when they have men in charge who know so much?"

"Well, the funny thing," said Thad, "is that you would have liked some of those chaps who went on the tour with me. They listened to what I had to say and they seemed anxious to find out what the problem was all about. But it's the men like Cassell who always manage to be Johnnyon-the-spot when recommendations are to be made to Washington."

"Did they get around to givin' the Utah boys a chance for their shootin', this fall?" asked Blakener.

"Don't worry, Blake," replied the deer stalker. "If the trapping and removal of the live deer did not result in the necessary reduction, why, then the hunters were to be allowed on the preserve. Oh, yes, the killing is to be conducted in a thoroughly sane and proper manner, along the lines of modern and approved principles of game management." Eburne's voice was bitter with sarcasm.

"An' what them Utah boys don't know about the 'principles of game management,'" growled Blakener, "would fill a book! They borrow a huntin' license, drive up to a water hole, kill the first dozen tame deer they see, load 'em into their cars, an' then head back for Utah—an' read up on the 'principles of game management' later."

"Blake, as I sat there and listened to those men telling how the Secretary of Agriculture in Washington would issue regulations, eliminate licensing system abuses, open and close sections of the park regardless of state lines, prescribe where the hunters would camp, it made me feel so helpless and hopeless that I became almost physically ill. Why, to open Buckskin to hunting under the 'principles of game management' would take more men than already are on the Secretary of Agriculture's payroll. It would take an army!"

Again Eburne lapsed into moody silence. "Did I say army?" he asked bitterly. "Well, the army is the only organization in which you are permitted to commit murder legally. The last recommendation of the committee was that if by trapping and hunting the deer on Buckskin were not reduced by 50 per cent in a reasonable time, it might be necessary to have the government officially destroy a large part of the herd, 'utilizing the meat and hides to the best available economic advantage.'"

Thad's imitation of the voice of the government official who had made the suggestion brought a roar of laughter from Blakener. He rose from his chair, knocked his pipe against the stone fireplace, and said, "If we rangers don't hit the hay we won't be able to keep our eyes on the two-hundred-an'-fifty square miles of the preserve the way we oughta, an' the Secretary of Agriculture ain't goin' to like that the least bit. I'm glad, Eburne, that you've got all this off your chest. Now you can sleep. It's a mess, but what can two rangers do about it? I'm kinda glad that I missed out on that tour last month. I couldn't 've kept my mouth shut the way you could. An' as for that hearin' over to the Rust Hotel, that woulda been just too much for me to take.

"I know you're goin' to leave the service. I've told you to many's the time. As for me, I'm too old to start anythin' else. I'll stick it out till I get my pension, an' then live in Flag or some'eres. But you're young enough to make your break now—for good. Then mebbe, too, this report will be filed an' forgotten, an' things'll go along as they were. The deer will oblige by starvin' to death."

It was the longest speech the old ranger had made in all his life. Thad knew that Blakener had shared his own feeling of futility and discouragement over the recital of the commission's report. He wished that he could accept it all as philosophically as the older man.

He took off his boots and rolled up in his blanket on the floor. "Well, partner," he said, "tomorrow is another day!"

15

MUCH to Eburne's disappointment and somewhat to his surprise, after the investigating committee had gone, he was ordered back to V. T. Park to resume trapping deer.

This prevented his hoped-for visit across the canyon, yet at the same time it somehow eased a strain that had steadily mounted since Patricia Clay had asked him to come to the El Tovar. Her invitation had been frank, direct, accompanied by a smile and a look which had haunted both waking and sleeping hours. But he feared that his imagination had run riot and garnered hopes farfetched and futile. This fear dominated him; nevertheless it did not kill the clear voice of his reasoning. Patricia knew how it was with him. She was not the woman to ask him to see her again unless there were hope for him.

Thus longing and doubt, uncertainty and faith wore on his mind until he was no longer his serene self. Only one thing kept him at the experiment of deer-trapping; and it was that he felt convinced his methods and patience would be less cruel than those of anyone else.

Blakener was absent again during part of the early fall, and upon his return he was full of information and rumor about the whole question of Buckskin Forest. Only one bit of news was encouraging to Eburne. McKay's deer drive proposition had gained rather than lost ground after the investigation.

Thad went on toiling at the deer trap, and he had just built one that he believed might prove more successful than any of the former ones when an early snow storm set in and drove all the deer on the east side of the mountain down into the lower cedar country, where buckbrush grew thickly.

In one day the snow melted off the desert and slopes, but it lingered on top of the plateau. Eburne abandoned the trapping of deer. He began to be discouraged with the work and felt that he would not be there another summer.

Mail arrived, containing both bad and good news. He was ordered to proceed at once to the west side of the preserve and patrol part of a district that was to be opened to permit the killing of deer. Eburne read the letter twice and swore roundly, to Blakener's mild amusement.

"What's fussin' you?" he queried. "I got the same orders. I'll have to go and dodge high-velocity steel-jacketed triple-expansion rifle bullets."

"Yes, but murdering these tame deer will *hurt* me. I'm irritable and perhaps morbid these days. It's quite likely I'll not be fair in my attitude toward these hunters who come in. Of course I'll obey orders and keep my mouth shut. But that's not being a good fellow."

"Thad, I've noticed that you're not your old self," replied Blakener, thoughtfully puffing his pipe. "You're thin. You don't eat and sleep as you used to. Reckon you need a change. Hang on till you've helped put McKay's deal over. And meanwhile cheer up. Everythin' always turns out for the best."

The good news that offset the bad came in shape of

a letter from Nels Stackhouse. To decipher it was a task, to grasp its content was a joy. He had been guiding Miss Clay and Sue all over the cattle country. They had looked at every ranch and salable piece of land around Flagstaff. Nothing entirely desirable, especially as to area, had been found as yet. At the time Nels wrote, they were going down to Oak Creek and then to the Verdi, where he believed Miss Clay would find what she wanted. He ended with the information that they would be at McKay's deer drive, if it was attempted, and if it was not, Eburne was to be invited to take a trip with them down into the Tonto Basin and southward, where the climate was mild in November.

Thad spelled the letter out a second time, and the last paragraph three times.

"Deer drive or no deer drive, it's all day with me, as Sue used to say," he muttered aloud. "I'll go!"

Eburne and Blakener with their pack-animals traveled across the plateau to the west side and somewhat north to the district described in the supervisor's order.

At Camp Ryan, where a number of forest service men had stopped on their way in, Thad learned that the deer situation had become exceedingly complex and involved.

The state governor had opposed the killing of deer on the preserve and had come out strongly in favor of McKay's driving the deer across the canyon. It appeared that McKay had met representatives of the state and forest service at Flagstaff, where plans for his big drive had been made.

There were two herds of deer during the winter season on Buckskin, one on the east, and the other on the west side. As McKay had to drive the east side, owing to the favorable topography of the land, his plan, even if successful, would not afford any relief to the congested west side herd. The state game warden, realizing the predicament in which the forest service was placed, endeavored to get the governor to permit the killing of deer. But he was unalterably opposed to such a measure, and Eburne openly championed him for it.

Thus an awkward and serious situation was precipitated. The forest service had endeavored to cooperate with the state and had secured the best possible advice on how to relieve the congestion of the herd. They determined to carry out this advice in the face of state opposition.

"That means the state game officers will try to arrest the hunters who kill deer, and we forest service men have to try to keep them from doing it," protested Eburne. He was not alone in this deduction.

"Exactly," replied one of the supervisors with a laugh. "And if you all get fired, which I suppose you will, you can qualify as first-class bootleggers."

But it was no joke to the rangers, especially Eburne, who had foreseen this situation from the beginning. He was disgusted to learn that automobile roads had been cut through to Jump Up, Bee Springs, and other points which up to now had been wild, isolated places. A crew of men were then at work clearing a road into Pine Hollow. Camps were to be made along these roads at places convenient to water, and here rangers were to be stationed to oversee the deer-hunting. They were to have native men there to rent horses, pack in dead deer, and otherwise look after the comfort of the visitors with guns.

Each camp was to be limited to about thirty hunters—to lessen the danger of their shooting one another and stampeding the herd. Rifles were to be kept sealed except during the actual hunting. No shooting near waterholes or from automobiles would be permitted.

It had been thought best, by those who controlled the issue, not to broadcast the news that Buckskin Forest had been opened to hunters. Eburne heard this plan openly called a deliberate favoring of the residents of Fredonia, Kanab, and other towns north. Flagstaff and Winslow were not to be let into the secret. The hunters were to be informed at a set date that they could kill three deer apiece at a charge of five dollars.

Eburne and Blakener were sent to Jump Up, the farthest camp, where there was a cabin and good water, with droves of deer browsing around like sheep. Next day, a clear, cold November day with a frosty nip in the atmosphere, hunters began to arrive in cars. They were all hungry for venison and keen to start out on the hunt. A few of them were old native cattlemen and horsemen who had not had a piece of deer meat for years. Eburne rather got the point of view of these men.

This crowd of about twenty-five men were like a bunch of wild boys eager to get in ahead of each other before the game was scared away. Eburne took a party of them out in the woods while Blakener guided others. Favorable locations were selected, but this was really not necessary, for there were deer everywhere.

"Wait for big bucks or good-sized ones, and be careful not to cripple any," were the instructions Eburne gave these hunters when he unsealed their rifles.

But the hunters were hot to kill. They had guns in their hands, and few of them waited to pick out large, choice deer.

Hardly had the guns been unsealed when Eburne, despite all he could do to prevent it, saw the first deer killed in his district, a two-year-old spike buck that stood fifty feet from the hunter and watched him very attentively while he loaded his rifle, leveled it, and shot. He missed! The deer did not seem frightened, but it turned away, looking back over its shoulder. A second shot struck it in the flank. With convulsive high leap, head and forefeet up, always a sign of mortal wound, the deer plunged away, soon to fall.

Whooping, the hunter ran to his fallen quarry. Eburne followed. The deer flopped and skittered around, eyes distended, mouth dripping blood—a terrible sight for any man equipped with intelligence or feelings. It was dying when Eburne reached its side, and the hunter was kneeling to cut its throat. Eburne saw that the bullet had struck in the back, to range forward and tear out the whole front of the breast. Heart and lungs had been torn to shreds.

"What—caliber shell—did you use?" queried Eburne, trying to speak naturally.

"Hundred and eighty grain soft-nose thirty government. Some bullet, I'll say. Look at that hole!" replied the hunter.

Eburne looked, and realized that he was unreasonable and perhaps absurd in his reaction, but for a moment he had a savage impulse to make just such a hole in this hunter.

He saw another deer shot out of that same tame troop before they loped off. It was a doe. The hunter overshot the buck at which he was aiming and struck the doe. It dashed off into the woods, followed by its fawn. Eburne trailed it by tracks and spots of blood, eventually finding it dying, with the little fawn standing by bewildered. As Eburne approached, the fawn ran off.

It was a grim business that Eburne had to see through, and after the first day he went at it with less personal distress and decided that since it was a job to be done, he must learn all he could from the experience.

Eburne's camp was crowded with its quota of men every day. Hunters would kill their limit in a few hours, sometimes in less time, often, where there was good marksmanship, in a matter of a few moments, have their game packed to the camp, loaded into their cars, and drive away to let other hunters take their place.

These cars, on the way out, were instructed to stick to roads most unlikely to be guarded by game wardens. Hunters from Utah—and most of them were from that state—were particularly liable to arrest. But many came from Fredonia, which, though mostly inhabited by Mormons, was in Arizona. Thus the state deputy wardens were embarrassed by the duty of arresting residents of their own state, and sometimes even neighbors.

Eburne received word one morning that the local deputy sheriff and two game wardens were on the way to his camp to make arrests. His orders were urgent to forestall these officers by warning all his quota of hunters and to get them started out of the woods at night. He rode all day, finding the hunters and cautioning them to hang up their game until night, then pack it into their cars and escape. Some cars left in the daylight over an old unused road and got out unmolested.

One party of hunters, not particularly worried about the muddle between state and federal authorities, left Eburne's camp next morning with nine deer. That evening others arrived with the information that the party with the nine deer had been arrested. Eburne and Blakener had to bear the brunt of much criticism and disgust over the way the affair was managed.

Another annoying circumstance for the rangers to put up with was the chagrin and complaints of hunters who hurriedly shot the first deer they saw and, after their limit, ran across much larger deer and finer heads.

Blakener summed the situation up in one terse statement: "It's a hectic mess!"

Eburne had much hard riding to do. Not only was it required of him to keep track of all hunters, to oversee their hunting wherever possible, to warn them of the imminence of officers, but he had to find the places where carcasses had been left, and he had to track the crippled ones. This last was a particularly bitter job, but he would have done it of his own accord. Fortunately not a great many deer escaped in a crippled condition, which was owing, of course, to the fact that, as they were tame and stood to be shot, most of those hit were mortally wounded.

All the hunters returned to the camp utterly amazed at the apparently innumerable deer. Old nimrods from

Utah, who had hunted on Buckskin many years before, expressed astonishment and sorrow at the condition of the range and deer. This was more objective proof of the overproduction of deer and destruction of deer food.

Does and fawns were found to be very thin, in poorer condition than those on the east side of the range. The biggest bucks had fairly good flesh, and a very few of these had fat over their kidneys. The heaviest deer weighed around two hundred pounds. The report of the old native hunters was that even the largest bucks killed were much smaller than those of years ago—a very significant fact to Eburne.

Over four hundred deer, that Eburne knew of, had been taken out at the expiration of the open season for shooting. The forest service had expected four thousand to be killed. But the lack of publicity, in the first place, and then the rumors about the activity of the game wardens, kept the expected number of hunters from risking it. Eburne's opinion was that what killing was done had not in the least benefited the deer herd, but he kept this out of his report.

The forest service made a report that the killing of excess deer could be accomplished without great injury to the herd; that the value of the meat and the pleasure furnished the hunters amply justified the continuance of the hunting season.

CHAPTER

16

*T*HE RUMORS Eburne heard about McKay's now celebrated deer drive were not ones to inspire him with very much hope or satisfaction. Men claiming to be in close touch with the forest service officials declared that the matter had not at all been definitely settled.

Eburne left his horses and pack outfit with Blakener, who was to meet him on or about December first at Kane, on the east side of the mountain. That was the date set for the deer drive. It was Eburne's plan to catch a ride out through Kanab to the railroad, go to the El Tovar for a day, and then on to Flagstaff, where he would join McKay.

At Kanab, where he stopped overnight, he was surprised that he did not get his discharge when he asked for a few days off duty, but was given the same patrol duty for McKay's deer drive as he had just exercised among the hunters.

The little town of Kanab appeared to be full of hunters with their deer trophies, strangers, forest service men, game wardens, and cattlemen. Eburne mingled freely with them and was not afraid to ask questions. In fact, he went so far as to appear unduly curious about people's opinions. But he found out that McKay's drive was not popular over here. Five thousand dollars worth of venison had already been packed through Kanab.

One rumor, overheard accidentally, could not be traced to any authentic source. This was from the lips of a stranger to Eburne, to the effect that if the forest service and state officials did give McKay the order to make the deer drive he would find it hard sledding.

"Where'd you get that?" queried Eburne sharply of the rough-clad, hard-faced individual he had taken for a stockman. He was standing on a street corner in conversation with other men of like aspect.

"Wal, ranger, I couldn't tell you if I would," replied the man, far from civilly. "The town's full of gab."

"That's a rather queer statement you made. I'll report it," said Eburne and passed on.

This chance bit of gossip and the appearance of these men recalled to Eburne, Dyott and his gang. There were insidious underground forces at work. Eburne could not conscientiously lay it at the door of the Mormons. He tried to find out where Dyott had been during the deer shooting season, but if any of those he asked really knew, they kept it secret.

There was planted then in Eburne's mind a suspicion that McKay would have more to deal with than the raising of funds, securing of riders and Indians, and the physical obstacles to driving the deer. The ranger had an intuitive flash of the utter hopelessness of McKay's cherished plan, but he refused to credit it and would not permit himself to be swayed by doubt and discouragement.

Two hunters from Lund took Eburne in their car to the railroad, where he took passage for Williams, arriving there the next day at noon. He had an hour before the branch train left for the Canyon, during which he talked to natives about McKay's deer drive. Here in Arizona everybody was keenly enthusiastic about it, and most of them approved of the governor's stand against opening the preserve to hunting. The deer drive was the sole topic of conversation at the station and in the stores. Feeling appeared to run rather high against those factions opposed to distributing live deer in the parts of Arizona long barren of game. One old Arizonan put it succinctly: "Thet thar Grand Canyon deer presarve is in Arizonie. It's not in Utah, an' them fellars over thar across the canyon, livin' in Utah an' votin' in Utah, oughtn't have power to do as they danged please. We hear they're most United States Government men, but thet's a lot of bull. The cowmen over thar have a lot to do about this deal."

When Eburne got on the Grand Canyon train his mood underwent a change. For weeks he had forced out of his mind certain thoughts, fancies, dreams in regard to Patricia Clay. He had learned that they were not conducive either to peace or good work. With a rush now they all returned; and he found himself face to face with the momentous query: What was he going to the Canyon for? Only one answer occurred to him, and its significance was staggering. He felt like a soldier who had done his duty and had burned the last bridge behind him.

The train puffed and labored up the grade from the flat desert country to the cedars and pines, winding along the side of a shallow valley. A thin covering of snow lay in shady places. As the train climbed, however, the snow areas increased until, at the station, the ground was all white. It was a clear, crisp winter afternoon, just cold enough to keep the snow from melting.

Eburne walked up the stairway and out to the rim before going into the hotel. Far across the haze-filled chasm he saw the jagged, fringed line of Buckskin Forest. How remote and inaccessible it seemed from this side!

As always, it gave him courage and calmness. He had not seen it for weeks and now realized what it had come to mean in his life. Even if circumstances removed him far from this cataclysm of nature, he would want to return now and then, as to a shrine. The Grand Canyon was his Mecca.

Then he went into the El Tovar. The lobby appeared comparatively deserted, most of the guests, no doubt, being out on rides and trips. Eburne had not been here for months, and the clerks were unknown to him. When he inquired for Miss Clay he was informed she was not there but had wired she would return that evening on the train. Eburne turned away from the desk, conscious of a double relief, that he was unknown, and that an ordeal both thrilling and portentous had been postponed for a few hours.

Eburne seated himself in one of the big leather arm-chairs in front of the open fireplace, where a bed of blazing logs gave forth a genial heat. When he stretched a palm to the warmth, he was surprised to see his fingers slightly trembling. He knew that this visit to the El Tovar was in some way, not now possible to divine, going to change his whole life. Already that life back there among the deer and the pines seemed vaguely far away. His thoughts had been like flying wheels, endlessly revolving, carrying him unconsciously far from the past. He had about settled himself comfortably, ready to surrender to these same thoughts, when a light, quick step attracted his attention, and out of the corner of his eye he saw a woman approach him.

"Why, Thad! Oh, I'm *so* glad to see you," she cried, effusively. Eburne gazed up with a start, to see a rather handsome young woman beaming warmly down upon him. Clara Hilton! He had absolutely forgotten her. Rising, somewhat confused, he reached for the hand she extended.

"Miss—Miss Hilton," he stammered. "How—do you do?"

"*Miss* Hilton?" she queried archly. "It used to be Clara."

"Well, Clara, then. You must excuse me," replied Eburne, recovering himself and shaking hands with her. "How are you?"

"Oh, I'm fine and dandy. Little sick of this job here," she returned. "I'd like to get out to California, somewhere away from this awful canyon."

"I suppose it's natural you should get tired of it. But isn't it of the job and the visitors instead of the canyon?"

"You said a lot, Thad. I sure do get weary of these tourists, especially these eastern ones who think they're so superior. What are you doing here?"

Eburne's geniality suffered a slight check and he answered rather at random:

"Well, I was just enjoying the open fireplace. Always liked that sort of thing."

"I suppose you're raving over McKay's deer drive and are on your way to meet him?" she asked rather sharply, with speculative eyes on him.

"Why, yes, I am, in a roundabout way, but my coming here has nothing to do with that."

"Come to see me, Thad?" she added, with a coquetry that did not hide a nervous, hungry eagerness.

"No, Clara, I didn't, I'm sorry to say," replied Eburne simply.

"Come to see your eastern friend," she asserted, with bitter change in tone and face.

Eburne's mind adjusted itself to the situation. How singular that he had utterly forgotten this young woman! He had been friendly with her at one time, not in a sentimental way, but kindly, and frankly glad to see her and talk with her. That she had appeared to respond more warmly than called for by his attitude had been the deciding factor in his failure to keep up the acquaintance.

"Yes, I'm here to see Miss Clay," he said, looking at her.

"*Clay?*" snapped the woman, suddenly losing her attractiveness. "Don't you know her name isn't Clay?"

"Pardon me, I don't believe I understand you," rejoined Eburne.

She flushed at his tone. "The party you mean is named Edgerton."

"No, her name is Clay. Miss Patricia Clay," he returned.

"That's what you think. And what we all thought here, for she's registered as Clay. But that's an assumed name, *I* believe."

Eburne gazed blankly at the woman. Succeeding his astonishment, there came a rush of conflicting feelings.

"Miss Hilton, you are making a serious statement," he said coldly. "Are you quite sure you can substantiate it?"

"Yes, I can," she retorted, angered at his tone. "But I don't have to. You can't bluff me, Thad Eburne. I don't see that it's any of your business, anyway. Just because you loafed around on the North Rim with this Edgerton woman and Sue Warren! She's made a fool of you. Oh, I heard all about your camping and riding—about the pet fawn Bo-peep you gave her. Why, Thad Eburne, you're a ranger at one twenty-five per month—a deer stalker—and this Edgerton party is a New York society woman worth millions."

"Please be lady enough to be impersonal as far as I'm concerned," returned Eburne. "You made a grave statement which I have a right to question."

"Oh, you have?" she flashed out maliciously.

"I question your right to discuss Miss Clay."

"Oh, I see. Old friends for new. You're sweet on her. You don't want to hear about her. You want to think she's sweet on you. Well, there are a lot of other sapheads who think the same as you, Thad Eburne," she added.

"You are adding insult to injury," returned Eburne, growing colder with the need to keep his temper. "I came here to ask Miss Clay to marry me. And I cannot permit you to demean yourself by any further—"

"My, but you're the ambitious ranger," she interrupted furiously. "Marry *you*? That woman! Why, you're out of your mind. And don't you insult *me*. I'm an honest girl. Nobody can even hint anything against my good name. But this woman you want to marry—why, everybody on two continents knows her disgrace. She's notorious. You poor fish of a ranger! You've mushed around your pet deer so much that you're not only out of the world but you're a love-sick fool.... Patricia Edgerton is a famous fashionable beauty. She's worth millions. She has had lovers galore. She ruined her reputation and had to leave New York. That's why she's parading under the name of Clay."

"You can't prove that," asserted Eburne hoarsely and low.

"I should say I can," fumed the woman. "Just you wait here." She strode, almost ran, to the stairway and started to ascend. Eburne did not move out of his tracks, but his gaze traveled to the fire and remained fixed there. He did not seem to be able to see or think clearly. He felt that he was waiting there for something dreadful to happen. Presently a touch on his arm aroused him. The woman had returned. She was panting. Her face was white. She seemed agitatedly aware of the presence of other people in the lobby, especially toward the office. She drew Eburne across the lobby and into the writing room. It was vacant. Then she halted, with one hand behind her back.

"Promise you'll give this back."

"I don't want to see what you have," he replied stiffly. "I followed you here to escape an undesired audience."

"You're afraid of the truth. Look here," she retorted and spread a newspaper before him on the desk.

Beneath his gaze lay the scandal sheet of one of the great New York dailies. Among the faces printed there shone Patricia's, the largest on the page, a likeness that struck him forcibly with its fidelity to her loveliness. No shadow of doubt! This was Patricia. She resembled a queen in royal raiment, her face proud, serene, lovely, her regal neck encircled with pearls. He had never seen her in anything save outdoor garb. Underneath the picture were printed words that he scanned with lightning-swift glance, the content of which he only half grasped before his sense of loyalty made him turn his eyes from the scandal sheet. But his reaction had been simple, natural, not the motive of a suspicious mind.

"What a vile lie!" he muttered through his teeth as he crushed the paper with firm hands.

Then all the tremendous forces of will and passion within him united to cast that ridiculous news story out of his mind. There was no truth in it! His code would not admit even the possibility that the girl he knew and loved ever had been involved in such a cheap scandal. He had spent hours alone on the rim of the Grand Canyon with Patricia Clay—or Edgerton, if that really was her right name; and he would have stalked his life and the salvation of his soul upon her honor. The poison of yellow journalism, both in newspapers and magazines, was something of which he was fully aware, isolated as his life had been. That was why he despised them so heartily. His mind went back to those summer days on the North Rim. He recalled the shadow in her lovely eyes. He remembered that evening at sunset when she had confessed that there was something secret she could not or would not divulge. But Eburne had gazed into her eyes with the searching and spiritual power of love, and what he had seen was sorrow and renunciation. Almost she had betrayed herself to him. It was some deed of sacrifice that had made her an exile. What it was he did not care to know until she was ready to confide in him.

Presently he got up, and unclenching his fists from the crushed paper, he made it as presentable as possible and refolded it. Then he went back through the lobby to Miss Hilton's desk. When she looked up to see him her face turned white.

"Have you showed this to anyone besides me?" he inquired curtly.

"Certainly—I—have," she replied haltingly but with a courage rising with the sound of her voice.

"How long have you had it?"

"Since last night. But I saw a copy of it some time ago. I didn't pay any attention to it at the time. But when this Edgerton woman arrived here in the spring, I remembered her face."

"Well, where did you get *this* paper?" queried Eburne as she hesitated.

"From a hotel guest who arrived last night from New York."

"Woman, of course. No man would carry around a thing like that and hand it over to you."

"Wrong again, Thad. Really you should wake up and hear the birdies sing. It was a man."

"Someone you knew?"

"Perfect stranger," she replied, growing tart and showing color in her cheeks. An irresistible propulsion was at work within her. How greedily her eyes devoured his face for signs of pain!

"You couldn't have got that from a stranger," he declared incredulously. "How could you?"

"That's my affair, Thad," she returned mockingly.

"Does Miss—does she know?" he asked in a low voice.

"Not yet!" she exclaimed, with a singular gleam in her eyes. Eburne had a revelation then, new in his experience—the passion of hate and jealously in a woman.

Abruptly Eburne whirled on his heel and strode away, biting his lips lest he speak the scorn he felt and the threat that burned within him. As he passed the office, he was aware of close scrutiny and whispers, the meaning of which he did not catch. He went to a far corner of an alcove-extension of the lobby, and here he sat in the shadow.

When comparative calmness returned, Eburne realized that Patricia would utterly ignore this calumny and those who chose to hear it or speak it. He could do no less. How it galled him not to be able to save her from covert, if not open, insult! But what would she care about the sneers of such persons as Clara Hilton or her chance acquaintances from the east?

As the afternoon waned to a close, guests of the hotel began to return from rides and trail trips, some of them weary, but all of them enthusiastic over some special feature of the canyon.

About dark, a motorcar stopped outside and a driver came banging in the storm door carrying bags and a robe. Then Eburne, from his corner, espied a tall, slender figure enter the lobby. Patricia! There was color in her cheeks, and there were snowflakes on the rich black fur around her neck. She walked briskly, pulling off her gloves, and she tarried a moment to extend chilled hands to the open fireplace. Then she passed on down the corridor and out of sight. Eburne became conscious of a relaxing of the tension that had bound him all day. How wonderful just to see her! He rose and went to one of the desks in the writing room—the very one upon which had been spread Miss Hilton's scandal-mongering newspaper—and sat down to write:

Dearest Patricia:

I was a long time keeping my promise to come to the El Tovar, but I am here at last. You will be interested to hear of the rest of my experiences with the deer investigation committee and among the tame-deer murderers on the west side of Buckskin.

No doubt you will have news for me from Flagstaff. I am on my way there, and must leave on tonight's train. I must make every effort to hurry to McKay.

I have a question of tremendous import to ask you, Patricia. Wherefore won't you please take dinner with me? I am anticipating the pleasure of seeing you, not as I know you, only in outdoor garb, like a boy, really, but as a woman in one of the beautiful gowns Sue raved to me about. Indeed, I have dreamed of you so long, and have conjured you up in so many enchanting visions, it seems wonderful that I am about to have the happiness of realizing one of them. In truth, I dare say I will not recognize you at all.

Faithfully,

Thad Eburne

This note he gave to a bellboy to deliver with a request for an answer. Presently the boy returned and said, "Miss Clay says she will take dinner with you in a half hour, sir."

Eburne drew a great breath of relief. It eased the feeling of oppression in his breast. She would see him! He had not expected anything else, nevertheless the fact that she wanted to see him too set his heart to pounding.

Gradually the lobby filled with guests dressed for dinner, chattering, laughing, calling out to each other. Eburne gave his chair before the fire to an agreeable old lady, who had appreciative eyes for his stalwart figure in its close-fitting ranger uniform. Then an elderly man, evidently with the woman, spoke genially to him and stood beside him, back to the fire. Eburne welcomed a little conversation, and the next quarter of an hour saw him cool and collected, confident of himself and that he could meet any situation. Meanwhile his eyes were keen to note newcomers to the lobby. And presently, when three men came sauntering down the wide stairway, easterners by the look of them and the cut of their clothes, Eburne had an intuitive flash that these were the guests he particularly wanted to observe. When they approached Miss Hilton's desk and she rose to greet them, effusively, it appeared, Eburne was sure he was on the right track. Casually moving over to the office desk, he glanced at the register until he had found listed together the names of three men from New York. Then, engaging the clerk in conversation, he took the opportunity deliberately to study the trio. Two were good-looking young men, not long out of college, with the keen, sharp, pale faces characteristic of New Yorkers. The third was older, past thirty, a well-fed, debonair person, whose smooth-shaven face bore a heat not from healthy exercise, and puffy lines not conducive to manly beauty. His hair was a little thin at the temples, his eyes were hard, his lips cynical and sensual. It was this individual who was talking to the vivacious and self-conscious Miss Hilton.

Eburne approached them in time to hear the stranger

say: "Give me back that newspaper, girlie. I'm leaving to-night for Los Angeles."

"Oh, here it is," she replied, stepping back to fumble in her desk. She produced the paper and handed it to him. "Strange you should happen along—someone who knew her."

"It's a small world," he said. "I knew Patricia Edgerton had come west and rather expected to run across her at Santa Barbara, Del Monte, or San Francisco. But not here. When did she leave for the coast?"

"I never said she left," returned the woman with an enigmatic smile. "She has been here on and off all summer and fall. Makes this her headquarters and has been gadding all over the desert. She's here now. Just got in."

"Here! Tonight!" he ejaculated in amazement. Then quickly he added, "You didn't use that paper for anything except identification?"

"You showed it to me. Why shouldn't I show it too?" she retorted.

"Oh say, now, all I wanted to find out from you was whether she really had been here," he returned, evidently ill at ease and resentful.

"Well, you were sure eager to hear all I could tell you," said Miss Hilton with an air of triumph at her cleverness. "And you told me that if Patricia Edgerton was really the Miss Clay who registered here it wasn't any wonder, considering she was a ruined and notorious woman. Now didn't you?"

The man stroked his chin and frowned as he regarded her closely, evidently the first time he had taken thoughtful stock of her.

"Miss Hilton, I fear I flattered you when I called you girlie," he said bluntly.

"You bet you did," she retorted with a dark flush. "You weren't above trying to flirt with me when you found out I thought I had a line on this Edgerton woman. But I was on to you, Mr. Errol Scott."

Eburne had halted a few paces distant from them, somewhat to one side of Miss Hilton. She seemed maliciously absorbed in her little coup.

"I was going to say 'stung,' but think I'll substitute 'scratched,'" he rejoined with a careless laugh.

Eburne moved forward, then, into range of Miss Hilton's gaze and he looked at her hard. She gave a violent start and stepped back in such manifest confusion at sight of him that Scott wheeled to see what had caused this sudden change. Eburne gave him the same steady look and then stepped out beyond the two young men, who had not, apparently, been interested in this byplay.

At this moment a tall, slender woman in a gown of silver sheen that captured radiance from every light about her came down the wide stairway into the lobby. Eburne's heart gave a great leap. He expected to see Patricia vastly different, and she was, but that lovely face was still the one of his dreams. Her free step, the poise of her head, the distinction of her carriage were the same. It was not the sight of her that lent Eburne his cool, easy command of himself, but what he knew.

Her dark gaze swept the lobby as she hesitated on the last step. Expectation and a slight smile of pleasure shone upon her face. Eburne felt a strong thrill of pride that he was the object of her search. Then she saw him— and he knew he had been right to come. As he started to advance, she stepped down to meet him.

The man Scott intercepted her as she was about to greet Eburne.

"Pat Edgerton! Well, of all people!" he burst out, with the gay suavity of one on familiar ground. "Somebody said you'd gone to Santa Barbara."

Eburne's eager step, his hand almost outstretched, were stayed as if by an invisible barrier. He saw her turn with a barely perceptible start to face the stranger from the East. She had recognized the voice before she saw the speaker. If Eburne ever was thrilled in his life it was then.

Her wonderful eyes seemed to dilate with a blaze of dark fire at a shock for which she had not been prepared.

"How do you do," she returned with hauteur, and, bowing slightly, she passed him, ignoring his proffered hand, to glide serene and proud up to Eburne.

"Hello Thad," she said, and with the words there came an indefinable change of poise, expression, tone. Her perfect command of the situation and the familiarity and warmth of her greeting freed Eburne from the awkwardness of the moment. He could not fail this woman.

He greeted her in few words and bowed over the hand she gave him.

"What a surprise," she continued. "I feared you'd forgotten your visit to the El Tovar. Here it is almost December. I've had such wonderful experiences since I saw you last ... How are you, Thad? You seem thin and worn."

"I'm well, but pretty tired," he replied. "And how are you?"

"Thad, I never had such health. Oh, this glorious West! So much to see and do! Can't you see the change in me? I was so thin and white."

"Perhaps I shall remember presently how you looked," he laughed.

"Let us go to dinner," she said and drew him toward the brightly lighted dining room.

As they walked in together, Eburne wondered at the suspended state of his emotions. He was listening calmly to her, and presently he was seated at a table near one of the windows, gazing at her.

"Now let me look at you," he said. "I want to be sure this is no dream." And he bent his gaze upon her with thoughtful concentration.

"Thad, you make me blush," she protested, with heightened color, and her eyes danced.

"Sue was right," was all he said. Yet to himself he confessed that a woman's beauty was not merely the classic lines of her face, it was how her hair was groomed, it was the contrast of the bare flesh of her neck and arms with the color and material of her gown—all these contributed to her loveliness.

"You might tell me what she said," declared Patricia.

"It's great to be with you," he rejoined, suddenly serious, "but before I give way to the sheer happiness of seeing you again—hearing your voice, let me ask you something. Who was the fellow you snubbed outside in the lobby? I know his name is Scott and he hails from New York. But is he someone you used to know?"

"It is Errol Scott. Yes, he belongs to a part of my life I would gladly forget. I seem to recall that he once did me the honor to ask me to become Mrs. Scott," replied Patricia. "He's a New York broker whom I met frequently in my rather mixed set. You heard him call me Pat Edgerton, did you not?"

"Yes, I did, but I assure you I was not curious about that."

"Well, it's my real name," she said frankly, with her eyes grave and dark upon his. "But he had not, nor ever had, the right to call me Pat. That was what my few real friends called me."

"Pat? How very unsuited to you! I prefer Patricia," he said, deliberately passing by the opening she gave him. "If you were called Princess Pat, like that beautiful English woman, it would be a little more felicitous." Here the waitress interrupted him, and there ensued a silence, during which Patricia withdrew her gaze from his. It thrilled him to see that she could not wholly control her agitation where he was concerned.

"I am not in the least hungry—that is, for food," he began again presently.

"Thad, you've been taking lessons from that incorrigible cowboy Nels," she said, shaking her head.

"In what?"

She did not reply.

"Patricia, you haven't forgotten how I—feel—toward you?" he asked gently.

"I'm afraid I haven't," she admitted. "But I—I believed you had gotten over it."

"One doesn't get over the kind of love I have for you, Patricia. If you could bring yourself to love me, you would know. Time and separation and silence—they only add to the *sureness* when you realize that you love a person."

Her white hands ceased movement, and she sat motionless, with downcast eyes, waiting for the words she knew were coming. Yet she made no move to check them. Leaning across the table, he took one of her cool hands in his and said in a tone that was little above a whisper:

"Patricia, will you marry me?"

She began to tremble. Her free hand came up to her face and she leaned her bare elbow on the table. Their faces were only a short distance apart. She looked straight at him with inscrutable dark eyes. But they were the eager eyes of a woman.

"No, Thad, I can't," she said simply and sadly.

"My dear, you told me over on the North Rim that you had neither husband nor lover nor ties of any kind," he protested. "Is it that I was mistaken about your caring for me—a little?"

"No. I do care. Please believe me, Thad. That was my confession when I asked you to come over. But I don't know how much."

"Patricia, even to know that you love me a little makes me the happiest and luckiest of men."

"Thad, please don't make love to me," she begged.

"I am not. I'm just asking a few simple questions and telling you some plain facts. *Why* can't you marry me?"

"It wouldn't be fair," she murmured.

"To whom?"

"You. And your mother—sister, all your family."

"Perhaps I would be the best judge of that. But I am asking you nothing, except to be my wife."

"No, Thad," she replied with white, trembling lips. "But I want you to know—you are the only man I ever wanted to marry."

"Patricia, isn't that a confession of love?" he asked.

"It must stand without any confession," she said, averting her face. "Thad, here we are in a public dining room, forgetting to eat our dinners, with people staring."

"What do I care for these people? I can't even see them. But one thing more—Patricia, I've given up my ranger work."

"You have!" she exclaimed in surprise. "When?"

"I made the decision a few moments ago. And I did it because I am going to follow you everywhere. I shall be like Nels. . . . Now forgive me for embarrassing you here. But I had to tell you."

She regarded him oddly, as if he had presented himself in a strange, new guise, but she did not offer further comment and went on with her dinner. Eburne made a pretense of eating. Presently they got back to conversation, this time about Sue and Nels and McKay's deer drive. Upon their return to the lobby, which was now well crowded with guests, Patricia said, "Let's have a look at the Canyon. I'll get my coat."

She returned bareheaded, with the black fur coat enveloping her. They went out together her hand tucked under his arm. The wind blew cold and sweet from the forest; the moon shone white through broken clouds. At the rim they halted to gaze down into the shadowy gulf. It had never seemed just like this to Eburne. He felt Patricia's hand close upon his arm. Then he turned to her as she gazed down into the depths. How pale and lovely she was! In the mystifying moonlight, standing like that, her dark hair blowing across her brow, her profile pure and cold, she seemed infinitely beyond him, yet he divined that he had won her love and some day would win her as his wife. The moment was beautiful and solemn, and when suddenly she felt impelled to lift her gaze from the Canyon to his face, life became intolerably sweet. The moment there beside that moon-blanched canyon had unconsciously wrung from her what she had denied him in the hotel.

"Patricia, you are lovely," he whispered, "and you are as good and true as you are lovely." He realized that he might have taken her in his arms right then, but he held back. "Come, it is too cold here for you. Besides, I have a train to catch."

She did not speak until they reached the steps of the El Tovar.

"My friend, you have made me happy—and unhappy too," she said, gravely looking down upon upon him with eyes like black stars. "I will see you in Flagstaff. Good night."

He bade her good night and wheeled away to stride down the plank walk to the stairway. Once he looked back. She still was standing where he had left her, but she had turned and was looking out over the moonlit canyon. His heart beat too high and full for his breast.

Below, the lights of the station gleamed on the snow; the engine puffed and steamed. Eburne reached the level of the platform.

"Talk of the devil!" exclaimed a voice. "There he is now, walking on air."

"For a deer hunter I'll say he's pretty smooth," answered a voice Eburne recognized as Scott's. "But it gets my goat that Pat should fall for him."

Eburne wheeled as in a flash and in two long strides confronted the last speaker.

"Deer hunters have sharp ears," he said caustically.

"Well, then, like all listeners they don't always hear good of themselves," retorted Scott thickly.

"I am indifferent to what I hear about myself, but about a friend—that's another matter," returned Eburne, stepping closer. "The familiar use of Miss Edgerton's pet name by you is offensive to her, and therefore to me."

"Why don't you keep your mouth shut?" demanded the man in harsh amazement.

Eburne quickly reached out and slapped him so hard that he sat down suddenly in the snow. He got up cursing and swung a cane at Eburne's head. Throwing up his arm, Eburne caught the force of the blow, snapping the cane like a pipestem. Then Eburne shot out his left hand to clutch Scott's coat collar.

"It's part of a deer hunter's work to deal with coyotes and skunks," said Eburne, shoving the man back hard against a post. "I think you're pretty much of a skunk. Packing around a dirty scandal sheet of a rotten newspaper to inspire gossip about a woman is just about as low-down as a man could get. So, Mr. Errol Scott, I'm handing you one for that!"

Eburne's wrath had gathered force with his speech, and he swung his fist in a sweeping arc, flush against the jaw of the surprised easterner. The blow sent Scott's head back with a sodden thud against the post. He dropped like an empty sack.

Eburne wiped his hands and turned to the man's companions.

"I don't think much of the company you gentlemen keep," he said curtly and strode away toward the train.

When he had found a seat inside, he looked out of the window to see the men bending over Scott's prostrate form. Just then the conductor shouted "All aboard," and the train started.

"Well, I can't say I'm sorry that post was there," muttered Eburne. "But I didn't mean to make him miss the train. I imagine, though, from the look and feel of my fist that he won't care to go back to the hotel to show his face to Patricia."

*E*BURNE arrived in Flagstaff at six o'clock next
morning, in the darkness of gray dawn. A nipping
cold wind blew in his face as he made his way to
the hotel. Flagstaff was situated high up on a bench of the
San Francisco Mountains, and winter already had set in.
Eburne reflected that McKay had no time to lose if he
meant to get his deer drive under way.

The hotel was about full of guests, which was somewhat unusual for Flagstaff at this season, and Eburne had
to accept what quarters were available. The snow squall
ceased while he was at breakfast, and the sun came out,
dazzlingly bright on a white-mantled world. After breakfast,
in the lobby of the hotel, Eburne began to question every
man he encountered. It did not take long to find out that
Flagstaff was strong for McKay's deer drive.

Gradually the lobby filled with men, natives and business people of the town, cowboys, ranchers, taxi drivers,
motion picture men, of whom there appeared to be many,
motorists on the way to California and others there for

the deer drive, and lastly a sprinkling of Indians.

Presently Nels Stackhouse and Tine Higgenbottom appeared, both as always picturesque in big sombreros, leather coats, overalls, and high boots. This morning, however, they were minus spurs and chaps.

"You ole deer chaser, put her there," drawled Nels, thrusting out a red paw.

"Howdy, Thad" was Tine's lazy greeting.

"Nice pert morning, boys," said Eburne, "and seeing you is good for my eyes."

"Say, Nels, he's sure rarin' full of pep," declared Tine to his comrade, and he winked.

"Thad, I'll bet you four bits you threw your pack at the El Tovar on your way over here," drawled Nels.

"Won't bet you, Nels," returned Thad with a laugh. "Don't start anything, for you know I always get it on you."

"Wal, I reckon you're here to help McKay, an' I'll say you've rustled up some job," said Nels.

"I'm anxious to get news. But first tell me, how's Sue?"

"Just grand. She'll be runnin' in to see you sometime."

"I'll sure be glad. And tell me, did you find a ranch that Miss—Miss Clay liked?"

"I'll say we did," replied Nels with beaming face. "Two sections, twelve hundred an' eighty acres, part in grass an' the most in timber. Six miles from town. Not a shack or a fence on it. Two big never-failin' springs, an' a dandy place to dam up for a lake. There's a deep, red-walled, wild canyon she just raved about. Fine elevation to build a house, an' a swell view of the peaks an' desert."

"You don't say!" ejaculated Eburne, sharing the cowboy's delight. "That's great news. I'm glad for her, and for you and Sue."

"Thad, you can ring me in on that," spoke up Tine with a grin. "I've got a new job. An' by golly, there's enough pine woods an' deer on this place to give you a job too."

Eburne joined in the hearty laugh, but could find no quick retort for the irrepressible Tine.

"Thad, you can bet I was plumb sick at first," went on Nels. "I just couldn't find a ranch she would have taken as a gift. We drove an' rode all over this country from Ash Fork to Gallup. You see I wanted to find a ranch with good roads, cleared land, fences, buildin's an' all that, so as to save Miss Clay a lot of money. Finally I got desperate an' took her out in the woods, to the wildest, roughest country around here. An' she was tickled to death. I told her it'd cost a thousand times more than it was worth to build a good road through this land, develop water, clear timber off, put up house, cabins, barns, corrals, fences, an' all the rest she wants. She never batted an eye. All she said was she could give deservin' men good jobs. An' she an' Sue have been drawin' plans to beat the band."

"Nels, I would have taken her to the uncultivated places first," responded Eburne. "Did she buy the land?"

"I'll say she did," declared Nels shortly.

"Drawing plans," mused Eburne. "I can appreciate the fun and happiness of that, especially when it is to make others happy besides yourself. But Nels, winter has come with a whoop. You can't begin that work till spring. What are your other plans?"

"We been waitin' on this deer drive," rejoined Nels seriously. "Sue an' Miss Clay are crazy to go. An' there are other women as keen about it. Me an' Tine haven't made a kick. Been waitin' for you. Thad, you'll have to put the kibosh on this deer drive for the womenfolk, at least those we are responsible for."

"Nels, you're right," said Thad thoughtfully. "It's too far and cold. We're going to get snowed in. They'd suffer too much hardship, for something we are by no means sure of. It'll be a great disappointment to them, but I believe it's up to us to prevent their going if we can."

"Say, why don't you tell Thad the *big* plan?" blurted out Tine. "Modest an' bashful, huh? Why, you used to have more gall an' brass than any cowpuncher—"

"Tine, I think heaps of you," drawled Nels in interruption, "but, you just got to look at me with respect."

"Thad, this here pard of mine is steppin' too high," complained Tine. "Every night Sue gives him lessons in readin', writin', an' Heaven knows what else."

"What's the big plan?" inquired Thad, with his hand going to Nels's shoulder.

"Wal, I've promised to go with McKay on the deer drive," replied Nels. "My bosses—I've sure got two now, one who pays me wages an' another who takes them away from me—they want me to help McKay. After that, Sue an' I are goin' to get married. We're to take a little trip to southern Arizona. Miss Clay will join us at Tucson, an' then we'll do much the same down there as we've been doin' round Flag, Aw, Thad, I've sure got mighty poor prospects. I'm feelin' awful bad."

"Bad nuthin'," retorted Tine in disgust. "Why, Thad, he whoops in his sleep, kicks me out of bed, an' yells 'James, fetch my boots.'"

When at length Thad did pin the boys down to sober talk about McKay and the deer drive, it was to have them confirm exactly what he had suspected. McKay was not getting anywhere with his preparations. He should have had trucks with grain and supplies, and saddle-and pack-horses already on the way across the desert.

While Eburne was listening to the practical opinions of the cowboys, McKay came stamping into the hotel, rough-clad and beaming, kicking snow off his boots, and bringing the breath of the winter outdoors with him.

"Mac, when do you start your drive?" began Eburne at once, drawing McKay to a corner.

"Wal, I aimed to start December first, but reckon I'll have to put it off till the fifteenth."

"Too late. You don't dare wait that long," rejoined Eburne earnestly.

"Few days more or less can't make any diff," said McKay, rubbing his bearded chin with a grimy hand. Honesty and toil seemed to sit well upon him. "I'm bein' held up by a lot of things. Sent to Globe for a truckload of wire. Have to wait for that. My brother's comin' from Kanab an' I've got to send him back to pick up Indians an' men. I'm waitin' for my son to come with another truck. I'm expectin' some of these Indian traders to talk about hirin' Indians. An' motion picture people are comin' to buy the picture rights to the drive. Then I'm tryin' to raise money."

"Mac, all this should have been done long ago," declared Eburne seriously. "You can't wait to do these things. They must be done at once."

"What's the rush, Thad?" he queried, in gruff surprise.

"If you wait till the fifteenth, you'll *never* pull off your drive. Mac, there are men working against you right now. All they need is a little time. I could not find out how or where or when they'll strike. But they don't want this deer drive to go over. Delay will be fatal. Besides there's the weather. When winter hits the east slope of Buckskin, as it has already hit here, you will be through. Absolutely. All your labor and expense for nothing."

"Eburne, I'm figgerin' on snow to help us make the drive," returned McKay stubbornly. "Besides, these here picture people want snow so the pictures of the deer will take pretty. No, the weather ain't worryin' me. Neither is that outfit over thar who's agin my drive. But a lot of things *is* worryin' me."

"Mac, have you made out a list of food supplies you'll need for your men and Indians? Grain, camp duffel, wire, burlap, gasoline, oil, cowbells, and the hundred-odd things necessary?"

"Grub for Indians?" echoed McKay, as if the idea had just struck him. "Hadn't thought of that. Wal, we'll kill a beef out thar an' give them a sack of flour."

"Mac, that would last a hundred Indians just one day," returned Eburne, trying to restrain his impatience. "It will take the Indians two days to get there from the gap, two days to get back, and say ten days for the drive. That is fourteen days, driving each and every one of which these

Indians will have to eat. Besides that it is a big transportation problem to move the Indians to and fro."

McKay scratched his grizzled head. "I'll be hanged if thar ain't a lot to think of. Eburne, I'm askin' you to help me."

"You bet I will. Here's all the money I can spare," replied Eburne, handing over a roll of bills. "Buy your grub and outfit. Get these started out today. Make the best deal possible with the picture people. Be quick. Every day gone lessens the chance of our success. Send trucks with grub to handle the Indians."

"But if I put off the drive till the fifteenth, I don't want the Indians out thar till then."

"You must *not* postpone the drive," declared Eburne with all the force he could muster.

"Wal, I'll see, but I reckon we can't get ready," said McKay.

"Then by all means give it up altogether. That's my advice. I know the country."

"Say, Eburne, I'll drive ten thousand deer across that canyon, an' all over the south side, an' right through the streets of Flagstaff," boomed McKay, slamming the table with a huge first.

"All right, I've had my say. Do it your own way. I'll help," said Eburne resignedly.

It was now indeed a forlorn hope. McKay was indomitable, a giant in strength, a man used to overcoming all kinds of physical obstacles, but he lacked wholly the organizing and executive ability to carry out such a tremendous project as this one.

During the next three days McKay changed his mind as many times as he listened to different persons who wanted to project their ideas into the deer drive. It was Eburne who got the machinery working. He could not, however, overcome the handicaps of unconsidered preparation and lack of funds, nor could he hurry McKay. As a matter of fact, somebody or something was holding up the trucks and the men McKay expected.

A circus in town would not have created the excitement that this deer drive did. Hundreds of people outside of Flagstaff came there to see it get under way or to participate in any way possible, but as they could not get any definite information as to the certainty of the drive coming off, or the date or place, most of them left with a conviction that the whole scheme was a fizzle.

Eburne saw how the confidence of the town people, McKay's own neighbors, was beginning to wane. Cowboys and cattlemen who had been keen to help drive the deer, just for the experience, gave up and went home. McKay had not been able to strike while the iron was hot.

At last, however, he got together twenty-five men, with horses and outfit, ready to start next morning. The plan was to travel across country to the canyon, go down Tanner's trail, cross the river, and up on the other side to the Saddle.

That day, trucks were started with supplies McKay had bought, but which Eburne knew would be pitifully inadequate. They were to go to Lee's Ferry, cross the Colorado there, continue on to Kane, and then up to the Saddle camp. They were then to return to one of the trading posts to fetch the Indians. If the roads were good, and if the drivers had unprecedented luck, all this might be accomplished in five days. McKay said in three! As a matter of fact, Eburne had a conviction that it could not be done at all. Instead of ten trucks that should have been sent, there were three, and two of them would never get as far as Kane on those desert roads.

That night a snowstorm arrived and increased in force until by morning a creditable blizzard was blowing. But McKay and his faithful followers departed, leaving some insurmountable tasks behind for Eburne to look after.

One of them was to deal with the trader Mobray, who, McKay had said, would handle the Indians.

"Mac never guaranteed nothin'," declared Mobray. "He sent me word to collect a hundred Indians an' go with them to Kane. I got the Indians bunched out at my post, eatin' me out of supplies. But I can't take them to Kane unless their pay an' keep is guaranteed. Two dollars a day, all the time they're out. An' the money's got to be sure or the superintendent of the reservation won't let them go. Here I find Mac gone, an' nothin' sure. What would you do, Eburne?"

"I'd risk it, but I certainly can't advise you to do that," replied Thad. "This sure looks like a cropper. McKay has spent all the money he could raise here in town. I think he expected to pay the Indians out of the money he got from the government for making the drive."

"But suppose he fails?" demanded Mobray in exasperation. "I'm out the grub an' clothes I've advanced. The Indians are out their wages."

At this juncture of the heated argument with the trader, Eburne became aware of several persons at his elbow, but he had been jostled by a curious crowd for days and he no longer had any interest in outsiders. It took quite a tug from a familiar hand to distract his attention. Then he turned to face Sue, rosy and bright, smiling at him. Nels and Patricia stood just behind her. Thad was immensely surprised and pleased. The worry with which he had burdened himself over this deer drive problem vanished as if by magic. It suddenly became nothing but a little work.

"Thad, I overheard some of your conversation with this man," said Patricia after the greetings were over. "You seem to be in difficulties."

The upshot of an explanation to Patricia was that she asked Mobray to go to the bank with her, where she would arrange to pay what money was due the Indians at the end of the drive.

During her short absence, the deer stalker had an argument with Sue about the inadvisability of women going on the deer drive. He had not by any means won it by the time Patricia returned.

"Thad, if you think it best, we will not go," said Patricia without hesitation. "We'll just have to swallow our disappointment. But I've had so many wonderful trips. Then I saw the deer. We must not be selfish, Sue, and handicap the men by our presence."

"It wasn't that, Patricia," whispered Sue, peering around to see where Nels was. "This cowboy friend of mine said he would show me who was boss, and that I wasn't going out there to catch pneumonia."

Eburne was tremendously busy the rest of that day, getting ready to start next morning with the motion picture men. Mobray had hurried out as soon as he was assured of his pay for the Indians. The snowstorm blew away and the sun came out warm and bright.

Thad had dinner with the girls and Nels, after which they went to the motion picture theater. When opportunity afforded, Patricia said:

"Thad, you remember the other night at the El Tovar?"

He laughed. "How could I forget it?"

"Didn't you see Errol Scott at the station before you boarded the train?"

"Why, yes, I believe I did, come to think of it," he replied slowly.

"Did you not have words with him?" went on Patricia.

"I might have said good evening or some such pleasant thing."

"Thad!"

"Patricia!" he returned in the same tone of voice.

"I believe you would lie to me," she said reproachfully.

"Most men can be terrible villains at times," he returned imperturbably.

"Thad, you're not going to tell me, then?" she asked. He wasn't sure whether she was approving or disapproving.

"Tell you what?"

"About your meeting with Scott."

"Why, Patricia, it wasn't much. Certainly nothing to interest you. I seem to have had an impression that he was a cad."

"Very well, Mr. Eburne," she continued. "Listen to this. That night, Scott was badly hurt and had to be taken in an automobile to Williams. They thought he had a fractured skull. But luckily he did not, and after three days he was able to go on to California."

"Indeed. I should imagine it impossible to fracture his skull," rejoined Thad laconically. "What happened to the gentleman?"

"Nobody seemed to know. His companions rushed him to Williams without explaining."

"He was a drinking man, and there was ice on the steps. He probably fell."

"Yes, he probably *did,*" declared Patricia with a low laugh. "It's a wonder he didn't fall clear into the canyon."

"That's true. A fat, heavy fellow like him, once he started to fall, might go a long way."

"Thad, you're incorrigible and also adorable," she whispered, squeezing his arm. "Listen to what I do know. That handsome young woman at the Canyon was smitten with you. She was horribly jealous, poor thing. Well, when she first saw me she suspected I was the original of a picture she had seen in a New York paper. When Scott arrived at the hotel she scraped up an acquaintance with him. And he had that paper with him. She got it from him and shoved it under everybody's nose, including yours ... And *you* never gave me the slightest sign you had seen it or—or knew of the notorious Pat Edgerton ... Oh, it was—"

"Pat," he interrupted softly, leaning close to look at her and whisper, "when I come back from this deer drive, will you marry me? I love you so desperately ... I want to go with you and Sue and Nels to southern Arizona."

"Oh—don't!" she faltered, and lapsed into an eloquent

silence. For moments he felt the quiver of her arm against his. Then the theater was darkened and the picture flashed upon the screen. She did not speak again until after the performance was over, and then it was to take up again the subject of the deer drive.

"Patricia, I wish you'd leave the El Tovar and come over here to stay with Sue," he said anxiously at parting.

"I have come, bag and baggage," she replied. "Poor Sue will tell you. Her little house won't hold my endless belongings."

"That is fine. I know you will be comfortable—and happy."

"Thad," said Sue, "we've shore got a dandy little open fireplace, a good lamp and table, and we're going to spend hours drawing plans for *two* houses, hers and mine."

*N*EXT morning a caravan of motorcars and trucks left Flagstaff on the long detour across the Painted Desert and canyon around to the eastern slope of Buckskin Mountain.

Eburne, with Tine Higgenbottom and a driver named Conroy, led the way. Behind strung out the cars of motion picture camera men and their assistants and a number of other ambitious adventurers. The morning was wintry but bright, and the pine forest through which the road wound for twenty miles was covered with a white mantle. On the low divide between the foothills they found the snow too deep for good travel, but they made it, and as they descended on the other side, the snow thinned out and at last disappeared about the edge of the cedars.

Thad viewed the hundred-mile valley of variegated colors with a deeply appreciative eye. He was glad for this brief renewal of his acquaintance with the desert, entirely aside from his interest in McKay and his sympathy for the deer. A new life stretched before him, somehow similar to this beautiful vista of winding, beckoning road and changing slopes and the rise and heave of the purple steps. This trip would be a hard, trying, and possibly disappointing adventure. He would do his best, as he had done in the past; he would welcome extreme exertion, bitter cold, privation, and whatever came. He would have preferred to be alone on this drive, for in the solitude of the journey there would have been an opportunity to turn his thoughts in contemplation to this new life and what it held for him. He found that this his isolation from people, his years of communion with nature, instead of leaving him unprepared and unready, had given him the patience and calm maturity to meet this most important crisis in his life. They had given him the knowledge that Patricia needed time to come to her decision. A woman was different from a man. It would not have mattered in the least if the tragedy of Patricia's life had been due to some blunder of her affections or weakness of her will. He saw beyond the fatality and frailty of human life to the true meaning of it and how the greatest thing a man could do was to love and believe and hope. All his lonely hours of contemplation had filled a treasure house of emotions from which he could now draw.

Tine talked incessantly, his range of conversation being unlimited in the extreme, from driving tame deer to photographing bull buffalo, and from the political crisis in Europe to the incredible imbecility of his friend Nels.

"By gum!" he ejaculated at length in profound disgust, "Thad, you've got the same way as Nels. I've took a tumble to myself. I see there's nothin' left for me to do but travel alone, or else get me a gurl."

Thereafter he directed his irrepressible and endless verbosity at the driver Conroy.

From Dead Man's Flat the road wound down over bare yellow and red slopes, descending rapidly to the Little Colorado. Here a halt was made to wait for the trucks. Eburne strolled around the trading post among the few

Indians present, and then out to the bluff above the river. The canyon of the Little Colorado began near there and had already assumed noble proportions. There was not the least sign of water anywhere; the river course was mud and sand, baked hard, and cracked. This was the first winter Thad had ever known or heard of in which the river had run dry. It brought to mind again the bitter drought on Buckskin, so cruel to the great herd of deer. The ranger reflected that if the deer had been left alone, free to answer to the call of nature, they would have migrated that season to another range, where water and browse were sufficient. But they had been isolated by man as well as by nature.

The trucks arrived safely, one by one, and the cavalcade once more headed across the desert. Beyond the river there lay a wide wind-swept gravel flat, miles in width, which merged in a zone of clay dunes, marvelous of hue: blue, heliotrope, lavender, purple. From there the going grew bad, so that travel became slow. Sand, rock, dry washes, slopes of adobe gave the driver all he could do to make five miles an hour. The sun began to slant to the western horizon, where the gray bulk of Kishlipie rose above the ragged red desert and the genial warmth took on a sudden chill. Northward the wandering buttes appeared slowly to sink beneath the horizon haze. There was a long two-hour stretch of sandy, gravelly, brushy desert, where the men had to walk and push and wait and try again.

Sunset brought them up out of the low wastes to a valley, bounded on the right by a great corrugated, many-hued escarpment, and on the left by an endless gray slope, dotted with the green of struggling foliage. Ahead, a ragged saw-tooth cliff poked its sharp silhouette over the bulge of the valley floor. Purple and gold clouds showed at the western horizon; to the east the sky was a magnificent spread of rose and bronze.

Soon, dusk mantled the desert, obscuring all save the high points. At dark, Conroy reached the Gap trading post, which belonged to Mobray. It got its name from a huge gap in the red barrier wall that shut out the north. Mobray was out collecting more Indians for the drive, as most of those who had been gathered there had already left in disgust. His wife and the young missionary who helped the trader gave the travelers supper and lodgings.

It was a lonely, wind-swept desert place, haunted by coyotes and visited by lean, dark-faced Navajos. Eburne made his bed out on the porch of the trading post; and found sweetness in the moan of the cold wind, and the white stars, and the bleating of the sheep.

They got started next morning before sunrise. The road climbed, at length, out of the sand and gravel, up through foothills of clay to a cedared ridge. Here, at another trading post, they found one of McKay's trucks broken down and empty. Eburne could not find out what had become of the driver and contents, but he assumed they had been taken along with the others. The incident, however, recalled his forebodings of disaster.

For hours after that, the car bowled along, now slow and then fast, upgrade through a narrow valley dominated by the jagged Echo Cliffs towering on the north. It seemed an endless road to Eburne. When they climbed out, at length, to the uplands once more, he saw again what he considered the most wonderful scene in all that country.

To the west, across the ridged ocean of bare, grassy desert, billowy and swelling, rose a horizon-long black and white plateau, standing up and out with most startling contrast to other landmarks. It was a vast cape, jutting out from the upflung red walls of Utah, and it extended far to the southward, breaking off abruptly in a wild and grand promontory that had been carved into the semblance of a riding saddle. The white was snow, the black was timber. In all the sweep of desert, these were the only colors not the stark, flaming ones of naked rock. How it thrilled Thad Eburne! For that black creeping escarpment, with his its gleams and patches of white, was Buckskin Forest. If he could have turned abruptly to the left and traveled as a crow flies, he would have reached Buckskin Forest and the Saddle in an hour. But that was not possible. Somewhere in the rolling, deceiving desert between here and there yawned the upper reaches of the Grand Canyon of the Colorado.

From the northern end of Buckskin there swept and zigzagged, by mighty and mounting steps, the leagues and leagues of the Vermillion Cliffs. On Eburne's right, the Echo Cliffs turned and notched the blue and ran for thirty miles to meet the opposite barrier, closing the apex of a triangle built as if for the gods of earth and sky. That triangle sloped toward the apex, descending first by sweeping undulations, grassy as a pasture, to grow wild with rocky steppes and at last be broken and bisected by a black wandering line—the Grand Canyon.

It was a scene of unparalleled grandeur, having no counterpart in all that vast canyon country. As the car wound down the rough, tortuous road, the miles slowly fell behind this triangle of upland country, and the two sides of colossal walls magnified all their striking characteristics. Distance had lent a purple-hazed enchantment, but proximity lifted the unscalable ramparts and made clear the true proportions of that incredible notch at the apex and that wandering black line, which grew to be a walled chasm.

All afternoon the car bumped down the road that seemed always about to end and yet appeared to be endless. And as the sun slanted behind, losing heat and brilliance, the vivid reds and golds and purples took on supernatural effulgence. Eburne found the scene in harmony with the thoughts that ran through his mind. He reveled in the sublimity of the natural wonders. But how puerile were they compared to the heights and depths of the new emotions that he had come to know in the last few months.

*　　　　　*　　　　　*

Sunset found the car winding under the denuded red wall, around into the split where the Colorado River broke through. The river there and its environment were what might have been expected from the approach. Across the river, in an oval valley, nestled a ranch, strangely beautiful to the eye weary of desert reds and grays. This was Lee's Ferry, famous for once having been the refuge of the noted Mormon, John D. Lee, instigator of the dread Mountain Meadow Massacre.

The ferry was a huge scow, operated on a cable and moved by the current. The river was so low that a wide sand bar extended halfway across the channel. To reach the scow, the car had to plow through mud and sand. Once aboard, the muddy red water swirled and roared and bellowed around the boat. When Eburne stepped ashore on the far side, he turned to see other cars waiting, and still others creeping like snails down under the beetling bluff. As dusk fell they were still coming.

The keeper of the ferry and an employee of the government lived at the edge of the oasis in flat stone houses. Here Eburne engaged meals for all, and what rooms were available. Most of the company of deer drivers would have to sleep outside on the ground.

The last of the trucks did not cross until late at night. Thad was told that the horses for the picture people, which had been sent on ahead in charge of cowboys, could not be ferried over in the dark.

All during Eburne's waking hours, and it seemed his slumbers, too, he was conscious of the changing but incessant roar of the river, now full and clear, then sullen and low, murmuring, moaning, thundering, but always sinister and threatening. It was an evil river, a destroyer, a merciless stream of water and silt, pouring the turbid flood through the black great walls! White stars blazed like beacons on the lofty rims.

Eburne, with a promise of reaching camp that night, urged all to an early start next morning. They crossed the peaceful oasis, a place to make travelers want to linger, and turned westward along the river bluff, then out on the lifting barren desert, on under the Vermillion Cliffs, creeping around the sharp curves, winding among grotesque monuments carved by wind and sand. It did not seem the same world that Eburne had faced the day before; but what the difference was he could not define. Now they were rounding stupendous corners of canyon wall, sky-high, cracked and seamed, with tottering ledges, vast sections of weathered talus, cliffs and caves, rims and crags, all rust-stained, gold-banded, dyed in vermilion hues.

Noon found them turning the last vast jutting wall. Before them a gray bowl-shaped valley lay open and bare, dotted by lonesome cattle, drawing the eye to rising flats and slopes that soon took on a tinge of snow and spotted patches of verdure. Above, grand, glittering, black as basalt, stretched Buckskin Mountain.

By three o'clock, Conroy had crossed the Valley. Looking back, Eburne could make out a dotted line of cars and trucks doggedly hanging on.

A little farther on they encountered the second of McKay's trucks. This one had lost a wheel. The bags of grain, bales of hay and wire, and boxes of supplies stood in a pile beside the trail. Two men were camped there on guard. They reported that the driver and his helper had gone on with others to fetch a truck back to pick up the supplies. Eburne could not get any more information out of them.

"Where are you from, anyhow?" he queried impatiently. "You did not come with this outfit."

"We're from Fredonia," was the reply.

"Where's your car?"

"Didn't have no car. We was ridin' hosses," added the older of the two, waving a hand toward the desert.

Thad thought this peculiar, to say the least. He did not see saddles in camp or horses out on the desert.

"I'll send a truck back for this stuff before dark," he said briefly.

"Them drivers said they'd have to go to Kanab for a truck."

Eburne pondered over this circumstance while his car climbed the last slope of the valley and turned west under the looming bulk of the black mountain. Here for miles the road was straight and level. Conroy made fast time. But soon there followed another gradual ascent, and then a beautiful sage flat, fragrant and purple, and after that gullies and ridges, until at last the cedars.

In another hour Eburne was gazing up at the banded rims of the Cocks Combs, gold with the last rays of the setting sun. Then came thicker beds of sage and clumps of cedar and patches of buckbrush rising out of deer-tracked snow!

The road ended at the head of a gulch, at a point that was known as Warm Springs, the site of the most remote ranger station on the preserve. There was a fine spring and pool of water. All about were signs of a large number of deer in the vicinity.

The ranger chose a camping place for the motion picture people on top of the cedar ridge above the ranger cabins. It was an ideal place to camp, even in cold weather. The view on all sides was something calculated to still the voice and dim the eye. Behind the camp rose the long, graceful slope, dotted with cedars, white-aisled between, reaching to black foothills that stepped up to the foot of the gold-barred, black-fringed rim. Buckskin loomed there, beckoning but unscalable. The level rim stretched on under the sunset-flushed sky to the great gap called the Saddle. This was the break through which McKay expected to drive the deer.

Like a colossal opened fan, the cedar ridges and slopes fell softly away from the mountain, spreading down and down to the level gray desert, in whose deceptive floor appeared a vast rent, as sharp and zigzagged as a streak of lightning. This rent was the Grand Canyon. It disappeared under the south point of Buckskin. Beyond, on three sides of the horizon, rose the dim purple walls, the cliffs of Utah to the north and the cliffs of Arizona to the east and south. The vast panorama made a noble setting for McKay's deer drive—a wild and gigantic stage for the romantic drama which was soon to take place wherever man was to help nature undo some of the ills which man and nature together had brought upon the great herd of gentle creatures who lived there.

Thad and Tine pitched Conroy's tent in a sheltered place in the lee of a clump of cedars. Then they gathered wood for a campfire. By the time this work was done, darkness had set in. There was nothing else to do but wait for the cars and trucks. Eburne remembered that Blakener was to be at Kane. It would be necessary to send him word by one of the drivers in the morning.

The cars arrived in fairly good time, but the trucks were late. The motion picture company had a cook and an abundance of supplies. When they sat down to a ten o'clock supper, they surely were a gay and hungry crowd. Eburne enjoyed eating with them. It was midnight before all of the tents were up and beds unrolled. As Eburne stretched out, weary and aching from the jolting car ride, he was too tired even to let his thoughts range as they were wont to do to a girl who had remained behind in Flagstaff because he had told her to.

He seemed to shut his eyes only to open them at dawn. Rosy light shone into his tent. The day promised to be glorious. There was no frost, but the air had a keen nip in it and was redolent of sweet sage and cedar. He got up to begin his tasks, the most of which for the present would be waiting.

After breakfast he went in search of McKay's first truck, which had been ahead of the two that had broken down and should have reached Warm Springs yesterday. It had not arrived. Not a man there had seen any sign of a truck. This occasioned Eburne more reflection, and all the conclusion he could come to was that this truck had gone off the road somewhere to the north of Kane.

"That truck is supposed to have two loads of supplies and four men from the trucks that broke down. Looks a bit fishy to me!" said Eburne to himself. "McKay surely hired a bunch of sapheads."

McKay and his party had been scheduled to arrive the day before from across the canyon. Thad had not really expected them. It would not surprise him if they were days late. The ranger was primed for disaster. This deer drive had as its incentive a tragedy; it had begun tragically, and so would it end. But as he reviewed the chain of blunders disasters, he became all the more determined to see the venture through to the end.

He walked around among the cedars adjacent to camp until he was tired. He saw numerous deer, and it struck him they were unusually wild for Buckskin deer. They were thin, too, and in poor condition. All the buckbrush he examined had been eaten bare, torn and stripped as high as a tall deer could reach. This variety of browse had been practically destroyed. Deer tracks were extraordinarily thick in the patches of snow throughout the cedars, but most of them were old. A large herd of deer evidently had been watering at Warm Springs until recently.

The next day was much like the day before, but late in the afternoon McKay with his outfit arrived.

"What a job!" he roared when he saw Eburne. "Two feet of snow on Tanner's trail. We lost three horses an' a lot of supplies. Had to relay across the river an' up to the Saddle. Where are my trucks?"

"Two broke down and the third seems to be lost," reported Eburne and briefly told the particulars as he knew them.

McKay cursed roundly, but in the main took the matter as a man to whom difficulties were omnipresent and who always came out of everything in the end. While his tired men pitched camp, he went over to try to induce the drivers of the motion picture company trucks to go back after his supplies and the Indians. They refused to start till morning.

"My brother Bill is comin' from Kanab with a truckload of stuff," said McKay. "I sent him word to fetch some Piutes an' hoss wranglers. He ought to be here. An' my son's got another truck on the way, or was to be. If we had thet wire we could put it up in a few days. Reckon there's some bad breaks I missed seein' before. Wal, I'll sure drive them deer, dinged if I don't."

Eburne reflected sadly that poor old McKay had missed many things which had been plain as daylight to the deer stalker. He was a practical miner and oil driller, cattle man and horse dealer, yet visionary in the extreme when it came to details.

Next day brought developments exasperating to McKay and more than ever indicative to Eburne. The supplies that had been guarded by the two men whom Eburne had accosted were gone. So were the men. It was impossible to tell that day whether or not McKay's first truck had picked them up. But when it finally arrived at the camp, with the two drivers in charge unable to give any information about either the missing supplies or the other drivers, the situation began to look serious to McKay.

Another day passed. That evening the truck that had gone to the Gap for the supplies and the Indians supposed to be there returned empty. The driver could not locate where the supplies had been taken, and Mobray would not be ready with the Indians for another day. So four wonderful calm and clear days passed by, utterly wasted. To Eburne it seemed to be tempting fate.

Late that night the cowboys with the troop of horses for the motion picture people arrived, all footsore and hungry. McKay had assured these men that one of his trucks would stop to leave grain and food with them. Nothing of the kind had happened—the drivers had not even had such instructions—and but for the kindness of the people at Mobray's, Lee's Ferry, and Kane, the cowboys would never have been able to complete the journey. They were disgruntled and pessimistic about the whole affair. Somebody at Kane had informed them there would be no deer drive.

Next morning, Thad was glad to see Blakener come riding in with Eburne's outfit.

"What made you so late, old-timer?" was the ranger's greeting.

"I was waitin' for you at Kane," replied Blakener with some irritation. "Some fellow in a car met Wilcox an' said he'd seen you at the Gap. You were goin' back to Flag. So I waited for some word."

Eburne threw up his hands. This might not be the last straw, but it was enough.

"Blakener, there's a lot of underhand work going on," he declared. "It's either just cussed maliciousness, or else it's pretty cunning propaganda. Have you run into anything queer?"

"Utah is against McKay's drive," replied Blakener. "The cattlemen are against it. All the loafin' riders an' horse hunters are against it. But I can't put my finger on any deliberate proof of their hinderin' it."

"Well, I'd gamble I can," said Eburne shortly. "But what's the use? You can't get an idea into McKay's thick head. Not to stay longer than you're talking! I can do nothing but stick along and see what happens."

"Thad, there'll be a lot of outfits comin' today to be on hand when the drive starts."

"They are in for disappointment."

"Wasn't this the day McKay set?"

"As far as I know it's no different from December first, second, third, fourth, fifth, sixth, and so on. This is the tenth. McKay assured the picture people he'd absolutely start today. But the Indians aren't here, the cowboys from Kanab are not here, the wire isn't here."

"Well, Thad, don't fret about it," replied Blakener philosophically. "You've sure done your best for the deer herd."

"I'm terribly disappointed," returned Thad. "I wanted to see this drive go through. We've had perfect weather. It can't last."

"Accordin' to the ache of my old bones there's a storm makin' now," said Blakener.

Eburne saddled his horse and, glad to be in the saddle once more, he rode out into the cedars on the scouting trip he had promised himself. First he headed down the slope toward the open sage flats. There were a few inches of snow covering most of the ground, and drifts in shady places. Tracks in snow were the same as printed words to him. There had been a considerable number of deer along this slope a week or ten days past. But they had moved. Thad found only a few fresh signs. Dead deer were numerous, most of which appeared to have starved to death. Some were bucks that had been gored to death in fighting.

When he reached the edge of the cedars, the snow failed, making tracks difficult to see, except in soft, bare earth. Everywhere he rode, the buckbrush appeared to have received the brunt of the hungry deer attack. Eburne rode south a mile and then turned west, encountering practically the same evidence he had already noted, except that he espied more deer. They ran off as if they had recently been shot at. Soon after that he espied tracks of shod horses. They did not appear to be fresh, and at length he dismounted to make sure. Some that he examined were fully ten days old. This did not cause the ranger any concern until after about an hour or so he began to be convinced that they were too numerous to have been made by rangers. There were no cattle on this slope. The only cattle on that end of the preserve were a few wild steers on Saddle Mountain. Sometimes cowmen rode out there to get some fresh beef, but these tracks had not been made by cowmen.

Eburne rode five miles up into the foothills under the rim. The higher he got, the deeper the snow lay and the more deer and deer tracks he saw. Most of the deer were browsing high. They would be hard to drive out of the rough brakes and thick brush. Eburne was quite astonished to find so many deer up there, when by all calculations they should be down on the lower, warmer slopes.

"Well, I've seen about seven hundred deer," he said to himself as he turned back toward camp. "And I still have one quarter of my ground to ride. Seven hundred in a strip a mile wide and six or seven miles long. That's a lot of deer. It would augur well for McKay's drive if it wasn't for all these infernal hitches. There are twelve or fifteen thousand deer on these cedar slopes between the Cocks Combs and the Saddle. If they were all low down we might make some progress toward driving them into Saddle Canyon, and so over the pass. But most of them are high up in the breaks. It's going to take time!"

The ranger returned to camp early in the afternoon. There had been many new arrivals. McKay's brother had arrived from Kanab, bringing four Piute Indians. He had been expected to bring at least twenty-five riders. Eburne casually interviewed him.

"Wal," he said, "I had their promise to come. But lately they just backed out. Reckon the feelin's pretty much again the drive over thet way. Somebody's done a heap of talkin', I don't know who."

So one by one the things McKay had counted on, either with or without reason, failed him. Still he went on deluding himself.

"Me an' some of the boys rode across them draws under the Saddle today," he declared in his big, lusty voice as he stood back to Eburne's campfire. "Seen a million deer, more or less. We edged them along a ways. Reckon they'll herd just like sheep, once we git them bunched an' started. We had the camera men with us, an' they shore threw fits at the places to photograph a bunch of deer runnin' along. . . . Wal, I'll stretch a line of men an' Indians from the foothills to the edge of the cedars. Men on hosses an' Indians with bells. We'll start back here five miles or so, where the Cocks Combs begin, an' drive this way, as far as camp. Next day we'll drive five miles more. Thet ought to bunch a big herd just under the Saddle. There's wall thet'll stop the deer from movin' on down. The third day we'll kind of corral them an' drive them up to the Saddle. Once over thet an' they've got to run down to the river. Trail or canyon. It don't make no difference to us."

"Mac, have you forgotten about the wire fence to go up in the several breaks along the trail?" queried Eburne casually.

"Jeepers, I reckon I had forgot thet," declared McKay perplexedly. "Wal, it'll take only a half day when the wire gits here. . . . I shore wish it'd come, an' them Indians, too."

19

D *ECEMBER* fourteenth arrived, with the unprecedented fine weather still holding.

Deer Drive Camp, as the motion picture wags called it, was a scene of color and action, noise and bustle. By the time the last truckload of Indians arrived, there were two hundred men in camp. Among them were Cassell, Judson, Settlemire, and game wardens, deputy marshals, sheriffs, tourists, rangers, wild horse hunters, cattlemen, Dyott and his gang, traders from the reservation, strangers from Utah, and last but not least, a Hopi truck driver. This Indian had spent three days and nights fetching the Navajos from the Gap.

Eburne cultivated the Hopi's acquaintance. He was an educated boy, small and sinewy, with clean-cut dark face and fine eyes. He wore a fur cap, which he set jauntily on his black hair. In the course of the ranger's friendly advances and inquiries, the fact came out that this Hopi had been approached at Lee's Ferry and Kane by strangers who made flattering offers for him to quit the job he was on and start at once on some errand for them. He said he had promised Mobray to get the Navajos to the deer drive and he was going to keep that promise.

"You're a straight shooter, boy," declared Thad with feeling, handing him a silver dollar. "You can eat at my camp. There won't be anything much to eat at your camp."

Dyott and his four men had a camp back of the Warm Springs cabin. Eburne strolled over there and up to their campfire.

"Howdy, men," he said coolly. "I see you've joined the procession."

"Yep, we reckoned it'd be some fun," replied Dyott, just as coolly, and he perked his huge head like a bird.

"The more the merrier. Of course you've got lots of friends in this crowd, and like them you're keen to help McKay make his deer drive," returned Thad with sarcasm.

"Wal, from all I hear you ain't any too popular either," said Dyott gruffly.

"Thank goodness!" declared the deer stalker fervently. "Dyott, you're an old-timer. Back in the days when you were the real thing, as cowman, or horse dealer—or just plain rustler—you'd have shied at a dirty job such as you've helped put over this fall and winter. I'll bet deep down in your heart you're ashamed of it now."

"Eburne, you shoot off your chin a lot fer a fellar who ain't got any half-hitch on his ranger job," rejoined Dyott with a leer.

"Dyott, I haven't any ranger job."

"Ha! You got fired, then, just as—"

"No. I quit. I beat them to it," interrupted Thad. "But ranger or otherwise, I still have a grudge to work out on you. *And* I'm no longer handicapped by forest service regulations. Savvy that?"

"Ahuh!" grunted Dyott, with his bushy head hanging thoughtfully. Then he looked up with a gleam in his deepset eyes. "Eburne, I gotta hand it to you fer bein' the kind of man I like. Listen hyar. I had as dirty a deal from these cattlemen as McKay's got. An' if they didn't hev the goods on me I'd shore give you a hunch. Thet's sayin' a lot, considerin' the whack you gave me on the head."

"Dyott, I don't want your hunch," replied Eburne, "but I'll shake hands with you on that straight talk.... There are a lot worse men than you."

From Dyott's camp Thad sauntered over to the ranger cabin, where Cassell, Judson, and others of the service were chatting with game wardens and deputies. Eburne found them all agreeable, pleasant to him, and full of questions about the drive. If any of them opposed McKay's plan, they assuredly were capital actors. The ranger inclined more and more to the conviction that the officials of the forest service would have been keen for the drive if only they themselves had originated it. The underground machinery of that cattle country, managing affairs at such long distance, operated perhaps a little too silently, secretly, and perfectly for them to comprehend. Eburne had the grace to give them the benefit of the doubt.

"I expected you to come to Ogden to report on the deer investigation," said Cassell.

"I mailed my report," replied Thad. "Then I got a few days' leave, went to Flagstaff, where I decided to resign from the service. Wrote you to that effect."

"You resigned!" ejaculated Cassell in surprise and heat. "Well, you saved us the trouble of dismissing you."

"Sure. I figured that. You don't want any rangers like me. I know too much about deer—and other things. Cattlemen, for instance, and how they *don't* obey the law. Tell your successor that, Mr. Cassell."

Eburne turned on his heel and went out amid complete silence. He was glad to have had an opportunity for that caustic little dig at the men who in the past had heaped so many indignities and injustices upon his head.

Then the ranger walked through the light snow up among the cedars where the Indians were encamped. They had cut large quantities of cedar and pine brush, which they heaped high in a circle, like a corral with a single opening. Around the inside edge they spread their blankets and sheepskins, and in the center they built a fire. Most of them were young stalwart men, eager for the deer drive and the big feast McKay's emissary had promised them. With their lean, dark heads and bronze, immobile faces, their blankets of bright hues, and their slow gestures and low, guttural voices, they formed picturesque and romantic groups which powerfully appealed to Thad. He wished Patricia might have seen these camps.

A vivid contrast to them was the camp of the motion picture men. It was like a prosperous little village where a circus was in progress. They had a cook and huge stores of food, tents and bales of blankets, utensils of every shape and size, and, lastly, many strange-appearing cases and stands and paraphernalia for their picture-making. This was an adventure for them, a thrilling and interesting hardship for which they had made full preparation and which they evidently were enjoying to the full. Eburne listened to their strange modern banter with amusement and with a feeling of how far and how long he had been absent from the world which they represented.

That night Thad heard McKay discuss his plans around two campfires, first with a crowd of forest service men and their visitors, and secondly with a miscellaneous group of the campers. In both cases he interrupted his harangues to stoop and draw rude maps on the ground. For some reason his first talk and map differed materially from the second.

Among the many remarks the silent and observant ranger heard made by disinterested men were two that stood out strikingly. An old deer hunter who had turned deputy sheriff remarked gruffly, "Wal, I come down Tanner's trail with him an' up to this Saddle. He can't do what he thinks he can. If you got a million deer started over thet Saddle, they'd all be gone out of sight before you got to Mancoweeps." The second remark was made by a thoughtful missionary who lived with Mobray and had spent years among the Navajos. "If I was doing it I'd let two of these old Indians manage this drive."

Before dawn next morning, the ring of axes awoke the echoes among the cedars, and bright fires soon blazed. The day broke clear and frosty, with a rosy east. By the time breakfast was over, the horses saddled, and Indians assembled, the sun had risen. No better day for a great drive could have been hoped for.

Mobray and the missionary had charge of the Indians. McKay led the forty or fifty horsemen; and they all went north through the cedars, making for a high green-spotted knoll that marked the northern end of the Cocks Combs. It took an hour or more of steady travel to reach it. Here McKay gave orders for Mobray and the missionary to take the Indians straight down the slope from this knoll and station a driver about every hundred yards. The men were to ride in groups up into the foothills. Eburne was given the job of climbing the knoll to shoot his rifle as a signal when all was ready and everyone in his position.

So the company parted, and Thad set out in the direction of the knoll. It was a foothill, steep on the side toward him, sloping gradually to the north. In spite of the easy climb, it proved to be higher than it looked. From the summit Eburne had a magnificent view in every direction. But withdrawing his eyes from the vast desert and the winding black canyon that bisected it, he concentrated his gaze on the topography of the ground at hand.

Between where he stood and the main slope of Buckskin there was a country so big and wild and wooded that a thousand riders could not have routed deer out of it.

Watching McKay, with a dozen or more riders, Eburne saw he was not trying to keep in line with the Indians, who had formed a picket line stretching straight down the slope.

"Haphazard in everything!" muttered Eburne. "Well,

I'll give him two days for his drive. Maybe only one, for I sure don't like those hazy clouds forming over Buckskin."

Gradually the riders disappeared, but Thad could still locate many by sound of hoof and voice. At length McKay's stentorian holloa from some high point made known to Eburne that he and his men were ready.

Thad dismounted and fired his rifle. The great deer drive was on!

He saw the Indian line, stretching down through open sage flat and cedar forest, begin to move forward with a jangle of cowbells and melodious Indian yells. The sights and sounds in the early morning air-stirred the ranger mightily. This vast drive was such a worthwhile, such a humane undertaking; what a pity McKay had not been able to measure up to the bigness of his idea! From the slopes above and the thickets of pine under the rim there rang out the long whoops and hoarse yells and good-natured shouts of the riders.

Eburne, calculating that it would be some little time before McKay's line worked down even with his position, remained where he was to watch and listen. And everywhere he gazed he espied deer beginning to move. Perhaps many had been standing motionless gazing at him and his horse, and because of their protective coloration against that gray background he had not been able to see them. Big bucks with wide-spread horns came into open places to look. Groups of does, some with fawns, appeared on the hillsides. Down below on the gradual slope, flashes of gray crossed aisles between the cedars. Deer were moving near and far, but it appeared to Eburne that they traveled in every direction except that hoped for by the drivers.

Soon Thad heard a line of riders coming down the thickly timbered slope opposite his position. They were throwing rocks, beating the brush, calling in every range of voice. Deer crossed in front of them going down; soon other deer ran in the opposite direction; next a mixed bunch of does and bucks moved diagonally back into the cedars.

"Looks to me like they just won't drive," muttered Eburne, his keen eyes roving everywhere.

Turning to keep in line with the Indians, who were now ahead of the riders, the ranger rode down the slope.

The first sign of deer he saw in front of the Indians was a little fawn. It evidently had lost its mother and did not know which way to go. It ran right into one of the Indians. He whooped and rang his bell, and ran quickly to try to catch the fawn. He did not succeed, but at least it appeared as though the Indians were having fun out of the drive. The next deer the ranger espied was a buck walking unconcernedly down the cedar slope, parallel with the Indians and right in front of them.

Eburne rode into a wash between the hills, where he got out of sight and sound of the drivers until he mounted the slope beyond. Along here, a chain of foothills extended steeply in the direction of the looming Cocks Combs, and more gently in the direction of the desert.

Adding his voice to the din, Eburne rode on, keeping to the highest points. He wanted to do his share of the driving, yet at the same time he wanted to see everything possible that was taking place in connection with the drive as a whole. To his dismay, he saw that McKay and his men were dropping back out of line. They could not have done otherwise, owing to the lay of the land. But even as they fell behind, they continued whooping at a great rate. The deer stalker recognized some high-pitched cowboy yells, such as were common on round-ups.

He came to a point where the ridge of the foothill sheered up and far to the right, reaching the proportions of a mountain. In one place it loomed so high that it concealed the Cocks Combs. The open sage slope changed to brushy cedars, with ravines and benches and outcroppings of ragged rock. At the base of this slope Eburne encountered a troop of deer, above him and a little to his right. They were working down almost in single file, and when they came close enough, he made them out to be bucks.

He counted forty—all bucks. Then, above them, appeared a line of does moving in the same general direction. The mating season had probably just ended, and bucks and does were now separating. Thad was at the extreme western end of the Indian line, and these deer were going behind it. He could not head them. So he waited to see what would happen when this large troop of deer encountered McKay's riders.

They passed within fifty yards of the ranger, coming close before he had time to ride up ahead of them. He calculated there were perhaps seventy in the two lines. The yelling evidently disturbed them, though they were not yet frightened. Eburne rode to an eminence so as to get a better perspective, and from there he saw more deer coming down the slope he had just crossed. Old bucks stood momentarily to gaze and then move on; groups of does, sleek and gray, yet too thin to be beautiful, nosed at the brush, walked, turned with long ears erect, distracted from the fading sounds of cowbells and Indians' yells to a new commotion closer at hand. A bunch of McKay's riders appeared in sight on a slope Eburne had just quit. They were yelling now at each other as much as to the deer. Eburne recognized McKay's booming voice, now hoarse, and strong with impatience. The deer were moving, but not forward.

Eburne was in time to see some riders race across an opening to head off half a dozen deer. They failed.

"Hyar they come!" yelled unseen riders.

"Head 'em off, boys!"

"Whoopee! All set! Let's go!"

"Ride 'em cowboy!"

So it appeared one troop of McKay's riders had raced down to the base of the steep slope, and another had gone up to the ridge, both in pursuit of bunches of deer. Eburne then saw the two lines of deer he had just watched pass him join others from the slope and all trot leisurely through the break in the line of riders and go out of sight in the cedars.

He waited for McKay to reach his position. Some of his riders arrived first. They had lost their loquacity and good humor. The work was hard, uphill and down, and inasmuch as it had been for nought, it was now becoming exasperating. Then McKay came along with six men. Eburne related briefly what he had observed.

"We can't keep up with the Indians," he shouted, his face grimy with sweat and dust. "The line's busted. Bill's lost in them brakes under the Cocks Combs. He's got ten men. I can't even hear the others. What'll we do?"

"Ride ahead. Catch up with the Indian line, and spread up the slopes as far as we can get," suggested Thad.

They rode on at a trot. McKay, with his best riders, including the cowboys, took to the slopes. Eburne, riding straight south, now with Blakener, found himself on a level sage flat, sparsely sprinkled with cedars and thinly patched with snow. They caught up with the Indian line. Deer were showing in increased numbers ahead of the Indians and working toward higher ground. Occasionally one would dash between the Indians, who now appeared close together. They had not kept their line formation.

"We'll soon have a good test of what we can do," declared Eburne.

"Looks so," called Blakener without enthusiasm or confidence.

McKay and his men had mounted the rugged slope, some of them as high as half a mile from the base. They were yelling, pointing, waving their hats, riding up and down as the exigencies of the rough ground demanded. Straggling lines of deer were moving in front of the Indians; and for a while it appeared that the drive was succeeding. As the Indians and riders forged ahead, the number of deer increased. But bucks, does and fawns, trios and sextets of deer, lines and groups, began to close in on one another; and presently Thad calculated there must be five hundred in sight.

"It's now or never!" yelled Eburne to the men within hearing of his voice.

The Indians at this upper end of the line seemed to realize that the test was about to come, as was evinced by the increase in volume and tone of their yells. Excitement gripped the riders. Even the horses caught the spirit of the drive. McKay's giant voice could be heard booming and echoing along the hills.

Now the wide-spread gray lines of deer were moving as if in unison and seemed about to mass. Suddenly they broke into a run, heading off the sage flat toward the slope. Indians and riders let out a yell. The sudden clamor roused the horses and frightened the deer. Reaching the slope, they bounded up and raced across the snow.

"Head 'em off!" pealed out McKay's stentorian voice.

The riders responded with a daring and speed that for a few moments augured well for the success of the movement. But the fleetness of the deer outdistanced the horsemen. Two thirds of that herd of deer streamed up the slope, one long bobbing line of gray and white, to pass beyond the riders; and wheeling back along the ridge, they flashed, leaped, darted in magnificent silhouette against the pale sky.

The other third, which consisted of the rear section of the herd, stampeded down the slope and straight at the riders. Eburne saw three horses narrowly escape being run down before the close-pressed mass of deer disintegrated. Blakener yelled a shrill warning to Thad and wheeled his horse. Then the ranger saw a line of antlers, heads, and ears, sharp-pointed above gray, sleek breasts and twinkling feet, bear swiftly down upon him. The sight was wild and beautiful, and he greeted the stampede with shrill yells of exultation.

"You won't trap! You won't drive! Run, oh! You deer! Run over the men who would steal your liberty!"

His horse became panic-stricken and, getting the bit between his teeth, he bolted and plunged forward in front of the deer. But swiftly as he ran, they soon caught and passed him. One old buck, with a forest of antlers on his head—horns with at least twenty points—passed so close to Eburne as to graze his stirrup. Then deer sped by him on both sides, bounding higher than his head, frantic to gain their freedom. For a few moments, deer appeared as thick as a herd of cattle. Then they passed on, gray rumps vanishing among the cedars. Eburne pulled his horse to a halt.

"By gum!" he panted. "That was—great—even if it was—bad for McKay."

Thad rode back to take his place in the line again. They rode on as before, McKay and his riders far up the slope, the Indians lost down among the cedars. This time the line advanced more slowly, more quietly, to flush in the next mile another troop of deer, and again to meet signal failure to drive them fifty rods consistently in the same direction. Another mile showed a like result. The deer ran up, down, through, but never before, that yelling line of men.

Gradually the Indians dropped behind the riders. There had never been a solid front presented to the deer. If there had been, it was Eburne's solemn conviction, the deer would have charged it, with perhaps serious results to the drivers.

"They are wild deer. They will not drive," he declared to Blakener, his voice ringing with finality.

But McKay drove his Indians and men to their limit; and at sunset it was a weary and disgusted cavalcade that made its way back to camp.

"We didn't do it right," roared McKay, his face back and seamed, his eyes glowing like furnaces. "We didn't keep in line an' close together. Tomorrow we'll drive them, shore as I'm a born sinner!"

Sometime late in the night Thad awoke. There was a moan out in the cedars, low, whining, mournful. The wind! The deer stalker had lain awake thousands of times listening to the music of the wind through the trees—soughing, sighing, rustling. But this was different. He raised his head and listened. It came again, accompanied by a tiny pattering on the tent. Tiny steely pellets of sleet! That wind was the storm-king of winter and it bore a menace.

Eburne had long ago resigned himself to the utter failure of McKay's drive. But because it had been such a wonderful idea, and because it might even have been accomplished with adequate preparation and a thousand Indians and cowboys, he had clung to a hope of at least partial success. That wind was now a death knell to any chance of driving a great herd. Poor McKay! He was already deeply in debt, and every day now would add to his burden.

Sleep would not come again. It was two o'clock in the morning. The wind lulled at intervals and then always returned a little stronger, with the strange irregular pattering of sleet or snow, and the desolate moans that were becoming higher and higher in pitch.

Toward morning he heard the Indians moving about, splitting dead wood. They knew. And the horses came back to camp, thudding under the cedars. They knew.

Eburne crawled out of his blankets in the gray of a winter dawn. It was bitter cold. His boots were like ice. He shook his comrade Tine rather unceremoniously.

"Wake up, you lazy deer driver," he said.

Tine sat up with sleepy eyes half opened. But in another moment his keen outdoor susceptibilities had grasped the change in the weather. "Storm, by golly! Winter has come an' the flowers lie in their graves!—Thad, my dreamy-eyed, locoed chevalier of the tall timbers—*me* for Flagstaff!"

"Tine, this seems to be a rare instance of your mind operating at an early hour," replied Thad grimly.

They bundled up in their heavy sheepskin-lined coats and went out. A cold wind was blowing in gusts, carrying fine snow, as sharp and cutting as particles of ice. The top of Buckskin Mountain was hidden in a gray pall of cloud.

Far down on the desert, beyond the edge of this storm cloud, the sun was shining, and the golds and reds and bronzes were more brilliant by constrast.

Eburne stirred around while Nels, who had slept under a cedar, and Tine cooked breakfast. Some of the more friendly Navajos answered the deer stalker's greeting with an expressive gesture and the words: "*No weyno!*" The prospects indeed were no good.

McKay's men sat or squatted or stood around their fire, eating breakfast, which appeared to Thad to be rather meager. They were not a cheerful lot.

"Mac, this is what I was afraid of," said Eburne briefly. "What we *might* have done I suppose we'll never know, but now we're too late."

"Aw, this little squall won't matter," returned McKay gruffly.

"I know this Buckskin. You don't. Winter has come. We're in for a blizzard and then zero weather."

"Wal, I've seen nice weather here right up to Christmas."

"Yes, down in the canyon, and even out on the desert. But we're high up here. If it snows hard tonight—and I'll gamble it will—you can't get these trucks out. We haven't grub supplies enough to stand being snowed in. The Indians haven't any grub left at all."

McKay seemed silenced by the ranger's deliberate statements. He kicked the campfire with a heavy boot.

"The situation is serious," went on Eburne. "You've got these Indians here on your hands. The motion picture trucks brought them. Not *your* trucks. Out of the nine you expected, you've got one. It's imperative that you think quick and hard, or some of us will have to do it for you."

McKay was a stubborn man. He did not seem to realize the plight of the Indians. His face was black as a thundercloud.

"We're goin' to drive deer, storm or no storm," he boomed.

Thad turned on his heel, pity and sorrow in his heart for McKay. Presently he was joined by Mobray and the missionary. They were inclined to be impressed by the ranger's size-up of the situation; and together they interviewed the young manager of the motion picture company. He saw at once the predicament of the Indians.

"Bet your life we'll get the Indians out," he declared. "We had hay and grain, supplies and boxes in those trucks. Most all gone now. And we can throw away a lot of stuff to make room. We're ready to pack whenever you say."

The generous attitude of the movie people relieved the situation as far as the Indians were concerned. Then Eburne trudged from one camp to another, finding, as he had expected there would be, a quick exodus of tourists, natives, and forest service men. Already they were packing. Cassell with his party had left right after breakfast.

Meanwhile it snowed intermittently. Riders and Indians stood around the campfires, or moved from one camp to another, as if to see what the other people were going to do. McKay finally had the horses brought up from the corrals and saddled.

About nine o'clock the clouds broke, the sun came through, and the snow ceased. McKay rallied Indians and men for another drive, this time toward the Saddle. Eburne marveled at the man's indomitable spirit and also at his stupidity and lack of consideration for those he had gotten into this mess. The lull in the storm, the warm sunshine, and the glimpse of blue sky were only short-lived. That heavy black pall hung over Buckskin like a mantle. Even the Saddle was no longer visible. Eburne knew that even halfway up to the Saddle the blizzard was raging now.

Nevertheless he mounted his horse, together with Tine, Nels, and Blakener, and made ready to join McKay's forces.

By the time the Indians and riders had received more elaborate instructions than those given yesterday, the blue sky had clouded over and a hard, thin, driving snow was falling. McKay strung his riders up the slope toward the foothills and the Indians down among the cedars. And so the second day of the drive began.

Southward from camp and toward the Saddle, the lay of the ground was uphill and cut by draws and ravines that soon deepened into V-shaped canyons. It was utterly absurd and simply impossible to drive deer over such country on such a day. Nevertheless the drive started.

As riders and Indians climbed, the storm increased, so that within a mile Eburne no longer heard the yells of the riders or bells of the Indians. It was significant that the Indians did not yell as enthusiastically as yesterday.

The snow now lay a foot deep on the slope, deeper in the hollows. Deer tracks were as plentiful as horse tracks in a corral. Whenever Thad raised his face against the bitter cold wind, with its stinging snow, he saw gray forms standing or walking or running. When he reached the edge of a canyon and sought momentary shelter behind a cedar, he could see them more clearly. Everywhere he looked deer were moving. Groups paused to look back and listen. They could see and hear what was beyond Eburne's ears. He saw a troop of over a hundred running along below him on their way up the canyon. Smaller groups appeared in open places, gray-spotting the white snow. Shadowy forms flashed across openings in the forest. The higher he climbed, the deeper grew the snow, the thicker the brush and trees, the harder and colder blew the wind, the more numerous were the deer.

He passed some of the picture men turning back, muffled up in storm coats, bending over their pommels, stiff with the cold. Eburne's face and ears and hands began to feel numb.

At length he reached the rim of the third canyon he had encountered. It was wide, deep, but not rocky, and the slopes were open. Across this canyon the snow came driving down from the gray heights with an icy, stinging velocity that was impossible to face. The ranger decided it was time to seek shelter. He believed he had gotten ahead of the line of riders and Indians. The roar of the storm drowned out all other sounds. It would be folly to cross this canyon. The Indians would never even reach it. He waited and watched the deer, there were perhaps a thousand milling up and down in the canyon. He drank his fill of that beautiful wild spectacle, because he knew he would never see it again. He doubted if such a sight would ever be seen by any man again. Another winter would find most of these deer dead.

Blakener, Nels, and Tine joined him there, having met while crossing the last canyon.

"The Indians are quittin'," yelled Blakener in his ear. "Poor fellows nearly froze. Some of them almost barefoot."

Nels had information of similar import: "Seen some riders turnin' back at that second canyon."

They waited there an hour. Part of that time was spent huddled over a little fire in the lee of a cedar clump. No riders appeared up the white-patched canyon slope, nor Indians from the opposite direction. Up here, five miles from camp, the snow was too deep for easy travel. It was still four miles farther up to where the trail crossed the Saddle. They could see that the blizzard was raging all along the Saddle. Eburne would have felt sorry for rider and horse essaying to make that pass today.

"Thad, old top," drawled Nels, his lips close to Eburne's ear. "I'm an easy-goin' cuss, but this is a wild-goose chase. An' I'm hankerin' for Sue an' that cosy little parlor with the open fire. Am I talkin', pard?"

"Lead the way back to camp, you horse-tracking cow-boy," shouted Thad, as if shouting would hide or quell the tremendous thrill which Nel's subtle speech had stirred in his heart.

It was a long, tough ride going back, even though the wind was behind them. Nels lived up to his reputation as a rider. The most striking circumstance of the return trip was the fact that Eburne saw more deer than he had seen going out. This, perhaps, might have been because the driving snow had made clear vision difficult. They drove deer out of cedar clumps and jumper thickets; they met deer at every turn; and, as always, these deer were moving in every direction. Thad saw them run off a hundred yards and halt. Drive these deer? It would have taken an army of men.

As the riders came down off the heights, out of the fury of the storm, they began to meet Indians, some resting, others standing undecided, and still more going back. A mile from camp, Eburne met an Indian who was limping. One of his tracks showed bloodstains. His moccasins were worn through. The ranger welcomed a chance to walk, so he gave his horse to the Indian.

Upon arriving at camp, he found all the picture men back, sitting comfortably around their campfire, and most of McKay's riders as well. None of the Indians, except the one Eburne had brought in on his horse, had returned. Six inches of snow had fallen, and the storm was reaching down off the mountain. It was two o'clock in the afternoon. Thad gave Conroy word to get his car ready and then busied himself rolling his bed and packing his effects. He could get some of the Flagstaff cowboys to fetch his horse and outfit in with theirs.

Tine and Nels cooked a quick meal, after which Eburne had them carry most of their food supplies over to the camps of the Indians. Presently McKay strode up.

"Wal, Thad, I'm licked," he said, extending a huge hand. "But the storm did it. . . . Much obliged for your help. I won't forget it."

He had lost the sullen vehemence, the indomitable passion, the blind confidence that he had exhibited earlier in the day. McKay had finally realized that he was whipped, and he took his defeat like a man. Just one more vicissitude of life had left him bloody but unbowed.

When, a little later, Eburne looked out of the car to take a last glimpse at Warm Springs ranger post, he happened to espy a pile of bales of wire that had been thrown under the cedars. McKay's wire for his fences! They had arrived two days before the drive; and McKay had forgotten them or just plain neglected to use them.

An hour later, looking down the slope from the edge of the cedars, Thad saw where the white snow line failed and the gray dry desert began, where the storm cloud broke off above and the sunlight streamed down.

*T*WO days' ride across the red barren lands brought Eburne's party to the summit of a ridge from which the San Francisco Range could be seen rising from a swelling desert tableland, its magnificent black bulk partly concealed in angry storm clouds.

At two o'clock that afternoon Eburne viewed the range again, from another ridge, this time against a mass of purple and gray cloud, dropping silver veils of snow. He began to grow a little apprehensive about crossing the divide. Behind his car were seven other cars and one truck. If the snow on the divide was not too deep they might make it.

When they reached Dead Man's Flat at five o'clock, they found themselves in a whirling snowstorm, and when the pines were reached, the cavalcade ran into a howling blizzard.

Conroy knew where the road ought to lie, and somehow he managed to keep on it. One foot of snow on a level did not halt him, but in the drifts the men had to get out and shovel, wade, stamp through, then return to shove the cars, one after another. Night fell shortly after they had left Dead Man's Flat. The gale of wind blew the dry powdery snow in blinding sheets. The air grew piercing cold. It took two hours of exceedingly hard toil to cross the divide. Then downgrade helped. But the last series of drifts had worn out the endurance of the men; and it was fortunate that a high-centered road was reached, which soon led into the main highway.

Thad had never been so glad in his life as when the lights of Flagstaff gleamed through the whirling sheets of snow.

"Conroy, you're a magnificent driver," exclaimed Eburne gratefully, as he and his comrades limped out of the car in front of the hotel.

Nels tugged at Thad's sleeve. He was a ludicrous-looking snow man, with icicles on his beard.

"Thad, I'm goin' in the hotel for a little," he said. "You run around to Sue's an' get the first crack at that open fire. Tell Sue I'll be there pronto."

Eburne could not very well run, because he was too stiff with cold and cramps, but he managed to plod through the deep snow around on the side street to the house Sue had rented. The blinds were drawn, but Eburne saw that behind them a bright light burned.

He tramped up the little porch and thumped on the door. He could feel the thump of his heart, too. A door opened inside, quick steps sounded in the hall. Then the outside door opened to disclose Sue. She started back in fright.

"It's Thad," announced Eburne, stepping over the threshold. "Frozen stiff, starved to death—but happy."

"Thad Eburne!" she cried joyously, and she pulled down his snow-covered head to kiss his cheek. "Oh, you snowy bear! I'm shore glad to see you. Is Nels all right? With you?"

"He'll be here pronto, he says," replied Eburne as he closed the door. "I think he wanted to clean up a little.

But I couldn't wait. I've got to *see* Patricia. Then I'll run back to the hotel and make myself presentable."

"She's in heah," replied Sue, with her hand going to a door in the dimly lighted hall. Then she whispered, "Let me give you a hunch. Be shore to grab her like a cave man before she can get over her surprise."

She flung open the door, letting out a flood of light. "Patricia, look who's heah!"

Eburne strode into the room, almost blinded by the glare, while Sue shut the door without entering. He heard a quick, low exclamation. His heart had not yet left his throat where Sue's extraordinary advice had sent it. Then he saw her. She was rising, lips parted, dark eyes dilating, one white hand pressed to her bosom. A magazine fell from her lap.

"Thad—is it you?" she cried.

How the rich, well-remembered voice rang through him.

"Yes, Patricia—all that's left of me," he replied huskily, finding it suddenly hard to speak. There was something subtly different about her, something softer in her face, sweeter and less aloof. "I just want—one look at you. Then I'll go make myself presentable."

"Oh, Thad, I didn't know you," she cried, gliding to him. "Why, you muddy, snowy, grimy, terrible man."

But his frightful appearance did not keep her from clasping his hand in both of hers, and then raising them to his muffled wet shoulders while she gazed up at him in a way to make him realize what Sue had hinted was no wild dream.

"Patricia, I'm—I'm all wet—dirty," he stammered, almost struck dumb by her nearness and the joy of surprise in her eyes.

"What do I care how wet and dirty you are?" she exclaimed. "But are you well—and all right?"

"Worn out, frozen—and starved—especially for sight of you," he replied.

"Well, here I am to—to look at."

"Are *you* well—and all right?"

"Indeed yes—and happy, Thad," she said tremulously.

"I'm glad," he said. He found that his voice, too, was a bit shaky.

He felt himself standing there like a fool, unable to think or act. How lovely she was! He trembled under the touch of her hands, still on his shoulders.

"But you don't ask why I'm happy," she said, with a shyness that he did not remember in her.

"It doesn't matter, so long as you are."

"But Thad—it has to do with you—something you asked me at the El Tovar. At dinner. Do you remember?"

"Every word."

"Well, I—I have reconsidered—and—and—if your offer is still open I may—"

"*Patricia!*" he whispered hoarsely.

"It is, then! Very well," she replied, suddenly composed, though a blush mounted to her cheeks. "I have a letter from an old friend—Alice, the woman for whom I sacrificed my reputation. You must read it."

"Patricia, I don't want—don't need to read it," he returned.

She regarded him with sweet grave eyes, in which shone a light that Eburne had never seen before.

"But, Thad—" she hesitated and slipped her hands a little farther along and over his shoulders. She was lightly pressing against him now, and a mist of joyous tears suddenly came into her eyes. "But Thad, this letter makes it possible for me to marry you!"

FINIS

Zane Grey, author of over 80 books, was born in Ohio in 1872. His writing career spanned over 35 years until his death in 1939. Estimates of Zane Grey's audience exceed 250 million readers.

Saddle-up to these

THE REGULATOR by *Dale Colter*
Sam Slater, blood brother of the Apache
and a cunning bounty-hunter, is out to
collect the big price on the heads of the
murderous Pauley gang. He'll give them
a single choice: surrender and live, or go
for your sixgun.

THE REGULATOR—Diablo At Daybreak
by *Dale Colter*
The Governor wants the blood of the
Apache murderers who ravaged his
daughter. He gives Sam Slater a choice:
work for him, or face a noose. Now
Slater must hunt down the deadly rene-
gade Chacon…Slater's Apache brother.

THE JUDGE by *Hank Edwards*
Federal Judge Clay Torn is more than a
judge—sometimes he has to be the jury
and the executioner. Torn pits himself
against the most violent and ruthless
man in Kansas, a battle whose final ver-
dict will judge one man right…and one
man dead.

THE JUDGE—War Clouds
by *Hank Edwards*
Judge Clay Torn rides into Dakota where
the Cheyenne are painting for war and
the army is shining steel and loading
lead. If war breaks out, someone is
going to make a pile of money on a river
of blood.